Jon Cleary

Jon Cleary is one of the statesmen of Australian storytelling. Born in Erskineville, Sydney in 1917, he has been a self-supporting professional writer since the 1940s, working in films and television in the United States and Britain. Seven of his books have been made into feature films and three have been adapted for television. A number of his recent Scobie Malone stories have been optioned for a television series. His most famous novel, *The Sundowners*, has sold more than three million copies, and his work has been translated and published in 14 countries. He has collected a number of literary prizes including the coveted Edgar Award, the Australian Literary Society's Crouch Medal for Best Australian Novel, and the Award for Lifelong Contribution to Crime, Mystery and Detective Genres at the 1995 inaugural Ned Kelly Awards.

W9-AOO-666

JON CLEARY

The Easy Sin

HarperCollins*Publishers*

HarperCollins*Publishers*
77–85 Fulham Palace Road,
Hammersmith, London W6 8JB

www.harpercollins.co.uk

This paperback edition 2003

First published by HarperCollins*Publishers* 2002

1 3 5 7 9 8 6 4 2

ISBN 0 00 713675 7

Set in Times

Printed in Australia by
Griffin Press

for Joy

Pride, Wrath, Envy, Lust, Gluttony, Avarice,
Sloth – oh, what a choice!

OLD SINNERS' HYMN

Chapter One

1

The apartment was big; and soul-less as an operating theatre. The walls, furniture and carpets were all white, as if the designer had been a graduate of Antarctica Tech. The paintings on the walls offered splashes of colour, but they were so abstract as to suggest burst blood vessels in the eyes of anyone looking at them. There were computers and phones in every room, including the bathrooms, as if the owner must always be available, even during ablutions or bowel movements. It was post-modern.

Errol Magee had no soul; or if he had, it had never bothered him. He had been educated at a private school where brutality by prefects had been considered part of social education and sodomy looked upon as a minor aberration of sexual education. He had been a brilliant student at school and university, his only blemish as an Australian his total lack of interest in sport. An only child, he had lost his parents during his first year at university. Paid-up Australians both, dismayed by his lack of interest in sport, they had taken up bungee-jumping in the hope of inspiring him into some excitement. Unfortunately, during a double-act in New Zealand, their rope had broken and they had plunged to their death in a splash that was like an explosion of their hopes. Errol had been dismayed by their death and its manner, but after six months he was over his grief and not looking back. That was ten years ago.

Now he was trying on his girlfriend's new Versace dress and jacket. The dark blue silk went with his eyes, which were his most distinctive feature. He was good-looking in an unremarkable way; his looks sort of crept up on an observer. He was short and slim

1

and the outfit, though a little tight, fitted well. Kylie was much the same build as himself, though with more on the upper deck, and he always liked the outfits she bought with his money. He undid his ponytail and let his blond hair fall loose; he looked at himself in the full-length mirror. Not bad, though the dress and jacket would have looked better worn with something else but his black Reeboks. Kylie's shoes were too small for him and, anyway, he always felt awkward in high heels, tottering around like a drunken drag queen.

He was not a drag queen; nor even a drag commoner. He was not gay nor bisexual nor perverted; he just liked dressing up. Which was one reason why he had never liked rugby at school, though today's one-day cricketers, in their fancy pyjamas, would have welcomed him. He had never told Kylie that he liked dressing up in her clothes. Everyone, he had read on the internet, had his or her idiosyncrasies, and this was his.

It had been another bastard of a day, everyone disowning the stuff-ups that had occurred. A year ago the stuff-ups had occurred singly and only occasionally; lately they had come in bunches, haemorrhoids of disaster. For almost three years he had ridden at the top of the rainbow, up there with all the other cyberspace millionaires; then the rainbow had begun to fade and he, like so many of the others, had begun to slide. But, because he had always been less vocal than so many of the others, his slide had been less remarked. He was not a modest man, but his mouth and mind were always connected, with his mind in control.

He had come home, glad to find that Kylie was out at another fashion show. She went to more openings than a battlefield surgeon; he occasionally tagged along, but always avoided the flash of the paparazzi's cameras; he was never there in the miles of smiles in the Sunday papers. He wanted to be alone tonight, to say goodbye to the apartment. His lease ran out in another week and he wasn't going to renew it. Twelve thousand dollars a month had once been chicken-feed; for a week or two, till he got out of the country, he would be living on chicken-burgers.

Which was what he had brought home for supper. He had eaten while looking at the ABC news, which was all bad news. He had sat in the ultra-modern kitchen, so sterile-looking that one wondered if food would taint it, and the tears had come as they hadn't since he was six years old when his father had yelled at him for not being able, for Crissake, to catch a bloody cricket ball. The tears were a mixture of self-pity and anger; the world had no right to treat him as it had. He wept for five minutes, then he got up and went into the en suite bathroom and washed his face. When he had come out into the main bedroom he had seen the open cardboard box on the bed, the Versace dress and jacket draped carelessly out of the box like an invitation. It had been enough.

He looked at himself now in the mirror, pirouetting slowly to let the full skirt flower out. Then he had glided, if one can glide in Reeboks, out of the bedroom into the big unlit living room. He drifted slowly around the room, touching furniture and objects as he had seen Loretta Young and Susan Hayward do in Late Late Movies as they said farewell to their Ole Kentucky Home and a Southern life gone forever. There was nothing ante-bellum in the apartment, though the computers in every room were now reminders of a war that no one had recognized at the time. Every computer had the same bad news of the day, like silent echoes of each other.

The apartment was on an upper floor in the block that was part of the man-made cliff that was East Circular Quay. Down on the harbour the ferries came and went at the wharves without fuss, like wooden governesses. Lights swirled on the dark waters, ghostly fish, and a lone night-bird went like a dark tic across the brilliance of the tall office blocks fronting the Quay. Two hundred yards across the water from Magee's apartment was a cruise ship. On an upper deck, night-glasses to her eyes, was Darlene Briskin. She was not a passenger, not at $160,000 the round trip; she had bluffed her way on board through the delivery hold as a casual waitress for tonight's big reception. Darlene was a planner, like

3

her mother, and had checked on this evening's programme aboard the SS *Caribbean*. She had also helped her mother to plan what was about to happen across the water.

She lowered the glasses, punched numbers on her mobile. Then: 'Go! She's alone!'

Errol Magee, in the apartment, did not hear Corey and Phoenix Briskin come in through the back door of the kitchen. Corey had been picking locks since he was twelve years old; the kitchen door was no problem. He and his brother wore ski-masks and surgical gloves; the ski-masks were battle-worn, but the gloves were new equipment. They went through into the living room and Errol Magee, as fey for the moment as Loretta Young in nostalgia, did not hear them as they crossed the thick white carpet. Phoenix came up behind him, wrapped the chloroform pad over his face and after a moment's struggle Errol was a dead weight. Phoenix grabbed him under the arms as he sagged.

'She's got no tits –'

'She's an ex-model,' said Corey. 'They don't have tits.'

'Not even when they're retired?'

'Pheeny, for Crissakes, shut up and bag her!'

While Phoenix pulled the big black garbage bag over the victim's head, Corey went round the apartment to the eight computers, including the ones in the bathrooms and the kitchen. On each he deleted everything he saw, then he typed an identical message on each screen. The surgical gloves left no prints on the keys. Their mother had planned that.

He went back into the living room where Errol Magee was now almost totally enveloped in the garbage bag. Phoenix, about to hoist the body over his shoulder, said, 'What's she wearing fucking Reeboks for? A model?'

'For Crissake, shut up – What's that?'

Juanita Marcos had just come in through the kitchen's back door. She was a Filipina with a flat pretty face and a history of choosing the wrong men. She had come in three times a week to clean the Magee apartment, re-locating the dust and managing not to flood the shower-stalls and the baths. She was paid twenty dollars an hour and didn't think she was overpaid, because this was the only job she had had since arriving from Zamboanga a year ago. And anyway Mr Magee was loaded; her live-in boyfriend, Vassily Todorov, had told her that and he knew everything about who had the money. Then this morning Miss Doolan, Mr Magee's girlfriend, the bitch, had given her notice.

'Go back,' Vassily had told her; he was a Bulgarian ex-communist and he knew all about capitalist bastards, 'and tell Mr Magee you want redundancy pay and sick-leave pay. Tell him you want two thousand dollars.'

'What's redundancy pay?' In Zamboanga she had never heard these esoteric terms.

'It's something capitalist bosses have to pay. Go now and tell him what you want or you will go to the Industrial Court.'

So Juanita Marcos came into the kitchen just as Corey Briskin came through from the living room. She saw him in his ski-mask and she opened her mouth to scream. He hit her with the first thing that came to hand, a copper-bottomed sauce-pan up-ended on the draining board. He was not to know, and she didn't know, that she had an eggshell skull. She was dead before Corey and Phoenix, the latter with the bagged form of Errol Magee over his shoulder, had left the apartment.

2

Fifteen minutes after the Briskins had departed, a man arrived in the Magee apartment with intent to murder, not to kidnap. He came in through the same door as the one through which the Briskins had departed with their baggage. He saw the corpse of Juanita Marcos on the floor, knelt down and felt for a pulse. He remained kneeling on one knee for a long moment, then he shook his head and stood up. He knew who Juanita was, but from observation, not from meeting her. He was a professional killer and he had a professional contempt for collateral damage.

He went quickly through the rest of the apartment, pausing only to look at the messages on the eight computers and shake his head again, this time in amusement.

When he left he had been in the apartment only three minutes. He had touched nothing but the still pulse on Juanita Marcos' throat.

Across the waters of Circular Quay he had been watched by a puzzled Darlene Briskin. She had been waiting for Errol Magee to come home and read the messages on the computers. Who was this stranger?

'You are looking at where you live?' The elderly man had appeared while she was concentrating, through the night-glasses, on the Magee apartment.

'No, my mother does.' She knew how to lie, she worked in a bank's customer service: *please hold, your custom is valued by us . . .*

'Very fortunate. I live in Essen, in Germany. Nothing to see. You are travelling alone?'

'Just me and my boyfriend.'

'Ach, a pity.'

Then her mobile rang. 'Excuse me,' she said and moved away along the deck. 'Corey?'

Corey gave her the bad news.

3

Malone read the messages, all the same, on the computers in all the rooms. Then he went back into the living room where John Kagal and Paula Decker sat with Kylie Doolan. The Physical Evidence team were going about their affairs with their usual unhurried competence; Juanita Marcos was zipped up in a body bag, ready to be taken away. Murder, and the solving of it, is a business.

Malone sat down opposite Kylie Doolan. 'You're the girl mentioned in the messages? The one they want five million dollars for?'

'Who else would it be?'

As if she wore the price tag round her neck. Kylie Doolan was a good-looking girl, an eyelash short of beautiful; it was her eyes, shrewd and grey, that distracted one from appreciating the rest of her finely chiselled face. She had thick blonde hair cut in a short page-boy style, a graceful figure and a voice cultivated a tone or two lower than its natural level. Malone found it difficult, even on short acquaintance, to like her.

'Miss Doolan, I don't mean to be rude – but why would you be worth five million dollars?'

'Because I'm Errol's girlfriend.'

He had known that; he had wanted to know what price she put on herself. 'And where would Mr Magee be now?'

'I have no idea –'

'There's a box with a half-eaten chicken-burger in the kitchen.' Kagal was sitting on the long couch beside Miss Doolan. Handsome and well-dressed, as usual, he looked more like an adviser than an interrogator. Malone always found him invaluable when questioning women, especially young women. 'Is that yours?'

'I never eat junk food. That would be Errol's. Or it might've been Juanita's. Though I don't know why she was here.' She glanced towards the kitchen as the maid, in a body bag, was carried out towards the front door. 'Are they going to take the – her – down in the front lifts?'

'You'd prefer she was taken down in the service lift?' said Malone.

For a moment she missed a step, without moving. 'No. No, of course not. I was just thinking of the other tenants, the other owners –'

7

'Should Juanita – that her name? – should she have been here this evening?'

Detective-Constable Paula Decker was from The Rocks station, the command that covered this downtown section of the city. The Rocks, short of staff, had called in Homicide and Malone, short of staff in his own section, had come down here with John Kagal, a junior sergeant. Tomorrow he would retire from the scene, go back to his office and leave the case to Kagal and another officer. And Paula Decker.

She was a tall girl: a high jumper, maybe, or a basketballer. She had pleasant eyes that, with her tallness, always seemed to be looking down. She had angular features that, had she been a man, would have made him handsome. She was dressed in a black trouser-suit and carried a handbag big enough to hold a year's crime reports. She was efficient and, like John Kagal, ambitious.

'Were you or Mr Magee expecting her?'

'No. I gave her notice this morning and paid her off.'

'You sacked her? She was unsatisfactory?'

'She wasn't exactly *brilliant*. She was lazy, but Errol trusted her and kept her on. No, I paid her off because we're not renewing the lease. Yes?' Kylie Doolan turned her head as Sam Penfold, leader of the PE team, appeared in the kitchen doorway.

Penfold ignored her. 'Inspector, I see you out here?'

Malone followed him into the kitchen. 'You come up with something?'

Sam Penfold had been coming up with something for twenty years and more. He was bony-faced with a hunter's eyes; he hunted evidence as other men hunted game. 'There are prints all around the place, but I'd say they're the owner's and his girlfriend's. What's she like?'

'The original Ice Maiden.'

'Never met her. We came up with this –' He held up a pad. 'It was in the sink, I thought it was a dish-rag. But smell it –' Malone took a sniff, reared back. 'Chloroform, right? It wasn't used on the dead maid. So who was it used on?'

'Mr Magee? What's that they say about the plot?'

'It thickens. I love it when that happens. It means PE guys like me don't become redundant. Another thing – on a chair out in the entrance hall, there's Magee's blazer, like he'd thrown it there when he came in. And his trousers and shirt are on the floor beside the bed in the main bedroom. No shoes, though. Mr Magee has been home some time this evening.'

When Malone went back into the living room Paula Decker was saying, 'Miss Doolan, there's a Versace box on the bed in the main bedroom, tissue paper on the bed – where is what was in the box?'

She should be in PE, thought Malone.

'I don't know. It was a new dress and jacket, I brought it home this afternoon.'

'How long have you known Mr Magee?'

'I don't know. A year, eighteen months.'

'Miss Doolan, what do you do?' asked Malone.

She gave him the full glare of the shrewd, challenging eyes. 'I decorate.'

'Decorate what?'

'Errol's life.'

Malone wasn't sure if he was supposed to laugh. He looked at Paula Decker and Kagal; they both appeared to be smiling at his naïveté. He looked back at the decorative Miss Doolan. 'In what way?'

'He shows me off.'

Malone pondered that one. She had a pre-loved look, like an expensive car. 'So you're more a decoration than a decorator?'

Her eyes scratched him. Then all of a sudden it seemed she decided to be patient with him, as if he were an Inuit from the remoter parts of Greenland. 'No, I work at it. The social pages on Sunday –'

Then John Kagal came to his rescue. 'Our boss isn't into the social whirl. He's still getting over the Bicentenary gig.'

Back in 1988: thank you, John. But he grinned benevolently.

Kagal took a pull on the rescue rope: 'Inspector, there's something I'd like to show you on the computers –'

Malone got up and followed him into the main bedroom. 'Look, I'm not interested in some feather-brained social butterfly –'

'She's no feather-brain, Scobie. I'd say she's as calculating as any girl I've ever come across.'

Malone said admiringly, 'And that would be a pretty wide circle.'

'Used to be,' admitted Kagal, safe in his conceit. 'Before I settled down with Kate.'

A relationship that had lasted longer than Malone had expected. Kagal had once confessed to Malone that he was double-gaited in his sexual preference, *fluid* as the gays called it, but he had been living with Kate Arletti, once one of Malone's Homicide detectives and now with Fraud, for five years and it seemed to be a happy arrangement. Malone, up to his belly in middle age, had given up guessing about the young. Including his own three young.

Then Norma Nickles came into the bedroom: *floating in*, as Malone always thought of her. She had been a ballet dancer before she had become Sam Penfold's most reliable assistant in Physical Evidence. She was blonde and attractive and looked *feminine* even in the police dark blue blouson and slacks.

'How are you two making out with Miss Doolan?'

'Have you spoken to her?' asked Malone.

'Only when I first came in. I told her we'd have to go through the entire apartment and she got a bit haughty about it.'

'If your boyfriend was missing, you've found your maid dead in your kitchen, kidnap notes on your computers, how upset would you be?'

'With the guy I just dumped, and no maid, not particularly

10

upset. But I see your point. Our Kylie's not going to need smelling salts.'

'You come up with anything?' said Kagal.

'Nothing that's going to help us much. But I could write you a character profile on Mr Magee and Miss Doolan. They're the original designer junkies, I think. The closets are full of designer labels. Alex Perry dresses, Blahnik shoes, Gucci handbags –'

'What about him?'

'Versace, Armani –'

Malone, who wouldn't have gone beyond K-Mart if allowed by his wife and daughters, who was a life member of Fletcher Jones and Gowings, thought labels, especially if worn on the outside, were like birdshit, something that should be scrubbed off.

'Spare me the details. Where does the money come from?' He looked around the apartment.

Kagal looked at him as if he had just arrived from the upper reaches of New Guinea. 'Scobie, Magee is I-Saw. *I-Saw*, for Crissakes.'

'Eyesore?'

Kagal spelled it out for him: 'I-S-A-W. Don't you ever read the BizCom pages in the papers? They have all the cute names, they're like twelve-year-old kids –'

'I'm not interested in BizCom or Information Technology, whatever you want to call it. I'm still getting used to faxes instead of telegrams –' He stopped at the look on Kagal's and Norma Nickles' faces. 'Righto, I'm joking. But no, I don't know who or what I-Saw is.'

Kagal didn't quite take him by the hand; but almost: 'I-Saw was started by Magee three or four years ago. It's a software programme for lawyers, worldwide. It's supposed to be, or anyway claimed to be, streets ahead of anything else in that field. It made Magee a millionaire, a *multi*-millionaire, almost overnight. On paper, that is – which is where most of these smart guys were, to begin with. I-Saw has started to go wrong over the last two or three months. It's got cases against it, geeks charging Magee pinched some of their programmes and adapted them –'

'What's wrong with that?' asked Norma, who had seen more larceny in ballet than any choreographer cared to admit.

Kagal looked at his boss. 'Is that the sort of principles they teach in Physical Evidence?'

'All the time,' said Malone and gave Norma a smile to show he didn't mean it. 'Go on.'

'I-Saw is on the point of going into receivership. I'd say that is one of the reasons Magee is giving up his lease on this –' He nodded around them. 'And why Miss Doolan sacked the maid this morning.'

Malone gave the matter some thought. 'So Mr Magee could've done a bunk, put those kidnap notes on the computer as some sort of joke against our girlfriend?'

'And killed the maid on the way out?' asked Norma, still practical-minded. 'Why?'

Malone knew it was a weak argument: 'Maybe he had a barney with her and thumped her with the saucepan. Any prints on it?'

'No. And I don't buy that argument.'

I'm losing the reins here, thought Malone; and said, 'Neither do I. You think of a better one?'

Said Kagal, also practical-minded: 'Why would he be wearing gloves in his own apartment? I mean if he put the messages on the computers as some sort of dirty joke against his girlfriend? Or did he put on gloves to pick up the saucepan to scone the maid?'

Malone sighed. 'You practical-minded buggers make me tired. Why don't you have a little Celtic imagination?'

'I once lived with an Irish ballet dancer.' Norma shook her head at the horrible memory. 'He'd get out of bed after sex to riverdance. All stiff arms and ratatatat with his feet.'

'Riverdancing in bare feet?' said Malone. 'You're kidding us. Righto, we put out an ASM on Magee, let The Rocks do it. We'll see what comes after that.'

He went back into the living room as a woman came in

the open front door and was halted by one of the uniformed men.

'Yes?' said Malone.

The woman looked around at all those who were staring at her. 'What's going on?'

'Who are you?' asked Malone.

'Caroline Magee.'

'A relative? His sister?'

'No,' said Caroline Magee. 'His wife.'

There was a gurgling sound from Kylie Doolan, like the last of the bathwater going down the plughole.

4

'We split up six years ago, in London,' said Caroline Magee.

'You're English?' asked Malone.

'No.' But the vowels had been rounded, she would *never* sing 'Tie Me Kangaroo Down, Sport'. 'We met there, were married for two years. I'm from Coonabarabran.'

Bush country: but she had brushed off the bindi-eyes and the paddock dust and the slow country drawl. She was a dark auburn version of Kylie Doolan, just a little sleeker, more sophisticated looking. But her eyes were large and frank, if still puzzled.

Malone had explained to her what had happened in the apartment. She had listened without comment, then just shaken her head. Whether in disbelief or expectation, it was hard to guess. But she did not crumble.

'Have you been in touch with your husband lately?'

'Yes, over the past couple of months.'

'Shit!' said Kylie Doolan.

Up till now neither woman had spoken to each other; indeed, Caroline Magee had hardly looked at Kylie Doolan. Malone, wiser than he played in the ways of women, had held off introducing the two till he saw how far the wife would undermine the girlfriend. He had learned a lot from an observant wife and two sharp-eyed daughters. A cop, he had also learned, could surround himself with less helpful company.

Caroline Magee looked at Kylie. 'And you are the girlfriend?' She made *girlfriend* sound like *bimbo*. The rounded vowels had spikes, like deep-sea mines.

Paula Decker and John Kagal sat silent; they had seen this before, but it was always worth attention. Women at odds with each other are more interesting than men in the same situation. There is more subtlety; or there was in this case. These two had been in training, though neither had known of the other.

'Yes. We've been together quite a while. Here.' Kylie looked around, staking out her claim, even though the lease had been cancelled. In, it seemed, more ways than one. 'He never mentioned you.'

'That'd be Errol. He always played things close to his flat little chest. Or has he put on weight?'

'You don't sound as if you've come back to – to take up with him again.' Kylie's tone also had spikes.

'No. He asked me to come back to help him.'

'In what way?' asked Kagal.

'I'm a computer software specialist. I taught Errol all he knows.' She was sitting on an upright chair, her knees together, her hands holding her handbag on her lap. Yet there was no prim stiffness to her, she looked totally relaxed.

'You knew he was in trouble?' said Kagal.

There was a slight hesitation. 'Yes.'

Kagal looked at Kylie Doolan. 'You knew, too?'

She had her hesitation. 'Ye-es.'

'Well, you have that in common.' Paula Decker had been silent up till now. She sounded as if she was unimpressed by both women. 'And Errol, too, of course.'

Caroline Magee looked at her. 'My interest in my husband is purely business. Or was.'

Kylie snorted, but Mrs Magee just ignored her.

Malone said, 'Where are you staying? Or were you planning to stay here?'

'No, she is not staying here!' Kylie had sat up as if she had been bitten by a spider or something else less welcome than Mrs Magee. 'No, no!'

'Of course not.' Caroline Magee's smile could have sliced rock. 'I'm at the Ritz-Carlton, just up the road. Errol booked me in there,' she added. 'He wanted me close by.'

Malone could taste the sweet-and-sour. 'Detective Kagal will escort you back there. You can tell Mrs Magee how much Sydney has changed in the time she's been away, John.'

'It'll be a pleasure,' said Kagal, who was the only one to have caught Malone's wink.

Caroline Magee stood up. 'You truly don't know where Errol is?'

'No, we don't know,' said Malone. 'I'm hoping he may call you at the Ritz-Carlton. You'll let us know, of course.'

'Of course.' She had an elegance to her that Kylie Doolan, no matter how many designer labels she wore, would never have. She had come a long, long way from Coonabarabran. 'Am I going to be under police surveillance?'

Malone wondered what she knew about police surveillance. 'Not unless you ask for it.'

'No, thank you.' She gave Kylie Doolan another false smile. 'Nice meeting you, Miss Doolan. Pity it's all over.'

She left with John Kagal. The PE team had moved out, the Crime Scene tapes were up, there were only two uniformed officers, Paula Decker and Malone left. And Kylie Doolan.

'What a bitch!' said Kylie.

'Errol really never mentioned her?' said Paula Decker.

'Never!' Kylie looked as if she was about to shiver apart with anger. 'How could he be so – so –'

'I think you'd better move out of here,' said Malone. 'For a night or two, anyway. Have you got someone you can stay with?'

Kylie looked around the room, then back at Malone. 'Yes, my sister. She lives out at Minto.'

Ultima Thule of the suburbs: about as far from these Circular Quay apartments as one could get. 'We'll get a police car to take you out there. We'll keep in touch. And if Errol gets in touch –'

'Out at Minto?' She pushed the suburb off the edge of the world. Malone wondered if Errol Magee knew as little about Kylie as she had known about him. 'He'll call here if he's going to get in touch with me.' She waved an angry hand, as if she suddenly hated (or was afraid of) the big apartment. 'There's a phone in every room with an answering machine – you noticed? Bloody computers with e-mail and faxes . . . The bastard!'

'Take care, Kylie.'

Malone nodded for Paula Decker to follow him to the front door. 'Get on to your boss, ask him to set up a watch on the switchboard at the Ritz-Carlton, in case Errol calls. They'll probably nominate a strike force, your command will be running it.'

'Are you staying on the case?'

He grinned wryly. 'We'll see. I think there are too many complications in this one for a simple-minded Homicide man.'

'I'd like to transfer to Homicide.'

He didn't ask why; he suddenly felt old and tired. 'Good luck.'

He left her and went home to Randwick, where there was no computer, no e-mail, no fax, only Lisa. Oh yes, there was Tom, his son, and *he* had a computer in his room; but Malone never looked at it, avoided it as if any virus it contained was the Ebola strain. There were the two mobile phones, without which no home today was completely furnished, but he looked on them as infectious. He consoled himself with the thought that he belonged to the last century, the further back in it the better. He wallowed in technology atavism.

He wondered if Errol Magee, linked to *his* world with every conceivable communication, would be heard from again.

Chapter Two

1

Shirlee Briskin was neat: everyone said so. Her blonde hair, her features, her dress: a neat package, said her doctor, a lecher, and her chiropodist, a lesbian lecher, swooned over her neat feet. In her house there was a place for everything and everything was in its place, or you'd better look out. In other people's houses she straightened the pictures on their walls. Her daughter Darlene, a cynic, told her she should have gone into government: she'd have had the country shipshape in no time.

Shirlee was also utterly amoral, though neat about it. She had not been innocent from the day she had first walked; she had gone from bad seed to full bloom in one step. She had learned the Seven Deadly Sins at convent school and thought them an ideal design for living. Her entire lack of morals and scruples was, in its own way, a sort of innocence. Or so she liked to think, when she thought of morals and scruples at all.

'What the devil got into you?' Her vocabulary, too, was neat; she never used four-letter words. 'How could you mistake a man for a girl?'

'Mum, it was fucking dark in the room –'

'Wash your mouth out.'

Corey Briskin sighed. He loved his mother in an off-hand sort of way, but you always had to be careful of the landmines of her temper. She, with some help, had planned the kidnapping of Errol Magee's girlfriend, but, like a good general, she had not come to the scene of the action.

'And that girl,' said Shirlee. 'Their maid, she's dead.'

'You were the one's been watching everything. You said she only came in during the day.'

'It was an accident, Mum.' Phoenix Briskin, without his ski-mask, wouldn't have attracted attention. He had such a plain face Shirlee sometimes wondered what she had been thinking about when she had conceived him. He had a thick neck and shoulders that could have carried an ox-yoke. 'She was gunna scream the house down if Corey hadn't clocked her.'

Shirlee looked at Darlene. 'Who was the bloke you said you saw come into the flat?'

'Got no idea,' said Darlene. 'All I could see was that he was wearing gloves. On a summer night, if you're wearing gloves, you're up to no good.'

'Corey was wearing gloves,' said Phoenix. 'So was I. Medical ones.'

'Pull your head in,' said his brother wearily. The resemblance between them was so faint one could be mistaken. Corey had a pleasant face, except for a certain caution about the eyes, as if he trusted no one. He was slim without being skinny and, where his brother was flat-footed, he moved with a certain grace. 'What we gunna do with Mr Magee? Can you ask a guy to pay for his own kidnapping?'

'Why not?' said Darlene, who had gone further at school than her brothers. 'There are self-funded retirees. Here's a self-funded kidnappee.'

'Let's talk sense,' said Shirlee, never without a supply of brass tacks.

They had brought Errol Magee, still drugged, to this house eighty kilometres south of Sydney. It was a timber house with a corrugated-iron roof, a turn-of-the-previous century relic; it stood in two hectares of partly-cleared, partly-timbered land that had somehow escaped developers and city folk looking for a weekend hideaway. Clyde Briskin, now dead by his wife's steady hand, had inherited it from his parents, who had inherited it from *their* parents. Clyde, though a drunk and a philanderer when he was not holding up service stations or in jail, had been a sentimentalist. In his will he had inserted a clause, as had been in his parents' and grandparents' wills, that the property was never to be sold. Shirlee, no sentimentalist, had nominated it as one of her reasons for poisoning him with fox bait.

Now she was glad they had not been able to sell the house. It was an ideal hideaway; there were no neighbours for at least a kilometre on either side. The road that ran past the property was a dirt track that led to a dead end against the Illawarra escarpment. Errol Magee could have disappeared off the face of the earth.

'I think you and me should talk to Mr Magee,' said Darlene. She was better-looking than her mother, but not a neat package; there was always the suggestion that something, physically or emotionally, was going to break out of her. But she had control, something else she had inherited from her mother. She worked for a bank, where control is endemic. 'We'll see how much he values himself.'

'Let me and Corey do it,' said Phoenix. 'We can scare the shit outa him –'

'Darlene and me can do that,' said his mother. 'Wash your mouth out. Here, Darlene, put this on.'

She had planned everything, even to the calico hoods to be worn when they were with Magee. They were pale blue, with round holes for eyes and mouth. 'Very chic,' said Darlene, slipping a hood over her head. 'Does it go with my yellow shirt?'

'Cut the crap,' said Corey, 'and get in there and tell him what our price is.'

Errol Magee was feeling sick: with the smell of the chloroform in his nostrils and with fear. Early this morning two hooded men had come into this room and taken him to the toilet, where everything had gushed out of him. They had brought him back here to the kitchen chair in this bedroom and rebound him with the brand-new leather straps. They had not spoken to him, just ignoring him when he had asked why the hell he was here. Then he had been left alone till now.

19

He looked up in surprise when the two women, hooded as the men had been, came into the room. He had heard voices somewhere at the back of the house, but he had not been able to tell how many there were.

'Mr Magee,' said Shirlee, nailing brass tacks to the floor, 'let's talk business.'

'Business? What sort of business?' His voice was a croak. His hands, bound together by a strap, were in his lap. In his blue dress, his knees bound together, he looked demure.

'Well,' said Darlene, 'we made a mistake, Mr Magee. We meant to take your girlfriend, not you. Do you usually mope around the house in drag at night?'

Magee felt even sicker, with embarrassment. 'No. No, of course not! It was – it was a joke, I was fooling around . . . What's going on, for God's sake?'

'We've kidnapped you,' said Shirlee. 'For money. Five million dollars.'

'American,' said Darlene, who knew the exchange rate. 'Not Australian.'

Magee looked at them; but the hoods were blank. 'You've gotta be kidding! I'm broke – skint –'

He was still sick with fear; but he was a good actor. He wouldn't tell them about the money hidden away overseas, not till they held a gun at his head and threatened to kill him. At the moment they were just talking a deal.

'Mr Magee,' said Shirlee patiently, 'you are worth seventy million dollars –'

'On paper,' said Darlene. 'Australian.'

'Christ, that was twelve months ago! Don't you read the papers?' But he had forgotten. There had been only rumours, buried away in financial columns, nothing in the headlines. He began to regret his closed mouth. 'My company is going into receivership –'

The two hoods turned towards each other. Then Darlene looked back at him. 'We're not financial wizards, Mr Magee, but do you

20

expect us to believe you could lose that much money in twelve months?'

He was dealing with financial idiots; or anyway, infants. He could feel his fear subsiding; a little expertise can stiffen a spine. 'Ladies –'

'Cut out the bullshit,' said Darlene.

Her mother's hood looked at her, but said nothing.

'Ladies, in IT –'

'What's that?' said Shirlee.

'Information Technology.' They were idiots, no doubt about it. 'In IT fortunes were made overnight. On paper, that is. And the millionaires went broke overnight. Throats are cut every day of the week. They started cutting my throat three months ago.'

'Who's they?' asked Shirlee.

'I'd rather not say –'

'Mr Magee,' said Darlene, 'I know what you say is true, about all those paper millionaires. But I don't think you are one of them. But for the record, who's been trying to cut your throat?'

'Are you in the game? IT?'

'No. But I'm not dumb, Mr Magee.'

He hesitated. It had disconcerted him to have these two women apparently running this kidnapping. He had felt threatened by the two silent men, but these two women, especially the older one, if she was the older one, had their own menace. He had never felt really safe with women, not with Caroline and the women between her and Kylie, but he had never felt *threatened* by them.

'The people who put up the venture capital. The Kunishima Bank, they're Japanese.'

'A *bank* is cutting your throat?' said Shirlee.

'Banks are expert at it,' said Darlene. 'You mean, Mr Magee, you've been playing funny buggers and the bank is foreclosing?'

'Something like that.'

'Not good enough,' said Shirlee and even beneath the hood one could see the jaw setting. 'Someone's gunna pay for you,

Mr Magee. All the money you've been worth don't just disappear into thin air.'

'Mum, let me handle this –'

Mum? He'd been kidnapped by a gang run by *Mum*? If he got out of this alive, nobody would believe him; or they would laugh him out of town. He had lunched with Bill Gates, had sat with leading lawyers in London, Paris, New York; the PM here in Australia had once called him Errol, like an old mate. And now Mum and daughter (he wondered what her name might be) were holding him to ransom. He was a snob, but that had been his mother's fault. She had never let him call her *Mum*.

'Errol,' said Darlene, like an old mate, 'someone is going to pay for you, so let's cut out the bullshit –'

'Wash your mouth out,' said the other blue hood.

'– and give us a name. What about your girlfriend Kylie?'

Somehow he managed a laugh. 'She'd put me on her credit card – that's all she ever uses. I told you, I'm broke –'

'All right, you told us that.' Shirlee was losing patience. She had neatly planned everything, like a Christmas package, and now all the string was coming undone. 'But it don't matter. You've got contacts, they've got money . . . I been reading about it, Big Business sticks together, it don't matter about the battlers –'

'You're battlers?'

'We won't be when we get the money for you,' said Darlene.

'Look, Big Business, as you call it, doesn't run a fund for kidnapped businessmen –' Then he shook his head, as if he had only just understood what he had said. 'Call my office, see what they can do.'

'We'll do that,' said Darlene and she and her mother stood up. 'You want some breakfast? Mum does nice sausages and bacon.'

His stomach heaved at the thought. 'No, thanks. Just some yoghurt and coffee.'

'Where does he think he is?' snapped Shirlee and whirled out of the room.

Darlene checked the straps that bound him, then fingered his dress and jacket. 'Versace?'

'Yeah. How'd you know?'

'I've been adding up what I'm gunna buy when we get the money for you. Try and get some sleep after breakfast.'

'Sitting up?'

'Imagine you're in economy class.' Behind the hood one could almost see the smile. 'You'll be back in first class, Errol, soon's we get the money.'

2

'What do you know about a software firm, I-Saw?' said Malone at breakfast.

Tom paused as he was about to bite into his second piece of toast and home-made marmalade. He was a big young man, bigger than his father, with a good blend of his father's and his mother's looks. He had recently graduated with an Honours degree in Economics and a month ago had started with an investment bank at 35,000 dollars a year, almost half of what his father was earning after twenty-seven years service in the police. He was already an expert on world economics, on how to run the country and an authority on other experts. He was still young, God bless him.

'Are we talking about last night's murder?' said Lisa. 'There is a golden rule in this house, in case you've forgotten. We don't talk shop at breakfast.'

Malone gave his wife what he thought of as his loving look. She was still beautiful, at least in his eyes, and had that calm command that was like oil on the family's occasional troubled waters. She wore no make-up at breakfast, was in shirt and slacks, always gave the appearance of being ready for the day.

'I am just trying to get some payback for all the years we've supported him –' He looked again at his son. 'What do you know about I-Saw?'

'I wouldn't put money into it,' said Tom. 'In fact, people are taking money *out* of it, if they can find suckers to buy their shares. Have been for some time. It's dead.'

'What killed it?'

'Hard to pin down. Too much ambition, not enough capital – it could be a dozen reasons. Errol Magee's not everyone's favourite character. Sometimes he's seen at the right places, but he never gives interviews or makes statements. There's virtually nothing about him on the internet, him personally, I mean. Everyone's heard of him, but no one knows him.'

'Except his girlfriend. And his wife.'

'He has a wife?' Lisa looked up from her Hi-Bran.

'What's happened to the golden rule?'

'Don't beat about the bush. You made a mistake, mentioning a girlfriend and the wife in one breath.'

'Never misses out on gossip,' Malone told his son. 'Righto, he has a wife no one suspected, least of all the girlfriend. She flew in yesterday from London. Mr Magee was expecting her, but forgot to tell the girlfriend.'

'What's she like?' asked Lisa.

'Who?'

'Both of them.'

'We're breaking the golden rule,' said Tom, grinning.

'Shut up,' said his mother. 'What are they like?'

'Good lookers, both of them.' Then Malone took his time. A man should never rush into explaining other women to his wife. He would have to explain that to Tom at some later date. 'They're out of the same mould, I think. Both calculating, but the wife would have the edge. More experience.'

'You must have spent some time sizing them up,' said Lisa, like a wife.

'Actually, I hardly looked at them. I made all that up.' Then he looked at Tom: 'What are the women like at the bank?'

'Calculating,' grinned Tom. 'I'm still looking for a woman with some mystery to her, like you told me –'

'He told you that?' said Lisa.

'You're still a mystery to me,' said Malone.

'Glad to hear it. Hurry up with your breakfast. It's wash day.'

Late last year she had given up her job as a public relations officer at Sydney's Town Hall and since then worked three days a week as a volunteer with the Red Cross. Claire, their eldest, was now married with a baby son and Maureen was living with a girlfriend while she picked and chose her way through a battalion of boyfriends. Tom, devoted to his mother's cooking, still lived at home, though there were nights when he didn't come home and his parents asked no questions.

'Find out what gossip you can about I-Saw,' said Malone.

'Am I on a retainer?' Tom was fast becoming an economic rationalist, a bane of his father's.

'I'll shout you a night out at Pizza Hut.'

'Investment bankers don't go to Pizza Hut.'

When Malone was leaving for the office Lisa followed him to the front door. 'Any more on the promotion? You said nothing last night.'

'It's going through.' He wasn't enthusiastic about it. 'I got a hint I'll be skipping a rank. How does Superintendent Malone strike you?'

'I'll get a new wardrobe.'

'There's a summer sale on at Best & Less.'

She kissed him tenderly. There are worse fates than a tight-fisted husband.

Malone drove into Strawberry Hills through an end-of-summer morning. The traffic was heavy, but road rage seemed to have been given a sedative. He was a careful driver and had never been a hurrier; he acknowledged the occasional but fading courtesy of other drivers and gave them his own. The day looked promising. He would turn the Juanita Marcos murder over to Russ Clements and relax behind his desk, mulling over the future.

He parked in the yard behind the building that housed the Homicide and Serial Offenders Unit and sat for a while in the car. In another month he would no longer be Inspector Malone, but Superintendent Malone. He would no longer be the co-ordinator of Homicide, but moved to a desk in Crime Agency at Police Central.

Strawberry Hills, named after the English estate of compulsive letter-writer Horace Walpole, though it had never looked English and had never grown strawberries, indeed had nothing to it but this large nondescript building in front of him, suddenly seemed like Home Sweet Home. In Homicide, whether here or in other locations – and the unit had been moved around like an unwanted bastard – he had spent most of his police life. It had not always been enjoyable; homicide officers were not sadists nor masochists. There had been times when he had wanted to turn away, sickened by what he had to investigate. But to balance that there had been the solving of the crimes, the bringing to justice those who had little or no regard for the lives of others. He hated murder and had never become casual about it. It was part of life and had to be accounted for.

As a superintendent in Crime Agency he would be at least one remove from it, maybe more.

He went up to the fourth floor, let himself in through the security door and was met by Russ Clements, who, he hoped, would succeed him. The big man, usually imperturbable, had something on his mind.

'I see you, mate? Before the meeting?'

There was always a meeting each morning, to check on yesterday's results, to assign new cases for today. 'What've we got? Something serious?'

He led the way into his office and Clements followed him. The big man, instead of taking his usual relaxed place on the couch beneath the window, eased his bulk into the chair opposite

Malone's desk. He looked uncomfortable, like a probationary constable who had made a wrong arrest.

'There were two more homicides last night, one at Maroubra, the other at Chatswood. The locals don't need us, they've got the suspects in custody. No, it's something else.'

Malone waited. He had a sudden irritating feeling that Clements was going to tell him something personal he didn't want to hear. That his marriage was breaking up?

'The job down at the Quay,' said Clements. 'The maid that was done in. Well, not her, exactly.' He shifted in the chair.

Malone, studying him, this man with whom he had worked for twenty-two years, said, 'What's eating you? You got ants up your crack?'

'No. Well, yes – in a way. The maid's boss, the guy who's disappeared, Errol Magee. We've got a problem.'

'We?' Still puzzled, he yet felt a certain relief that Clements' problem was not a domestic one.

'Well, me.' He looked out at the bright day, then back at Malone. 'I invested in Magee's company, I got in when it was floated.'

'So?'

'You're not helping me, are you?'

'I'm listening, but you're taking a long time to get around to what's worrying you.'

Clements looked out the window again. He was not a handsome man, but there was a certain strength to the set of his big face that, for the truly aware, was more reassuring than mere good looks. Right now, though, all the strength seemed to have drained out of him. He looked back at Malone. 'I invested sixty thousand dollars.' Almost a year's salary for a senior sergeant. 'I've done the lot. The receivers are moving in on I-Saw, it's gunna be announced today.'

Clements had always been a gambler, first on the horses, then, when he married, on the stock exchange. But he had never been a plunger. Or so Malone had always believed.

Malone shook his head. 'Sixty thousand? You and Romy've got that much to spare?'

'It's not gunna bankrupt us. But no, we don't have it to spare. Not for gambling – which, I guess, is what she calls it. I just got greedy. I thought things had settled down in the IT game, the mugs had been sorted out – you know what it was like a coupla years ago.'

'Only what Tom told me. I was never into companies that weren't going to show any profit for five, ten years. That were paying their bosses half a million or more before they'd proved anything. I'm short-sighted, I like my dividends every six months. One thing about the Old Economy, as I gather you smartarses call it, it had little time for bullshit. Does Romy know you've done that much?'

Again Clements looked out the window, then back at Malone. 'No. Not yet.'

'Ah.' As wives say when told something they don't want to hear. 'I can hear her say that. Ah.'

'No, it'll be Ach! She'll all of a sudden be Teutonic.' Romy, his wife, had been in Australia just over twenty years, but she was still proudly German. She liked Bach, Weill and Günter Grass, three strangers Clements avoided, and occasionally tartly reminded him that not all Germans had been Nazis. They were an odd match but genuinely in love. 'Even when I tell her that I was aiming for a trust fund for Amanda.'

Amanda was the Clements' five-year-old daughter. 'When did you dream that up, the trust fund?'

Clements grinned weakly. 'Is it that obvious? Okay, when I first put the money into I-Saw, all I saw . . .' He paused.

'Go on. Forget the puns.'

Clements grinned again, but there was no humour in him. 'All I saw was I was gunna make a million or more. It was gunna zoom to the top, like Yahoo. It was designed to help out lawyers, and lawyers are like rabbits. You get two lawyers in an office and pretty soon you've got four or six or a whole bloody floor of them. My stockbroker told me we couldn't lose.'

'How much has *he* lost?'

Again the grin, shamefaced this time. 'He cashed in at the end of the first day's trading, made 40 per cent. He didn't tell me. I hung on, I was gunna make 1000 per cent.'

Malone pondered a while. This could not have come at a worse time; he had already recommended Clements for promotion. The Service had had a rough period, with Internal Affairs sniffing around like bloodhounds, and matters had only settled down in the last few months. But the media and the Opposition in Parliament were always out there, prowling the edges like hyenas, waiting to score points, scandal-chewers. He and Clements had always been honest cops, but they were always wary of outsiders. It came with the wearing of the blue.

'Righto, you're not going to have anything to do with the murder. You're out of it. Entirely. But I want you to find out all you can about Mr Magee. He could've arranged his own kidnapping, if he's in the shit financially. He might also have killed the maid. Has Forensic come up with anything more?'

'Not so far. John and Sheryl are with the maid's boyfriend now. They're in the interview room. He's a Bulgarian.'

'I'll leave him to you for the time being. When you're finding out what you can about Magee, stay out of the picture yourself. We don't want feature stories on you in the *Herald* or the *Mirror*. You know, Greg Random has backed up my recommendation that you take over from me.' Random was their senior in Crime Agency. 'Don't bugger it up.'

Clements stood up slowly, as if his joints had set. 'You're not very sympathetic, are you?'

'You said yourself you were greedy. What do you want me to do – bless you?'

'I'll be glad when you move out.'

Malone hummed, 'You gonna miss me, honey, when I'm gone –'

They grinned at each other. The glue of friendship still held fast.

'I'm gunna take half an hour off and duck over to see Romy.'

'You're going to give her the bad news in the morgue?'

Romy was the Deputy-Director of Forensic Medicine in the State Department of Health and second-in-charge at the City Morgue. She earned more than Clements and, like Lisa, kept an eye on household accounts.

'I wanna get it off my chest.'

'Good luck. I've got two females to interview, Magee's girlfriend and his wife. Do I toss up?'

'Take the girlfriend. She'll always tell you more than a wife.'

They grinned at each other again, further glued by domestic chauvinism.

As Clements left, Malone saw Kagal and Sheryl Dallen come into the main office. He signalled them and they came in and sat down opposite him. They had no look of excitement on their faces.

'Mr Todorov doesn't think much of the New South Wales Police Service,' said Kagal.

'Or any police service,' said Sheryl Dallen. 'I just wonder whose side he was on back in Bulgaria.'

Though not a lesbian or a man-hater, she always had reserved opinions about men. She was attractive without any distinguishing good looks, except that she always looked so healthy; she worked out three times a week at a gym and was on first-name terms with every muscle in her body. Just looking at her sometimes made Malone tired.

'He doesn't seem too upset by what happened to his girlfriend,' said Kagal. 'He's already asking if he can claim worker's compensation for her murder.'

Kagal always added distinction to the office. But his looks, his sartorial elegance compared to Malone and Clements, never hid the fact that, like Sheryl Dallen, he was a bloody good detective.

'Keep an eye on him,' said Malone. 'Could he have had a hand in the kidnapping? Things went wrong when his girlfriend somehow got her skull bashed in?'

'Maybe,' said Sheryl, 'but it's a long shot. But we'll put him on the list. Do we put surveillance on him?'

'Let The Rocks do that.' Never deprive another command of work. 'Has the maid got any relatives?'

'In the Philippines. We're trying to get in touch with them.'

The paperwork of murder: 'Try and unload that on The Rocks, too. In the meantime keep looking for Mr Magee. Though he's ostensibly been kidnapped, he's our Number One suspect for the moment. Unless you've got another candidate?'

They shook their heads, got up and left his office. He sat a while, trying to stir up energy and enthusiasm; suddenly he was in limbo. Was this what promotion did to you? He remembered that Greg Random, though a melancholy man at the best of times, had once told him that his devotion to police work had evaporated the day he had been promoted out of Homicide. Maybe there was a rung in the ladder of upward mobility (where had *that* phrase gone to?) where your foot found a natural resting place, where you really didn't want to go any higher. But then (and he had seen it happen too often) there was the danger of growing fat and lazy on that rung.

He stirred himself, reached for his phone and called Detective-Constable Decker at The Rocks station. 'Inspector Malone, Constable.' He was always formal with officers from someone else's command; he expected the same treatment for his own officers by other commanders. 'What's with Miss Doolan?'

'I left her with her sister, sir, out at Minto. Macquarie Fields are keeping an eye on her, Minto is in their area. Any progress at your end, sir?'

'No.' Was she keeping score? Or was he becoming sensitive

31

in his late middle age? 'I'm going out to see Miss Doolan now. I'll keep you up to date.'

'You want me to come with you, sir? I think I built up some rapport with her.'

He hesitated, then said, 'No. I'll be in touch, Constable.'

'Yes, sir.'

It was always the same, the territorial imperative, the defence of one's own turf. David Attenborough should bring the BBC Science Film Unit down here to study the wildlife in the NSW Police Service. Beginning with ageing bulls . . .

He had no sooner put down the phone than it rang: 'Scobie? Sam Penfold. Norma has been back to the Magee apartment, something about the computers worried her.' He paused: Physical Evidence were becoming actors.

'Get on with it, Sam. Forget the dramatic pauses, I get enough of that on TV.'

One could almost imagine Penfold's grin at the other end of the line. 'Just effect, mate, that's all. Norma looked again at the keys on the computers, all of 'em. On all the keys the prints were the same – we surmise they were Magee's own. Evidently no one but him used the computers. On the keys that tapped out the ransom note, on all the computers, there were no prints or they were smudged. As if he'd worn gloves. Did he have something wrong with his hands, dermatitis or something?'

'I wouldn't know, Sam. I'll ask Miss Doolan. I should imagine it's not easy to type with gloves.'

'Unless they were thin gloves. Surgical gloves. Ask Miss Doolan if he ever wore those.'

'Righto, Sam, thanks. You fellers take care of Norma. She's useful.'

'Some women are. Don't quote me.'

Malone took Sheryl Dallen with him out to Minto. She drove and he sat beside her, his feet as usual buried in the floorboards. He was not a car man; he had never envied Inspector Morse his Jaguar or that American detective of long ago who rode around in a Rolls-Royce. All travellers have attitudes; in a car his was nervousness. Sheryl drove as he imagined she exercised, purposefully and keeping her pulse rate up; and his. They talked of everything but the case, as if to mention it would sully the shining day through which they drove. Summer was going out like a fading benediction.

It was a long drive, almost fifty kilometres, on roads clogged with traffic. Heavy vehicles bore down on them like ocean liners; speed-hogs, driving not their own but company cars, sidestepped in front of them without warning. Sheryl swore at them and Malone buried his feet deeper in the floorboards.

They passed a military camp, strangely deserted but for a squad of soldiers marching stiff-legged to nowhere, training for wars not yet declared. A tank rolled without warning out into the road before them, right in the path of an oncoming 10-ton freight truck. Malone sat up, waiting for the coming crash, but somehow the two leviathans managed to avoid each other.

'Pity,' said Sheryl and drove on.

Minto lies in what was once rolling farm and orchard country. It was first settled almost two hundred years ago and only in the last fifty years has it grown to being a populated suburb of the nearby small city of Campbelltown. Its name was another example of the crawling, sucking-up, brown-nosing, call it what you will, that distinguished the early colonists. In 1808 officers of the New South Wales Corps, rum-runners that the Mafia would have welcomed as Family, deposed Governor William Blight and assumed control of the colony themselves. Then they decided they had better curry some favour with someone in authority. They chose to nominate the Earl of Minto, the nearest high-ranking British official, as patron of the new settlement south of Sydney. That Minto was Viceroy of India, was 7500 miles from Sydney and hadn't a clue what went on below the Equator, didn't faze the crawlers. They knew an easy target when they heard of one; they were years ahead of the traps of mobile phones and e-mail and faxes. That a settlement of less than forty people was named, supposedly as an honour, after a man viceroy to 200 million was a joke that nobody spread.

The suburb lay on the slopes of gentle hills, a mix of would-be mansions on the heights, new villas, modest older and smaller houses and cramped terraces built by the State government and blind bureaucrats in the late 1970s. There was a shopping centre, with the new patrons, McDonalds, Pizza Hut and Burger King flying their pennants above it. There were several parks and playing fields and two schools that had large open playgrounds. It was better than Malone, trapped in the mindset of inner Sydney, had expected.

Malone had got the address from Detective Decker and Sheryl found it as if she came to Minto every day of the week.

There were half a dozen cars parked in the street, only one of them occupied. Malone got out and walked down to the grey, unmarked Holden. The young plainclothes officer got out when Malone introduced himself.

'Detective-Constable Paul Fernandez, sir. We're doing two hours on, four hours off, just one man at a time. Are you expecting anyone to try and snatch Miss Doolan?'

'We don't know. You know what happened?'

'We got it through on the computer.' He was tall and heavily built and at ease. And bored: 'There's not much market for kidnappings around here, sir.'

Malone grinned, though he was not amused. But you didn't throw your weight around with the men from another's command. He knew how boring a watch could be. 'Have you spoken to Miss Doolan?'

'No, sir. Our patrol commander had a word with her, he said she didn't seem particularly put out. I mean about the kidnapping.'

'That's Miss Doolan.'

Sheryl waited for him outside the gate of Number 41. It was a weatherboard house that had a settled look, as if it had stood on the small lot for years; but its paint was not peeling and the small

34

garden and lawn were well kept. There were cheap security grilles on the windows and a security door guarding the front door. On its grille was a metal sign, *Welcome*, like a dry joke.

The door was opened by a larger, older, faded version of Kylie Doolan. 'I'm Monica, Kylie's sister. You more coppers?'

Malone introduced himself and Sheryl. 'May we come in?'

'You better, otherwise we're gunna have a crowd at our front gate. They're already complaining about your mate over there in his car.' She led the way into a living room that opened off the front door. 'But I suppose you're used to that? Complaints?'

'Occasionally.' Malone hadn't come here to wage war.

The living room was small, crowded with a lounge suite, coffee table, sideboard and a large TV set in one corner. The sideboard was decked with silver-framed photographs, like a rosary of memories; Kylie was there, younger, fresher, chubbier. Hans Heysen and Elioth Gruner prints hung on the walls; someone liked the Australian bush as it had once been. The whole house, Malone guessed, would have fitted three times into the apartment at Circular Quay.

'Kylie's in the shower,' said Monica and waved at the two suitcases by the front door. 'She's going back to the flat, where her and What'shisname –'

'Errol Magee,' said Sheryl, and Malone wondered just how much interest Monica, out here in the backblocks, had taken of Kylie in the high life.

'Yeah. Siddown. You like some coffee? It'll only be instant –'

Malone declined the offer. 'We're here to talk to Kylie. How's she been?'

'Itchy. It's a bit crowded here, we only got two bedrooms. There's me and my husband and our two girls, they're teenagers. Wanna be like their aunty,' she said and grinned, but there was no humour in her. 'Ah, here she is.'

Kylie Doolan stood in the doorway, wrapped in a thick terry-towelling gown, barefooted and frowning. 'What are you doing here?'

Malone ignored that, nodded at the suitcases. 'You're going back to the apartment?'

'Yeah. It's too crowded here.'

'Thanks,' said Monica, drily. 'Any port in a storm, so long's it's not too small.'

'Well, it is. I'm not ungrateful –'

'Put a lid on it, Kylie. You thought you'd got outa here, outa Minto, for good. But they hadda bring you back here to be safe –'

Malone and Sheryl sat silent. Listeners learn more than talkers.

Monica turned to them: 'She always wanted to get away from here, from the time she was in high school. Now she's got my girls talking like her –'

'Don't blame me, they've got minds of their own. You'd of got outa here if it hadn't been for Clarrie –' Her voice had slipped, she sounded exactly like her sister.

'Clarrie,' Monica told the two detectives, 'he's my husband. She never liked him –'

'That's not true – he was just – just –' She flapped a hand.

'Yeah, he was *just*. He never had any ambition, he never looked beyond the end of the street. But he was – he is *solid*. He's a pastrycook,' she was talking to Malone and Sheryl again, 'he works in a baker's shop in Campbelltown. He's good and solid and he loves me and the girls –' Suddenly she buried her face in her hands and started to weep.

'Oh shit!' said Kylie and dropped to her knees and put her arms round her sister. 'I'm sorry, sis. Really.'

The room seemed to get smaller; Malone felt cramped, hedged in. He was no stranger to the intrusion into another family, but the awkwardness never left him. He waited a while, glanced at Sheryl, who had turned her head and was looking out the window. Then he said, 'Get dressed, Kylie. We'll take you back to town.'

She hesitated, then she pressed her sister's shoulders, stood

36

up and went out of the room without looking at Malone and Sheryl.

Sheryl said, 'Monica, did she ever talk to you about Mr Magee?'

Monica dried her eyes on her sleeve, sniffed and, after fumbling, found a tissue in the pocket of her apron. 'Not much.'

'She say anything about him being kidnapped instead of her?'

'She laughed. We both did. But it's not something to laugh about, is it? The maid dead, and that. God knows what's happened to him. You find out anything yet?'

'We're working on it,' said Malone; you never admit ignorance to the voters. 'She ever talk to you about how much he was worth? And now it's all gone?'

Monica raised her eyebrows. She would have been good-looking once, Malone thought, but the years had bruised her. He wondered how tough life had been for her and Clarrie and the girls. Wondered, too, how much she had envied Kylie.

'It's all *gone*? He's broke? I read about him once or twice, he wasn't in the papers much, but I'd see his name and because of Kylie . . . He was worth *millions*!'

'All on paper,' said Sheryl.

Monica laughed, with seemingly genuine humour, no bitterness at all. 'Wait till I tell Clarrie. He'll bake a cake –' She laughed again; she was good-looking for a moment. 'He won't be nasty, he's not like that, but he'll enjoy it. He's not worth much, but it's not paper, he brings it home every week –' She shook her head, then said, 'What's gunna happen to Kylie?'

'I don't know.' Crime victims had to be dropped out of one's knowing. It wasn't lack of compassion. It was a question of self-survival.

'I don't mean in the future, I mean right now.' She was shrewder than he had thought. 'Will she be in –' She hesitated, as if afraid of the word: '– in danger? I'd hate to think I'd let her go back to that –'

'We'll take care of her, there'll be surveillance on her. Eventually –' He shrugged. 'Is she strong?'

'Too strong. She's always known what she wanted.'

'What was that?' said Sheryl.

'Money, the good life, all that sorta stuff. That's the way it is these days, isn't it?' She said it without rancour, resigned to a tide she couldn't stop. 'I see it in my own girls and their friends –'

Malone changed the subject: 'Where are your parents?'

'Dead, both of them. Ten years ago, when Kylie was seventeen. Dad went first, a stroke – he was a battler, always in debt, it just got him down in the end. Mum went two months after, like she'd been waiting for him to go and didn't want to stay on. Both of 'em not fifty. They were like Clarrie and me. Kylie never understood that, you know what I mean?'

'Yes,' said Malone. 'But you've got your girls.'

'Sure,' she said. 'But for how long?'

Then Kylie came back. Malone, who wouldn't have known a Donna Karan from a K-Mart, recognized that she would always dress for the occasion: any occasion. Her dress was discreet, but it made the other two women look as if they had just shopped at St Vincent de Paul. In Monica's case, he felt, the contrast was cruel.

But it seemed that the cruelty was unintentional. Kylie kissed her sister with real affection. 'Say goodbye to Clarrie and the girls for me. I'll call you.'

'Look after yourself,' said Monica.

'Sure,' said Kylie and one knew that she would. Always.

Sheryl picked up the suitcases and Kylie looked at Malone. 'Is that how it is in the police force? The women carry the bags?'

'Only Detective Dallen. It's part of her weights programme.'

He grinned at Sheryl and went ahead of her and Kylie down the garden path. Behind him he heard Kylie say, 'How can you stand him?'

He was out of earshot before Sheryl replied. He went across to Detective-Constable Fernandez, who got out of his car as he approached. 'There'll be no need for further surveillance. I'll call your commander and put it on the computer. We're taking Miss Doolan back to town.'

Fernandez looked past him. 'She doesn't look too upset, sir.'

'Like I told you, that's Miss Doolan.'

Fernandez nodded. 'They'll always be a mystery to me, women.'

'Never try to solve them, Paul. You might be disappointed.'

He went along to his own car. Sheryl had put the suitcases in the boot and she and Kylie stood waiting for him.

'Kylie, did Errol ever wear gloves?'

'You mean in winter, against the cold?'

'No, medical gloves, surgical ones. Did he have a hand condition, dermatitis, something like that?'

'God, no, nothing like that. He had beautiful hands, too good for a man, almost like a woman's. Why?'

'Oh, something's come up. Righto, Sheryl, can you find your way back to town?'

'We just head north, sir. We'll hit either Sydney or Brisbane.'

Serves me right for being a smartarse with a junior rank.

They drove Kylie Doolan back to Sydney. She sat in the back of the car looking out at the passing scene with eyes blank of recognition or nostalgia. She had drained Minto out of her blood.

3

'Before we take you back to your unit –'

'Apartment. Not unit.'

'Apartment, unit, flat,' said Malone. 'What's the difference?'

'Size. Location,' said Kylie. She could sell real estate, he thought. She could sell anything, including herself. 'If I'd stayed in Minto, I'd be living in a flat. Or a unit.'

'Righto. Before we take you back to your *apartment*, I think we might drop in at I-Saw's offices. Where are they?'

'In Milson's Point,' said Sheryl, chopping off a road-rager trying to cut in on her. 'They have a whole building there.'

He might have guessed it; Sheryl always did her homework. 'Milson's Point? When my wife and I were first married we lived in Kirribilli, the other side of the Bridge. In a unit.'

'He's a real card, isn't he?' Kylie said to Sheryl. 'Okay, let's go to I-Saw.'

'Who dreamed up that awful bloody name?' asked Malone.

'Is it any worse than Yahoo, Sausage, names like that?' She was defensive of I-Saw; after all it had kept her in luxury. 'It was a game in the early days, dreaming up smartarse names. There were four-letter ones that almost got on to the companies' register.'

'It's no longer a game,' said Sheryl, taking the car over the Harbour Bridge.

'No,' said Kylie and was abruptly silent.

Milson's Point was another of the original grants to early settlers; modern-day developers wince at the luck of James Milson. He was a farmer from Lincolnshire, who, to his credit, couldn't believe his own luck. Today the Point and its neighbour, Kirribilli, are the most densely settled area north of the harbour. The ghost of James Milson occasionally stands on the Point, beneath the grey rainbow of the bridge, and looks across at the city skyline. Standing behind him, more solidly fleshed, are developers and estate agents wondering how much higher they can push property prices.

Errol Magee had had the sense not to call his building I-Saw House. It had a number, was twelve storeys high and stood between two high-rise blocks of units – excuse me, apartments. Other high-rise buildings ran down to the water's edge, a wall of cliff. Gulls cruised the upper storeys as if looking for ledges on which to nest.

Sheryl, true to her training, parked in a No Standing zone. The three of them got out of the car and went into the building and up to the executive floor. There was no one in the lobby and no one in the lifts. Malone had the abrupt feeling that he was entering a shell.

The executive floor was like none that Malone had ever been on. A receptionist lolled in a chair behind a desk on which were two computers. Behind her were empty work-stations, yards from which the horses had bolted. In the far distance two men sat behind a long table.

'Can I help you?' She was in her early twenties, jeans and a plaid shirt open almost to her belt. She was pretty but appeared to have done everything she could to avoid the label. 'Oh, it's you, Kylie! Hi.'

'These are the police, Louise. Who's in today?'

The girl looked over her shoulder towards the far distance, then turned back. She hadn't risen. 'Just Jared. You want to see him?'

'No,' said Malone, 'she doesn't want to see him. I do, Inspector Malone. Now do you think you could stir yourself and tell Jared we're here and that I'm not a patient man? Right, Detective Dallen?'

'Oh, boss,' said Sheryl, 'you have a terrible temper. Better do what he says, love.'

The girl looked at Kylie as if to say, *Where'd you dig up these two*? Then she got up and sauntered down towards the end of the room.

Malone looked at Kylie. 'Are they all like that who work in IT? Rude and laid back?'

For the first time since leaving Minto she smiled. 'No. But she's a mathematical whiz, she's not really the receptionist. The girl they had had manners.'

'Where's she now?' Malone looked around. 'Where's everybody?'

Kylie shrugged, the smile suddenly gone. She's more worried than she's letting on, thought Malone.

Then Louise, the mathematical whiz, came back. 'He'll see you.'

Malone, Sheryl and Kylie travelled the huge floor, walking between the work-stations that, empty, looked like stylized roofless caves. As they came to the end of the room the two men at the long table stood up.

The taller of the two men came round the table and put out his hand. 'I'm Jared Cragg.' It sounded more like a rock-heap than a name, but Malone, who remembered the good old days of Clarrie and Joe and Smithy, kept his face expressionless. He couldn't imagine this soft-faced, slimly built man being called Craggy. But the soft paw was much firmer in its grip than he had expected. 'It's about Errol? Oh, this is Joe Smith.'

Malone couldn't believe his luck; he shook hands warmly with Smithy. 'Yes, it's about Mr Magee.'

'Well, basically, he's a bastard.' Cragg couldn't have been more than thirty, but he looked as if his last ten years had been flattened and stretched like strudel dough. His eyes were tired and disillusioned, they had none of the spark of the New Economy. 'Have you caught him yet?'

'Caught him?'

'Well, he's basically done a bunk, hasn't he? He knew who was coming in today. Mr Smith is from Ballantine, Ballantine and Kowinsky. The receivers.'

Smith was middle-aged in every way: dress, looks, demeanour. He made Cragg in his dark blue shirt with button-down collar and no tie, his off-white cargo pants and his trainers look like an over-the-hill teenager. But he was good-humoured, as if he had decided that was the only way to combat the depression of throwing businesses out on the street.

'My men are down in the finance department,' he said. 'When we came in this morning all Mr Cragg's staff just up and left, as if we'd come to fumigate the place. No offence, Mr Cragg. It's the way we're always greeted.' He smiled as if to show it was water off a platypus' back. 'One gets used to it.'

42

'It's a regular business, receivership?' said Malone.

'Like cremation,' said Smith and smiled again.

'Who ordered the cremation?'

Smith hesitated, but Malone's look told him: don't hedge, mate. 'The Kunishima Bank. They're Japanese, from Osaka.'

'And what have you found?'

'It's too early to say,' said Smith, hedging. 'But the losses are considerable, otherwise we wouldn't be here.'

Malone looked back at Cragg. 'What do you think happened to Magee?'

Cragg ran a pondering hand over his head. His hair was cut to such a short stubble that it looked like dust; Malone waited for him to look at his hand to see if any had come off. He, too, was hedging. 'Well, basically, from what I read in the papers, the joke on the computers about a ransom for Kylie –' He nodded at her as if she were no more than a prize doll on a sideshow stall.

Malone wondered who had told the media about the messages on the computers. 'You don't want to believe everything you read in the newspapers. So you think he killed the maid on his way out, just as an afterthought?'

'No!' Kylie up till now had remained silent in the background. 'Errol wouldn't hurt a fly –'

'He's hurt three hundred workers,' said Cragg. 'All of them downsized without, basically, any redundancy pay. He's a bastard,' he repeated.

'You haven't answered my question,' said Malone. 'You think he killed the maid?'

'Well, no-o . . .' Cragg all at once looked lost: not just for words, but as if the scene he looked out on, the rows of work-stations, had abruptly turned into a landscape he didn't recognize. 'No, I know it doesn't sound like him – basically –'

'Of course it doesn't!'

Malone motioned for Kylie to keep quiet. 'Could *he* have been kidnapped?'

'Why? Why would anyone want to kidnap him and ask for a

ransom?' Cragg frowned. 'Jesus, everyone's known for the past week we're broke –'

'Maybe one of your staff, or several of them, thought there was some money hidden that would pay for him?' Sheryl had picked up a nod from Malone. Two interrogators were always better than one. It was Malone's old cricket strategy, different-type bowlers from opposite ends. 'Is there any money missing?'

The last question was directed at Smith; he shook his head. 'Too early to tell.' Then he added undiplomatically, 'There often is.'

'Where would it be?' Kylie had lapsed back into sullen silence, but now her nose pointed to the scent of money.

Smith shrugged. 'Anywhere in the world. I'm not saying there *is* any, but if there is our clients have first call on it. They are the major debtors.'

Malone gave Cragg a hard stare, taking over the bowling again. 'Did you know the state of affairs?'

Cragg spread his hands, like a man pushing away cards he had been dealt that had no value. 'I'm not a money man. I came in here two years after Errol had got it off the ground – he wanted my technical experience. I worked in Silicon Valley for two years – I came back here and I could take my pick of jobs. Errol made the best offer.'

'You've got options?' said Sheryl and again after a slight hesitation Cragg nodded. He seemed off-balance with the two-pronged attack. 'On paper you'd have been wealthy. Did you sell when you saw the share price going down?'

'What business is it of yours?' He was growing angry.

'We cover every angle,' said Malone and waited.

Cragg hesitated again, looked at Smith, then back again at Malone and Sheryl. 'Well, basically, yes –'

Then Malone saw the woman come in the door at the far end of the long room and pause by the reception desk. He was long-sighted, but it was a moment before he recognized Caroline Magee. She stared down towards the group, then turned and was about to disappear when Malone called out, almost a shout, 'Mrs Magee!'

'Mrs Magee?' said Cragg. 'Who's that, his mum?'

'He doesn't have a mum,' said Kylie. 'It's his bloody wife!'

'His wife?' Cragg looked at Kylie as if she had suddenly become an unwanted refugee. 'He has a *wife*?'

'I wonder if she controls any of his assets?' said Smith and looked like a prospector who had just come on an unexpected reef. Then he saw Malone look at him and he smiled yet again. 'Sorry. Just a thought.'

Caroline Magee came leisurely down through the desert of work-stations. She has *style*, thought Malone; the sort of style Kylie Doolan would never achieve. She was dressed in a dark-green suit with a cream silk shirt under it; a heavy gold bracelet on her wrist and a thin gold chain round her neck were the only decoration. The dark auburn hair was sleek on her head and the large hazel eyes were cautious but confident. She smiled at Malone, ignoring the others.

'Hello, Inspector. What do we have – good news or bad news?'

'No news so far.' Malone introduced her to Sheryl, Cragg and Smith. Kylie had stepped back a pace or two, as if into a frigid zone. 'Has he contacted you?'

'Not a word.' Then she turned to Cragg. 'Errol mentioned you, Mr Cragg. Said you held the company together.'

Smith laughed; he was the most jovial accountant Malone had ever met. Cragg gave him a sour look, then said, 'I think Errol was kidding, Mrs Magee. While I was holding it together, he was basically pulling it apart.'

Caroline nodded agreeably. 'That would be Errol. Wouldn't it, Miss Doolan?'

Kylie thawed, but only a degree. 'He always treated me okay.'

'One can see that,' said Caroline, spraying freezer. Then she turned to Smith. 'Will there be any debt?'

'Oh, I should think so.' Christ, thought Malone, I bet he goes to cemeteries and dances on graves. 'Perhaps you could spare me half an hour for a talk?'

She returned his smile. 'Forget it, Mr Smith. There's nothing in my name nor with my signature on it. Did he have you sign anything?' She drew Kylie in again from Antarctica.

Kylie suddenly looked pinched, even sick. 'Only for credit cards.'

'Jesus!' Cragg ran his hand over his head. 'He's left us all holding the can!'

'Not me,' said Caroline.

Then Sheryl, who had been silent up till now, said, 'Did he ever talk with you about places he'd like to go to, to live in retirement?'

'Like Majorca? It's a little crowded there, isn't it? But then, it's easier to get lost in a crowd, isn't it?'

Malone wondered what sort of man Errol Magee had been that neither his wife nor his girlfriend appeared too upset at his disappearance. But then as he and Detective Constable Fernandez had agreed, women were a mystery.

'We'll find him eventually, Mrs Magee,' he said. 'We sometimes have unsolved murders on our books, but when we know who the murderer is, we usually find him. No matter how long it takes.'

'So you basically think he killed the maid,' said Cragg.

'We never use the word *basically* in Homicide, Mr Cragg. With us, it either is or it ain't. Not basically.'

'I don't believe Errol killed Juanita,' said Kylie.

'Neither do I,' said Caroline.

They looked at each other as if they had heard disembodied voices. They will never be friends, thought Malone, but they'll defend Magee if only because they want to get to him before we do. And he began to wonder if the women, separately, knew more than they were telling.

Then the computer on the table behind Cragg began to print

out a message. Malone stepped round Cragg and read it: *There's a call for you, Jared. They won't speak to anyone but you.*

He looked towards the far end of the room. Louise had sat back from the computer on her desk and was looking towards them. Crumbs, he thought, they even talk to each other on the screens. 'It's for you, Mr Cragg. The phone.'

'Thanks,' said Cragg sarcastically and picked up one of the three phones on the table. 'Put them through, Louise.'

Then: 'Yes, this is Jared Cragg. Who's that? Who?'

Then he looked at Malone, nodded at a second phone and reached across and pressed a button. Malone picked up the second phone.

'Look –' Cragg was showing no agitation; Malone, watching him, had to admire him. 'How do we know you've got Mr Magee?'

'He was the one who gave us your name,' said the woman at the other end of the line. It was an Australian voice, Malone remarked, no accent. Over the past few years the police had started to divide crims up into ethnic groups, much to the loud disapproval of ethnic groups. 'He's all right, Mr Cragg. He hasn't been harmed – not so far. He said you'd be able to raise the money we're asking. Five million dollars, US.'

Cragg raised his eyebrows at Malone, who gestured at him to keep talking. 'US? Why US?'

'You know what the Aussie dollar is like, Mr Cragg. Up and down like a yo-yo. Five million, American.'

'Mr Magee knows we don't have that sort of money right now, US or Aussie. He would've told you that, right?' There was silence at the other end. 'Right? Well, I'm confirming it. Name a reasonable sum and I'll see what we can raise.'

'You can raise the five million. Try your partners, the Kunishima Bank. I'll call back at five this evening. Have the money by then.'

'Just a moment,' said Malone, cutting in. 'This is Detective-Inspector Malone, of Homicide. Put Mr Magee himself on.'

The woman laughed, a pleasant laugh. 'You're kidding, aren't you? Get lost, copper. This is between us and Magee's company.'

'Did you kill the Magee maid? That puts it between you and me.'

There was a moment's silence, then the phone went dead.

Cragg said, 'Can you trace that call?'

'Maybe the area, but not the actual phone. Sheryl, get them started on that.'

'Right away, sir.' She checked the number of I-Saw, then went quickly down to the reception desk.

'Did you recognize the woman's voice?' Malone asked Cragg.

'A *woman*?' Kylie's voice rose. 'Holy shit, he's got *another* woman?'

'It's getting crowded,' said Caroline Magee and there was just a hint of a smile around her lips.

Malone ignored them both. 'If they're demanding ransom for Magee, if they *do* have him, why the pantomime of the ransom notes on the computers for Miss Doolan?' But he was talking to himself; he wasn't looking for an answer from the others. 'Could the woman on the phone be someone who works here?'

'I didn't recognize the voice,' said Cragg. 'You still think someone from here organized all this?'

'I don't know. We consider every possibility and then start eliminating them. I still think the strongest possibility is that Errol organized his own kidnapping and it all went wrong when the maid was killed. Maybe the woman is in on the scam with him —'

'Bastard!' said Kylie.

Malone had been thinking aloud, something no cop should ever do. He realized it and tried to get his thoughts and his tongue under control. He looked at Caroline: 'Did he ever mention another woman to you?'

'Only Miss Doolan,' said Caroline and made it sound as if *Miss Doolan* were no more than *graffiti* on a wall.

Malone swallowed his smile, turned back to Cragg. 'I want a list of everyone who's worked here in the past twelve months.'

'Everyone?'

'Everyone. It shouldn't be any problem, Mr Cragg.' He nodded at the deserted work-stations, every one with its own computer. 'Not with Information Technology.'

He spoke with the sarcasm of a troglodyte who still scratched sketches on the wall of his cave. Cragg and Smith looked at him as if they saw him exactly like that.

'Can we help?' asked Smith.

'Just see no money goes out, five million or even a dollar. No ransom, unless you talk to us first. We'll be in touch.'

He walked down the long room to where Sheryl waited for him at the reception desk.

'They've started the trace,' she said. 'But they're not hopeful.'

'Good,' said Malone, but entertained no hope. 'Have you got Louise's full name?'

'Louise Cobcroft.'

'Why do you want my name?' Louise was standing at her desk, antagonism in every line of her slim body. She had drawn her hair back, holding it in place with a headband, and it improved her looks, showing the fine bonework in her face. Her eyes were almost glassy in their severity. 'What's going on?'

'Louise, you stayed on the phone when that call came through for Mr Cragg. I saw you, you listened to every word. Do you usually do that on your boss' calls?'

'No-o.' She backed down, but only an inch.

'Did you recognize that woman's voice? One of your workmates, for instance?'

'No, I didn't.'

'Why were you so interested in the call? Did the woman mention Mr Magee when she first came on the line?'

'No-o.' She was looking less and less confident.

49

'How well did you know Mr Magee? Did you work closely with him?'

'Yes.'

'How close?' said Sheryl, coming in at the other end of the pitch. She's learning, thought Malone, she's going to be a good change bowler.

'We'd work at night together –'

'That all?'

Suddenly all the stiffness went out of Louise. She glanced down towards the far end of the room. The group there were looking in the direction of Malone and the two women. Louise sighed and turned back to Malone and Sheryl. 'Okay, sometimes we'd hold hands –'

Malone grinned. 'How tightly?'

Unexpectedly she smiled; it changed her whole face, made her very attractive. 'It was nothing serious . . . He had Kylie. But now and again one thing would lead to another . . . You know how it is –' She looked at Sheryl, not at the old man beside her. 'Basically, just one-night stands.'

'Here amongst the work-stations?' said Malone.

'No. Up till yesterday the work-stations were in operation twenty-four hours a day. He'd take me home . . .'

'Did he hold hands with any of the other women on the staff?'

'I don't know. He might have . . . And that's all I'm going to tell you. Here comes Kylie. Don't tell her.'

'You talking about me?' said Kylie as she reached them.

'Only sympathetically,' said Sheryl, reacting quicker than Malone. 'You must be terribly hurt by what's happened to Errol.'

'Oh, I am,' said Kylie, and sounded as if she might also be pleased. 'What's going to happen to you, Louise?'

'Oh, I'll be okay,' said Louise, settling back into her chair. 'In this game you're always ready to jump. It's the nature of it.'

'Basically,' said Malone and then from another age asked,

'Don't you ever think of long-service leave and superannuation?'

'What are they?' she said, but gave him the pleasant smile again.

4

Darlene hung up the phone and stepped out of the phone-box into the glare of the Sutherland street. She put on her dark glasses and stepped under the shade of a shop awning. She only knew this southern suburb from passing through it on the way down to the bush cottage. She was a stranger here.

'We've got to get right away from where we usually are,' her mum had said. 'We don't make any calls from anywhere near home. I dunno whether they can trace phone calls, but we're not gunna take any chances. Don't use your mobile.'

Shirlee had organized them all, right after breakfast. First, she had spoken to Phoenix, who always wanted to argue: 'You go back up to Hurstville and check in at Centrelink, tell 'em you're still looking for a job. Then go and bank your dole cheque –'

'Ah shit, Mum –'

'Wash your mouth out,' she said, washing dishes.

'Well, for Crissakes, Mum, we're gunna be rich – why the fuck – why the hell've I gotta worry about my dole cheque? Or fuck – or Centrelink? I'm not innarested in a job now.'

'We don't arouse suspicion, that's why. So none of the nosy neighbours back in Hurstville can talk –'

'Mum,' said Corey, lolling back in a chair at the breakfast table, 'why d'you think anyone's gunna suspect us? You think they got guys out there, watching Pheeny don't turn up at Centrelink?'

'As for you,' said his mum, the general, 'you be certain, you go back to town, you walk around like you got a sore back. Men on workers' compo, the insurance companies, they got private

51

investigators watching you like hawks. I seen it on TV a coupla months ago.'

Corey worked for a haulage company as its chief mechanic. A week ago he had conveniently strained his back and had gone to a doctor, recommended by one of his workmates, who, for the right consideration, would give a death certificate to a glowing-with-health gymnast.

'How long we gunna give 'em to make up their minds to pay the ransom?'

'Four, five days, a week at the most. They're gunna bargain. I been reading about Big Business, them takeover deals. They bargain for weeks. They do something, I dunno what it means, it's called due diligence.'

'Mum,' said Darlene, putting on her face, looking at it in her vanity mirror, wondering what she would look like when she was a million dollars richer, 'this isn't big business. It's a ransom, five million dollars. Petty cash to them.'

'You been working too long at that bank,' said Corey. 'You dunno what real money means.'

She put away her mirror and lipstick. 'We can't sit around here looking after His Nibs, feeding him, taking him to the toilet . . . I'll give 'em a deadline. I'll call 'em today, give 'em till five o'clock. They want more time, I'll say till five p.m. tomorrow. That'll be the absolute deadline.'

'And they don't come through?' said Corey. 'What do we do then?'

'We do him,' said Phoenix and nodded towards the front of the house.

His brother and sister looked at him and his mother paused at the kitchen sink, a wet plate in her hand. 'I think we'll have to talk to Chantelle.'

Chantelle was their contact, the one who had told them where the money was. Or where they had thought it was.

Now Darlene paused under the shop awning and wondered if she should go on into the city. She had phoned in first thing this morning to the bank and told her boss she was not well, but would be in at work tomorrow. *Bloody women*, had been his only comment and he had hung up in her ear.

She was worried that the police were already on the case; but that was because of the stupid bungle, the killing of the maid. Sometimes she wondered at the intelligence of her brothers. Corey had all his marbles, but at times he could be as cold-blooded as their mother. Pheeny was two or three marbles short and she wondered how he would keep his mouth shut after they had collected the ransom money and let Errol Magee go. But that was in the future, down the track, as Pheeny, who never thought beyond tomorrow, would say.

She and her brothers had been petty crims ever since their early teens. They had never been encouraged to take up thieving; but neither had they been discouraged. Their mother, and their father when he wasn't doing time, had looked upon it as part of growing up, like acne, or in her own case, period pains. Darlene herself had never felt any conscience; if money or clothes or make-up was there to be taken, it was taken. She had never stolen from workmates, but that had been only because it was stupid. Her mother, in the only piece of advice she had given on how to get ahead in the world, had told her that.

She had never gone in for breaking and entering, as Corey and Pheeny had, but that had been more laziness than conscience. Their father had used guns in his hold-ups, but Darlene had never thought much of him anyway, let alone loved him. When her mother had told her, almost off-handedly, that she was getting rid of their father, she hadn't enquired how or why. He would not be missed, she had told herself, and that had been true.

Shirlee had supplemented the family budget with stolen credit cards, ATM cards and shoplifting. None of them had ever been caught, not even dumb Pheeny. Of course, Clyde had been caught and jailed half a dozen times, but that was to be expected; he had been a loudmouth and thought he had flair. Flair and the loud mouth had landed him in jail and, finally, in a grave.

Shirlee had been firm about one thing: no drugs. She knew the money that was in drugs, but that had been her one moral principle: no drug dealing. And Darlene had always admired her mum for it, as if she were a volunteer aid worker. The family had gone on, making adequate but constant money to supplement what Darlene and Corey earned by working, and then had come this *big* opportunity.

Now she walked back to the railway station. She passed a newsagent's and saw the billboard: *E-Tycoon On Run.* She smiled and a young man, passing her, paused and smiled back. She looked at him, puzzled, then gave him a glare that sent him on his way. She had had half a dozen boyfriends, but they had been only passing fancies, one or two good in bed but none of them a long-term prospect. She would wait and see what she could attract with a million dollars.

In the meantime Chantelle needed to be consulted. She bought a ticket, went out on to the platform and waited for a train. A few minutes and then a loudspeaker announced: 'The 10.48 for Central is running fourteen minutes late. Good luck.'

She had enough sense of humour to smile at the thought of taking a train, no matter how late, to discuss a ransom of five million dollars.

5

'What did you do?' asked Lisa.

'I should have done a lobotomy on him,' said Romy. 'When he told me –' Her voice trailed off.

The two women were having lunch in the pavilion restaurant in Centennial Park. They were surrounded by other diners: women, children, a few older men who looked like retirees: it was not a restaurant that catered for serious dining or serious deals. But both Lisa and Romy Clements looked serious.

Romy picked at her crab salad. She was a good-looking woman edging towards that mark where her age and her measurements might complement each other. She had an air of quiet confidence and competence to her that made her a success in her job; but today she was a wife and it was a long time since Lisa had seen her so – not unconfident, but unsure.

'Why are men so desperate for money?'

'Come on, Romy. Not just men. Women, too. I don't think *we* were – not my generation.'

'Nor mine.'

They sat a moment in satisfied contemplation of their generation's lack of greed. Out beyond the windows of the restaurant the huge park, a green oasis, was restless with horse riders, cyclists, joggers and a swarm of small children shredding the air with hysterical laughter. At a nearby table a young mother was telling a three-year-old boy not to stuff his mouth so full. The boy looked at her uncomprehendingly, as if to tell her that was what mouths were for.

'What are you going to do?'

'What can I do?' Romy chewed on a piece of crab. 'The money's gone. It won't bankrupt us – but I felt like bankrupting him. Cutting his balls off with a scalpel.'

Lisa smiled. 'That would have –'

'I know.' Romy, too, smiled; but wryly. 'Cutting off my nose to spite my face . . . The irony is, this morning they brought in the girl from the Magee apartment, the one he killed. I did the prelim autopsy on her. That was just before Russ came out to the morgue and told me what he'd done. Then I called you. I hope you didn't mind?'

Lisa reached across and pressed her friend's hand. The Dutchwoman and the German had bonded almost from the moment they had met, civilized Europeans amongst the Australoids. Both of them were better educated than their husbands, had more sophisticated tastes; yet both were happily married and each knew she had made the right choice. If either of them were nostalgic for their heritage, they never told anyone, not even each other.

'I didn't say anything to Russ,' said Romy, 'but my father was greedy.'

Her father had died six months ago in jail, where he was serving a life sentence for murder. She rarely mentioned him, ashamed of him and his deed but bound to him by childhood love when he had been a doting father. She had gone four or five times a year to visit him in jail, coming back home and saying nothing to her husband. And Clements had never questioned her about the visits. It had been he and Malone who had arrested her father.

'Russ isn't greedy,' said Lisa. 'Not really.'

'Yes, he is. Or was. He told me he wanted to make the money to set up a trust fund for Amanda, but I didn't believe him. And he knew I didn't.' She pushed her plate away from her. 'Why am I eating? I can't taste anything.'

'Sixty thousand dollars?' said Lisa. 'Are you tasting the money?'

Romy frowned at her. 'What sort of question is that?'

'I'm Dutch, darling – we're supposed to be careful with money. Not as careful as Scobie – but who is? If he lost sixty thousand dollars, you'd be doing a post-mortem on him at the morgue.'

She looked out the big glass walls again. These 500 acres, 'a countryside in the midst of a city,' as the originator of the park called it, were only five minutes walk from her house and she came here often on her own. She found isolation here, even amongst the riders, the joggers, the cyclists and the picnickers; her own space, as her daughters would have called it. She would sit beside one of the small lakes and watch the ducks bobbing their heads and the swans with their question-mark necks and sometimes doze off under the warm blanket of the sun and forget the world that, though it rarely touched her and the children, was where Scobie lived his working life. Where murder and greed and betrayal signposted the city in which they lived, where even this 'countryside' had known murder to shred its peace.

She said abruptly, surprising herself, 'He's up for promotion.'

'Who?' Romy was adrift in her own thoughts.

'Scobie. He says Russ will probably take over Homicide.'

It was Romy's turn to stare out through the glass walls. 'Do you ever wish that they had some other job? Traffic or Fraud, something without murder to it?'

'Often. But would you give up Forensic, cutting people up to see how and maybe why they died?'

Romy took her time. 'No-o.'

'Then we put up with what we've got. You could have chosen much worse than Russ.'

Romy pulled her plate back in front of her, picked at the crab salad again. 'I still could cut his balls off.'

A boy about seven paused by their table. 'Whose balls?'

'Yours. Get lost,' said Romy and started to laugh. Lisa joined in.

Diners at other tables looked at them, two very attractive women sharing a happy day out on their own.

At a far table a mother said to her seven-year-old son, 'What did the lady say to you?'

'She said she'd cut my balls off.'

'Serves you right for speaking to strange women,' said his father. 'Remember that, when you grow up.'

He looked across the restaurant and wondered what sort of exciting sex life those two good-looking women led.

'What are you looking at?' said his wife.

'The ducks,' he said and went back to his long black coffee, which did nothing for the libido.

Chapter Three

1

Malone and Sheryl Dallen delivered Kylie Doolan back to the Magee apartment, where Paula Decker was waiting for them. Malone had phoned her before leaving Minto and she had sounded as if she was jumping at the chance to being involved in the Magee case again.

'I'll move in with Miss Doolan,' she said, looking around the apartment like a prospective buyer. 'My boss okayed it.'

'Nobody asked me,' said Kylie.

'Miss Doolan,' said Malone; his patience with women had been long learned, 'this is for your protection. You may still be on the kidnap list.'

She stared at him as if he were threatening her; then she abruptly turned and went into one of the bedrooms. It was the wrong room. A moment later she came out and went into the main bedroom.

Malone looked at Sheryl and Paula Decker and shrugged. 'Don't let her out of your sight, Paula. I'm going to make a call.'

'The toilet's that way,' said Sheryl, nodding.

'A phone call,' he said and saw her grinning. She was enjoying working with him and he with her, but he would have to see she kept her place. Maybe the word had already got around that he was on his way out of Homicide. The Police Service had always been secretive, even about official business, and the times had not changed.

He went into the kitchen. The chalked outline of Juanita Marcos' body had been scrubbed out; the kitchen looked almost too spick and span, like a magazine advertisement, to have ever been used; all that was missing was the copper-bottomed saucepan that had killed Juanita Marcos. The ransom message on the kitchen's computer had not been scrubbed out, but it was almost irrelevant now, like last week's grocery list.

He checked his notebook, dialled a Harbord number, a beach suburb north of the harbour. 'Hello? Blackie? Inspector Malone.'

'G'day, Mr Malone.' Blackie Ovens had been a stand-over man, an iron-bar expert, who had worked for Jack Aldwych for almost fifty years, one way or another. He was now valet, butler, chauffeur and general handyman to the old retired criminal boss. 'The boss ain't here. He goes in once a week to the office, to talk with Jack Junior.'

'How is he, Blackie? I haven't seen him in almost a year.' He and the old crim were almost friends, as cops and criminals often are, but never social friends.

'He's getting old, Mr Malone. But ain't we all? He's really slowed down, spends all his time reading. Reading *books*. He sent me out the other day to buy – whatyoucallthemthings? Bookmarks. Like he used to send me out once to buy bullets. Don't tell him I said that.'

'You know me, Blackie. I've never grassed on a mate in my life.'

'We're mates?'

'We are now, Blackie. Phone him and tell him I'm coming. They still in the AMP Tower?'

'Yeah. Up there with all the respectable ones.' He laughed, dry as wind on dust. 'Makes you laugh, don't it?'

'Not in Sydney, Blackie.'

He hung up, left Sheryl and Paula Decker with Kylie Doolan and walked round the quay, along the colonnade under the expensive restaurants where IT millionaires once, and some still did, dined, and up the hill, past the Police Museum where he had once worked when it had been a police station, to the AMP Tower. This end of town was where most of the city's tallest buildings had been erected; buried beneath them, somewhere down there in the foundations, were the colony's beginnings. Jack Aldwych sat in his office forty-five floors and several basement floors above the ghosts of crims of long ago. The ghosts never bothered him, as Malone well knew.

'Scobie, I'd begun to think you'd forgotten me!'

'Never, Jack. I've got framed running sheets on you on my office wall. Hello, Jack,' he said to Jack Junior and shook hands with both men. 'Still a great view from here.'

'We deserve it,' said Aldwych, but his smile was self-mocking rather than smug.

Landfall Holdings, which covered a multitude of companies and several sins, occupied the whole of this floor. This corner office, that of the managing director Jack Junior, had a view of the harbour that made the view from Magee's apartment look like a small postcard.

The receptionist, an elegant brunette who was the granddaughter of one of Aldwych's old brothel madams, brought Malone coffee and gave him a smile that her grandmother would have charged him for.

'Thanks, Valerie. How's your grandmother?'

'Fine, thanks, Mr Malone. She's in a nursing home, reminiscing with some of her old clients.' She widened her smile to include all three men and went out.

'A treasure,' said Aldwych. 'Just like her grandmother. So what can we do for you, Scobie?'

'Seven or eight years ago, Jack, maybe nine, you had a run-in with a Japanese bank, the Kunishima Bank.'

'What a memory,' Aldwych said to his son; then he looked back at Malone. 'That in your running sheets on me?'

'No, Jack. I'm just relying on memory. They were a bit suspect at the time, weren't they?'

It was Jack Junior who answered: 'Yes. But they've established a steady reputation since then. They work quietly, no blowing their own trumpet.'

'What's their main business?'

'Investment. They're also into venture capital. This is something to do with I-Saw, right?'

'You're as sharp as your old man,' said Malone.

'I taught him,' said Aldwych and for a moment actually looked like a proud father. Which would have shocked some of his old colleagues and some cops. 'What's on your mind?'

'They've sent the receivers into I-Saw.'

'That's no surprise,' said Jack Junior.

'What else is on your mind?' Aldwych had been a successful crim because his mind had always been two steps ahead. Which was why, having turned respectable, he was so far ahead that no one could accurately guess his wealth.

Malone always liked dealing with the old man; at cricket he had always enjoyed bowling to a formidable batsman. 'We're not sure whether Errol Magee, of I-Saw, was kidnapped or whether he's pulling a scam. That's just between us, okay?' He trusted Aldwych, who could have run any intelligence organization, but he wasn't sure about Jack Junior. Honesty, and Jack Junior had the reputation of being honest, can breed leaks. 'But whoever's behind it, whether it's Magee or someone else, they're asking five million ransom. They suggested the Kunishima Bank might come good.'

The two Aldwyches looked at each other, then the father looked back at Malone and shook his head. 'No way, Scobie. They wouldn't bail out Buddha.'

'Why?' said Malone and tried to look innocent, no mean feat for a Homicide cop. 'The *yakuza* still run it?'

'As I said, what a memory.'

'Jack, I worked on that case eight or nine years ago. They were just getting started, but we knew the *yakuza* had something to do with them. They're much more respectable now, right?'

'Yes,' said Jack Junior. 'But the *yakuza* still runs them. It's their money behind the bank.'

Out on the harbour there was a faint bellow of protest from a ferry as some idiot on a water-sled shot across the front of it. A window cleaner abseiled down outside, like a suicide who had changed his mind and was trying to slow his dive.

Then Malone slowly nodded his head. 'You rich buggers really know how to complicate things.'

Aldwych grinned. 'Not us, Scobie. I thought you blokes would of known.'

'Fraud probably does. Homicide, we don't go looking for extra worries. Have the *yakuza* gone in for stand-over stuff out here?'

'Not the way they do, or used to do, in Japan. They don't pack company AGMs and threaten shareholders,' said Jack Junior. 'Nothing like that. But yes, behind scenes we've heard they apply pressure.'

'And Securities and the A-Triple-C haven't enquired into them?'

'If they have, none of it has got into the media.'

'These blokes are sophisticated, Scobie,' said Aldwych. 'And rich. Some bloke wants to shoot his mouth off, they either make him disappear or they buy him off. Either way, he disappears.'

'Would they buy Errol Magee, pay the ransom?'

'I doubt it,' said Jack Junior.

'Have you had any dealings with them?'

It was a delicate question and Malone did his best to ask it delicately. Once again the two Aldwyches looked at each other, then Jack Junior said, 'They approached us once when they heard about a project we had going. We said no.'

'Politely,' said Aldwych with a grin.

Malone took his time, observing the two men. They were both handsome, the father more ruggedly so: he had been scarred by razor, club and bullet. Jack Junior was smoother, immaculately dressed, expensively barbered. There was no mistaking their relationship, but Aldwych had got older, even somehow smaller, since Malone had seen him last. Or was it that the old man had lost the menace he once had? For twenty years he had boasted he had retired but not reformed and one had been prepared to believe him. But now he looked – *soft*? Malone wondered.

'Can you give me the name of someone to see at Kunishima? Someone with clout.'

'Mr Okada.' Jack Junior had hesitated a moment, but his father had nodded at him. Aldwych might have retired, but he was still the boss. 'He's not *yakuza*, but he knows where the money comes from.'

'Is he likely to open up on Mr Magee?'

'Good luck, Scobie,' said Aldwych and in his smile there was a hint of the gang boss he had once been. 'You could read my face when we ran into each other –'

'Like an open book, Jack.'

'It's not like that with a Japanese face. Good luck.'

2

Malone stood outside the AMP Tower for almost five minutes before he took out his mobile and rang Clements at Homicide. 'Meet me outside the Aurora building in twenty minutes. We're going to talk to a man at the Kunishima Bank.'

'You told me I was to stay off the case –'

'I need you, mate, you're the finance expert.' He explained what he had learned in the last half-hour.

'Do we mention the *yakuza* if we're getting nowhere with this Mr Okada?'

'Let's see how we go.'

He walked up Macquarie Street, past the brass plates of hundreds of doctors whose consulting rooms looked out on the Botanic Gardens; you could stand by a window and be told you had six months to live and look out on the greenest spot in the city where life came out of the earth year after year after year. He found a bench and sat on it, soaking up the sun. It would never have occurred to him to spend the time having a coffee; his throat and taste buds were never as dry as his pocket. Starbucks would never have come to Australia if there had been a nation of abstainers like him.

Clements arrived within twenty minutes in an unmarked car. He parked it in a No Parking zone, the Police Service's refuge, and walked back to where Malone sat waiting for him. 'You think we're gunna get anything outa this Okada guy?'

'We've come up against dead-ends so far. Another one won't make any difference.'

'Now you're about to be promoted, are you losing your – what's the word? – *enthusiasm* for this case? You'd rather leave it to me?'

'I'll let you know,' said Malone, non-committedly.

The Aurora complex is a Renza Piano-designed project that stands where a black glass block, known as the Black Stump, had once stood. The Black Stump had housed government departments, or their senior officers; the State Premier's office had been on an upper floor. There Malone had begun the journey that had taken him to London to arrest the Australian High Commissioner for murder and where he had met Lisa. As he passed through the doors of the Aurora building the Celt in him sensed the past, like fog on the terracotta walls of the foyer.

The Kunishima Bank had two floors high up in the building; it never had to worry about hoi polloi coming in off the street to make a deposit or complain about bank fees. The receptionist was Japanese, though not a geisha; she was as smart and modern as Valerie at Landfall Holdings. She was polite but firm: 'Mr Okada never sees anyone without an appointment.'

'Miss,' said Malone, equally polite, 'this is a police badge I am showing you. Now tell Mr Okada we'd like to see him right away, *immediately*, or all hell is going to break loose.'

Her look was as dead as a blank computer screen; then she turned and went into an inner office. 'All hell is gunna break loose?' said Clements. 'I must remember that one.'

'I heard a TV cop say it the other night.'

The receptionist was gone for several minutes and Malone started to become impatient. Clements picked up a business magazine from a side table and leafed through it. 'It says here, globalization is the new imperialism. History just repeats itself, it says.'

'Everything repeats itself,' said Malone, who believed it.

Then the receptionist came back, gave him and Clements a small bow and said, 'Mr Okada will see you.'

Mr Okada was a Westernized Japanese. He was short and broad with thinning black hair, like a splintered helmet. He wore a double-breasted blue suit, a white shirt and, though Malone didn't recognize it, an Oxford University tie. With him were two other men, both small and thin and immaculately dressed. Real bankers, thought Malone, and wondered which one was the man from the *yakuza*. For he was sure that was the reason for the delay in seeing him and Clements.

'This is about Mr Errol Magee?' Okada came straight to the point, but with a smile. He had lively eyes that suggested he might have a sense of humour, but he wasn't going to start joking, not yet. Malone hadn't expected him to be so blunt, but maybe he had become Australianized as well as Westernized. Circumlocution was not a local habit, except with politicians. 'You have found him? Safe, I hope?'

'No, Mr Okada,' said Malone and looked at the other two men.

Okada smiled again. 'Forgive me. Mr Nakasone and Mr Tajiri.'

The two men were not thoroughly Westernized; they bowed, faces impassive. Malone almost bowed in return, but checked himself and just nodded.

'No, we haven't found Mr Magee yet. We aren't even sure if he was kidnapped or arranged the kidnapping.' He waited for a reaction, but there was none. *You can't read a Japanese face* . . . He went on, 'There was a call from a woman this morning, asking for five million dollars ransom. We don't know

65

whether she is part of a kidnap gang or whether she is in collusion with Mr Magee. She suggested you should be approached for the ransom.'

The impassive faces cracked. There was merriment from Okada and even Nakasone and Tajiri smiled. 'Oh, Inspector –' Okada got his merriment under control. 'Our bank – ransom Mr Magee? Why?'

'The woman must have got word from someone. Mr Magee, maybe?'

All five men were seated, on opposite sides of a large desk; like delegates at an international conference. This was a corner office, like Jack Junior's, with a view over the Botanic Gardens and out to the heads of the harbour. It was not furnished Japanese style: there was thick carpet on the floor, the desk was big and heavy with a leather top, the chairs leathered with comfort. Only the Japanese prints on the walls suggested Okada might pine for home.

'Mr Okada –' Clements spoke for the first time: taking up the bowling. 'We're from Homicide –'

'Homicide?' All three looked puzzled.

'Yeah, Homicide. You heard or read about the murder of Mr Magee's maid?'

'Oh, the maid.' Okada sounded as if a budgerigar or some other household pet had been despatched. 'Oh, of course. So she is your interest?'

'Part of it, Mr Okada. If she hadn't been killed, we would not be on the case. But now we are, we have to cover every aspect of it. How much did Kunishima invest in Mr Magee and I-Saw?'

Okada on the surface was thoroughly Westernized; but he had read the teachings of Yamamoto Jocho in *Hagakure*. He knew the dignity of the closed mouth; but it had nothing to do with wanting to be a *samurai*. A closed mouth told no secrets; it also gave one time to think. Despite the suddenly impassive face, Malone and Clements could see that Mr Okada was thinking. Deeply.

'I'm afraid that is confidential,' he said at last.

'No one can be more confidential than we are,' said Clements.

Okada smiled again, as if surprised that a police officer could have a sense of humour. 'I'm sure you can, Sergeant. But we are in different territory –'

'No, we're not, Mr Okada –'

Malone wondered if he should step in, but decided to wait and give Clements his head. The big man had knocked down stone walls before, not always with a sledgehammer. Nakasone and Tajiri had shifted a little uneasily in their chairs. *Go for it, Russ* . . .

'You see,' said Clements, 'we've done due diligence on your bank and its investments here. I-Saw is your only bad investment. Three hundred million dollars, your original investment, has gone down the drain.'

'Then why are you asking?'

'Because in Homicide we're like you bankers – we like everything confirmed. It helps in prosecution.'

Okada was impressed. 'How do you know so much, Sergeant?'

Malone got Clements out of that one before the latter might be tempted to explain how he had lost sixty thousand dollars: 'You'd be surprised how much investigation we have done before we got to Kunishima.' And how little the investigation had produced. 'We don't want the Securities Commission getting in our way – and I'm sure you don't, either. So let's talk friendly, just between ourselves, and see what we come up with.'

Okada stared at him, not hostilely, then he looked at Nakasone, who said something in Japanese. Okada listened, nodded, then looked back at Malone. 'Mr Nakasone is from our head office in Osaka. He doesn't speak English.'

Not bloody much he doesn't, thought Malone. He had read too many faces, Japanese or otherwise, to know when a conversation was not understood. Nakasone and Tajiri had understood every word that had been said since he and Clements had come into the office.

'So what has he suggested? From head office?'

'He has suggested we co-operate –'

Up to a point: it wasn't said, but Malone read it.

'Mr Magee has been less than honest with Kunishima. As you may know –' Okada looked at Clements, as if recognizing he was the businessman '– the share price for I-Saw has gone down and down over the past six months. We bought from anyone who wanted to sell, but we couldn't prevent the slide. Then we found that one of the biggest sellers was Mr Magee – he had shares under other names. But the money wasn't coming back into I-Saw. It had just disappeared. Forty million dollars.'

'Gone overseas?' said Clements, sounding unsurprised.

Okada nodded. 'We presume so. But where?' He spread his hands, a Mediterranean gesture; Nakasone looked sideways at him, as if he had emigrated. These fellers don't trust each other, thought Malone. 'Switzerland, Hong Kong, the Bahamas, the Caymans? Who knows? We are searching, but so far, no success.'

'If we find Mr Magee,' said Malone, 'what do you plan to do?'

Okada looked at Nakasone and Tajiri, said something in Japanese; all three men smiled. Then he looked back at the two detectives. 'Persuade him to tell us where the money is.'

'So you won't pay the five million ransom, even to get him back to persuade him to tell you where the forty million is?'

Okada continued smiling. 'As you Aussies say, no way, mate.'

Only then did Malone say, 'And what about your backers, the *yakuza*? What will they say?'

Suddenly all the smiles were gone; the faces turned to stone. A gull appeared outside the big window, fluttering close to the glass as if trying to mate with its own reflection. Then, as if frightened by the atmosphere inside the room, it abruptly swept away.

'You see, Mr Okada,' said Malone, 'as Sergeant Clements has said, we've done due diligence.'

'Un-due diligence, I think, Inspector. You are wrong, very wrong.' The *r*s were indistinct, he had slipped back into his nationality.

Malone, like most of his countrymen, was impressed with foreigners who spoke English so well, even if they had some difficulty with certain letters. He was also impressed that Nakasone and Tajiri appeared to have understood what Okada had said.

'I don't think so, Mr Okada. We have our sources.'

The three bankers looked at each other. The question could be read on the unreadable faces: what sources? where? Then Okada looked back at Malone: 'This meeting is over, Inspector.'

He stood up and bowed, suddenly no longer Westernized, and Nakasone and Tajiri followed suit. Malone hesitated, then he and Clements rose.

'We'll be back, sir. Take that for granted.'

He turned abruptly, rudely, and walked out, followed by Clements. Neither of them spoke as they crossed the reception area nor in the crowded lift as they went down to the lobby. There Malone paused and let out his breath, as if he had been holding it for the past several minutes.

'What do you think?'

'Like you said, we'll have to come back –' Clements led the way out into sunshine; it was like a blessing. 'I think Okada is genuine, a banker. The other two –'

'Nakasone probably is, too. But Tajiri –'

'Don't *yakuza* cover themselves in tattoos? He had skin like a baby.'

'He had eyes like a snake . . . Remember the Casement case? The last time we heard of Kunishima? The feller in that we were chasing, his name was Tajiri. Is that a *yakuza* name?'

'I dunno. Are all Malones cops?'

'Righto, you've made your point. He was the one I was watching when I mentioned the *yakuza*. He was the one who showed no reaction, nothing. He doesn't need tattoos to tell me where he comes from.'

Clements grinned. 'Maybe they've given up on tattoos, now all the idiots are into it. We'll keep an eye on him.'

They walked down to their car and Clements said, 'You think they'll do Magee if they get to him before we do?'

'We'll have to see that they don't.'

There was the usual parking ticket on the unmarked car. Clements tore it up and dropped it down a grating. They smiled at each other, glad of small consolations not due other voters.

3

Errol Magee, still in his blue dress, still bound to his chair, sat in the darkened room and began to wonder if he would get out of this place, wherever it was, alive. There was a callous coldness hidden in the blue hoods that came in every so often: the two men and Mum. The younger woman, the daughter, had left the house –' She's gone to talk to your friends at the bank,' Mum had said.

Fat chance, he had thought but didn't voice it. Unless Kunishima offered to pay the ransom, then reneged on it once he was turned over to them. Then, he knew, his life wouldn't be worth ten cents. He trembled at the thought and almost wet himself.

He began to wonder where he was being held. Obviously somewhere in the bush; the outside silence told him that. Occasionally the silence would be broken by the squawk of parrots, something one didn't hear in the apartment at Circular Quay; once he thought he heard a cow or a bull bellow, but he wasn't sure. He was not and never had been a bush person; Centennial Park was his idea of the Outback. He was not interested in conservation nor in the welfare of endangered species. Once, when approached for a donation, he had asked an animal rights lover if she felt deprived, materially and emotionally, because there were no more brontosauruses. He had been shocked when she broke his nose with her flailed backpack. It had cost two thousand dollars to repair the damaged nose and from then on he had steered clear of anyone remotely connected with the bush.

The door opened, letting in some daylight from the hallway. Corey Briskin, anonymous inside the blue hood, came in. 'You wanna go to the dunny?'

'I could do with another leak.'

'You got a weak bladder or something? This is the second time in an hour.'

'I'm scared of you lot. You'd be pissing, too, if you were in my place.'

'Relax, sport.' Corey undid the straps. 'We're not gunna do you. What would you be worth dead?'

Magee didn't know whether it was the relaxed attitude of this kidnapper or whether it was just that they were having a conversation, of sorts; all at once he felt less scared. 'Nothing. I think you're going to find out I'm not worth much more alive.'

Corey chuckled inside the hood. 'Wrong thing to say, sport. Okay, on your feet. No funny stuff or I'll have to clock you.' He held up a bunched fist. For the first time Magee noticed the tattoo on the back of the hand: a woman's lips opened in a smile, the teeth yellowed by the hand's tan. 'I'm not squeamish about it.'

'I can believe it,' said Magee and managed to make it sound complimentary.

Corey led him down a short hallway to the bathroom. On the way Magee remarked that the house seemed sparsely furnished; so this wasn't where they lived permanently. Corey said, 'When you're wearing a dress, do you sit down to pee?'

'Till I was brought here, I'd never had to pee when I was in a dress.' He lifted the front of the dress and relieved himself.

'You're not a poof. What makes you go in for that sorta thing?'

'I dunno. Like you say, I'm not a poof. I don't even think I'm weird. It's just – I dunno.' He shook the dress back into place, then looked down at it. 'You got something you can lend me, I can change into? If Kunishima comes up with the ransom money, I don't want to be turned over to them in *this*.'

Corey smiled inside the hood. 'That'd be something in the *Financial Review*, wouldn't it?'

Magee remembered reading once about the relationship that had grown between kidnappers and kidnappees in the terrorist days in Beirut. He had been in London then and there had been a Lebanese working in the same office whose father had been kidnapped and killed. So there could be a relationship verging on friendship, yet it could still end in murder.

He couldn't imagine himself ever becoming friends with this lot, but the atmosphere had certainly improved since this morning. Maybe it was just this one guy; the other one, who had sounded younger, was another case altogether. Mum had sounded as cold and hard as any woman could get to be; and he had known a few in his time. The younger woman (these guys' sister?) had sounded as if she might have a sense of humour. The atmosphere might improve, but he was kidding himself if he thought they would be *friendly*. With him, who had never encouraged friendships.

They went back to the room. 'Do you have to tie me up?'

'Sport, we're in business. Do you trust people in business?'

He hadn't, but he wasn't going to say so. 'Most of the time, yes.'

'Not here, sport. Sorry. Here –' Corey had gone to an old-fashioned wardrobe, taken out a pair of jeans and an old wrinkled football jersey – 'get outa that dress.'

Magee pulled on the jersey and jeans. 'South Sydney?'

'My old man played for them years ago. Don't get any ideas about trying to trace us. A thousand guys played for Souths. You follow league?'

'No, I'm not a football fan. I'm not sports-minded.'

'How come you know that's a South's jersey?'

'I-Saw did some research for the lawyers when they were

trying to wind up Souths.' The club had been dropped by the league's administrators and there had been huge demonstrations by the club's supporters. He had not understood the supporters' anger, but he was sure his parents would have. His father, though not a rugby league fan, would have been writing letters to the newspapers decrying the death of real sport. 'I wish you'd believe me. I-Saw is broke. Skint. If you hadn't grabbed me, I'd be on the dole next week.'

'Errol –' Corey was tolerant, like a master to a pupil. He began to tie Magee up again. 'I think you're having us on. Don't stretch your luck. If that bank of yours don't come good, you're in the shit, sport. There. Comfy?'

'Up yours,' said Magee, suddenly brave out of desperation and despair.

Corey chuckled behind the hood. 'That used to be South's old motto.'

He went out, closing the door again. Gloom settled on Magee and the room.

Out in the kitchen Corey took off his hood. 'Mum, what we gunna do with him if, like he says, there's no money?'

Shirlee Briskin was making corned-beef-and-salad sandwiches. She had once worked in a delicatessen, when Clyde had been doing time again, and she made sandwiches with professional skill. 'If he gives us trouble, we'll have to get rid of him.'

Corey, occasionally, had trouble accepting his mother's approach. He had dug the pit in the timber up behind the house and buried his father after his mother had poisoned him. He had never had any time for his father, but he would never have *killed* him. He might have beaten him up and told him to get lost, but he would never have *murdered* him, certainly not with arsenic fed to him over two days. The police had never come near them, because the family had never reported Clyde's disappearance. Some of the family's friends had asked what had happened to Clyde and they had been told that he, you know what a bastard he was, had gone off with another woman and Shirlee, dry-eyed, was glad to see him go. One or two of the women friends had nodded and said, *good riddance*.

He remembered the agony, spread over two days, in which his father had died. It had been messy, with vomiting and diarrhoea, but his mother had attended to all that, telling his father he must have eaten something and should be more careful. Clyde had wanted to go to a doctor, but Shirlee had said, no, she'd get the doctor to come to him. The doctor, because he wasn't called, never had.

When Clyde was dead, Shirlee had cleaned him up, wrapped him in his best suit, and told Corey to go up into the timber and dig the grave. Pheeny, only sixteen then, had helped him, silent and puzzled, asking no questions, just doing what their mother ordered. Then they had carried the body up to the grave and dumped it in it. Their mother had followed them, lugging a suitcase and with other of Clyde's clothes slung over one arm.

'Bury them with him,' she had said. 'I'm gunna tell people he's left us and run off with some woman. You keep your traps shut, understand?'

'What we gunna tell Darlene?' Corey had asked.

Darlene had not come down to the house that weekend. She, like Corey, had no time for their father, but Corey doubted she would have stayed in the house while their mother killed him.

'We tell her the truth. She'll understand.' Then Shirlee had looked down at the body lying crumpled at the bottom of the pit. 'I dunno why I ever married him.'

'You had us,' said Corey defensively.

She turned her head towards him and Pheeny, but in the darkness he couldn't see her face. 'Yeah. I suppose I owe him that.'

'Thanks,' Corey had said sourly and walked off down through the timber. 'You fill in the hole, Pheeny.'

That had been four years ago. Shirlee had told Darlene the truth about their father's murder, making no excuses, telling it flatly, take it or leave it. Darlene had taken it; Corey had been unable to read her face. She had never talked about it with him or Pheeny and gradually their father had faded from memory, a ghost who never haunted them.

Mum had kept them together ever since. He looked at her now, as domestic as any mother could be, and said, 'I'm not gunna be in any killing of that guy in there. I decked that maid of his, I didn't mean to kill her, and I've got that hanging over my head. You wanna get rid of Mr Magee, you and Pheeny and Darlene can do it. Count me out.'

She arranged the sandwiches neatly on a plate. 'Please yourself. How's he behaving himself?'

'Still trying to tell us he's broke. I'm beginning to think if we'd snatched his girlfriend, insteada him, he wouldn't of come good with the money. I think we might of been sold, whatdotheycall it, a pig in a poke.'

'I don't think so,' said Shirlee emphatically. 'Chantelle knows where the money is. Here, have a sandwich. You want tea or coffee?'

Corey put two of the sandwiches on a second plate. 'I'll feed him.'

Shirlee looked at him shrewdly; sometimes she wondered how much of herself was in her kids. 'You're not starting to feel sorry for him, are you?'

'No,' said Corey and wondered if what he felt was regret for his own life.

4

Malone looked at Clements across the roof of their car.

'You go back to the office, keep digging into Kunishima. I'm going down to the Ritz-Carlton, see if I can have a word with Mrs Magee.'

'What's she like?'

'I think she'd have saved the *Titanic* if she'd been there. Controlled, I think is the word.'

'She's all yours, then. Right now I'm in the grip of a controlled woman. I tried to call her at lunchtime, but they said she'd gone out to lunch with Mrs Malone.'

'They're conspiring against us. No, not *us*. You. Lisa will be talking to me when I get home about husbands, no names, no pack drill, who lose thousands of dollars on shonky investments.'

'She wouldn't, would she? My friend Lisa?'

Malone grinned. 'Don't expect me to defend you, *mate*.'

Clements gave him the middle finger and Malone, still grinning, went off down Macquarie Street to the Ritz-Carlton. The sunshine was still bright, the passers-by seemingly unworried. Half a dozen of them, strangers to each other, came towards him, all of them identical, water-bottles to their mouths, mobiles to their ears. Nobody, it seemed, could remain unconnected to someone, anyone, for longer than five minutes. I'm getting old, he thought, and felt no regret, just a comfortable smugness.

'Yes,' said the clerk at the Ritz-Carlton, 'Mrs Magee is in. Who shall I say is calling?'

'Detective-Inspector Malone.'

The clerk nodded as if detective-inspectors came to the hotel all week long. He spoke to Caroline Magee on the phone, then gave Malone the room number.

Malone rode up in the lift, sorting out what questions he would ask and finding them a jumble.

Caroline was waiting for him with the door open, smiling like a good hostess. 'Inspector, come in. I didn't expect to see you again so soon.'

'You expected to see me again?'

She led him into the room, taking her time. It was not a suite, just a bedroom with a small lounge space that looked out across the Botanic Gardens to the distant harbour heads. Malone could only guess at the price: five hundred dollars a night? Caroline Magee, it seemed, was not short of a quid or two.

'Naturally,' she said at last as she sat down and motioned him to take a seat. 'Isn't that the way the police work? Always coming back?'

'It's the only way we know. Persistence.'

'Plod, plod, plod?'

'We try to be a little more light-footed than that. You've had experience of the police before this?'

'No-o.' He noticed the slight hesitation; then she went on, 'Only for traffic offences. In the UK.'

'Never out at Coonabarabran?' he asked with a smile.

She returned the smile. 'Never. I was just a young girl then, never in trouble.'

Then he pitched a beanball: 'When Errol asked you to come out here, did he tell you he had something like forty million dollars salted away somewhere?'

She didn't duck; nor looked surprised. 'I find that hard to believe.'

'Oh, we have it on good authority. He stole it.'

'The Kunishima Bank? Well, well.' She rolled her eyes, only slightly, at her ex-husband's rash cheek. 'Forty million?'

'You knew nothing about his plans?'

'Plans?'

'He knew I-Saw was going down the gurgler, so he must've been preparing for it for quite a while. You don't grab forty million just like that −' He snapped his fingers. 'Not unless you're holding up a bank or one of the armoured-car companies that service banks. What plans were you going to discuss with him, if he was planning to do a bunk?'

'Am I under suspicion or something?' She gathered chill round her like a wrap.

'What makes you think that, Mrs Magee?'

She gave him another smile, this time no more than a dental inspection. 'All right, you are just covering every possibility. No, Errol told me nothing about stealing money or doing a bunk anywhere. I thought I was coming out here to help him salvage something from the wreckage. All I knew was that everything was in a hell of a mess.'

'Did he tell you why?'

'No, but I guessed. Too much optimism, over-expansion. It's an IT disease, Inspector. Dotcom spread quicker than Spanish 'flu. Or Hong Kong 'flu or whichever is the latest strain. Everybody wanted in, whether they knew anything about it or not. Errol was – *is* a salesman, not an IT genius. He sold himself, and the world out there was full of suckers. I-Saw was a good idea, but Errol – and he wasn't the only one – he thought it a Vision, with a capital V. It wasn't. It was just a good idea.'

'Was he a ladies' man?'

'You mean was he charming and sexy? No, he wasn't. But he always had girlfriends, even during our marriage. I told you, he was a salesman.'

'What did you see in him?' She was a remarkably attractive woman the more one looked at her; some women never improve beyond one's first impression of them, but Caroline Magee seemed to gradually show a different facet of herself, like a dancer unwrapping veils. Malone had seen a photo of Magee and he could not help but wonder what she had seen in the small, nondescript man.

She gave him the dental display again. 'Have you ever asked your wife what she saw in you?'

He considered that for a long moment; and was surprised at the answer: 'No-o. No, I haven't.'

'What women see in a man, outside the obvious – I don't think you can put a finger on it. I thought I saw something in Errol, but I was wrong – and I knew I was wrong in the first twelve months. He was a pain in the arse to be married to. Why do you ask if he was a ladies' man?'

'There's a woman involved in the ransom bid . . . Whom did you work with in London?'

'A firm of stockbrokers, Greenfield and Co.'

'And you resigned to come out and help Errol out of his mess? You must be a bit narked, now. Giving up your job –'

'No, I took extended leave, two months. I knew Errol well enough not to give up a good job on the basis of a promise.'

'What was the promise?'

'A bonus, plus salary, if I helped him work out his problems.'

'A big bonus?'

'Big enough. But it's all just a busted bubble now.'

'You'll stay till we find Errol?'

'Of course. I just hope you find him –' A slight hesitation: 'Alive.'

'I hope so, too. We may want to charge him with murder.'

If she was shocked at that, she did not show it. 'The maid? I don't think Errol would have done that. He's a coward at heart.'

He couldn't help the barb: 'And you still loved him?'

She wore a breastplate: 'No, I didn't. I *thought* I did.'

He looked around the room, then back at her. 'You'll be staying on here?'

'Only till the end of the week.' The smile this time was friendlier. 'I had hoped to stay in Errol's apartment. But I don't think Miss Doolan would agree to that. We have shares, as it were, in Errol, but I don't think we're partners.'

The smile widened, the chill gone now, and he found himself liking her.

'You'll go back to England?'

'Of course.'

'You don't think this is the Lucky Country?'

'Of course it is. Lucky it has prospered as much as it has, considering the idiots who run it.'

'You've become a Pommy.'

'No, just someone far enough away to get the big picture. Or the capital B, capital P, Big Picture. I'm long-sighted, I take the long view.'

'So do I. I stay at home and try to convert the ones who don't see beyond next week or the next election.'

'How much success do you have?'

'Very little. But I'm Irish, we're used to banging our heads against the wall.' He stood up. 'Will you wait till we've found Errol?'

She looked at him, a half-smile now. 'I don't love him, Inspector. But I'm not heartless.'

'Sorry. When you leave the hotel, where will we find you? Back at Coonabarabran?'

'No, that's a long way behind me.'

'No folks? Parents or siblings?'

'You ask a lot of questions.'

'It's our nature, otherwise we'd never get any answers.'

'I have a brother, but I've lost touch with him. There's nothing to keep me here.'

'Except Errol.'

Again the hesitation, then: 'Yes, except Errol.'

'We'll be in touch, Mrs Magee. We don't want to lose you.'

She said nothing to that, just opened the door. The chill was back.

Chapter Four

1

'We've been forgetting one thing,' said Clements. 'The dead maid. The corpse. What brought us in, Homicide.'

Malone nodded. 'Yeah, I know. But you haven't met all the suspects. A greedy lot of buggers who make you forget what'shername. Juanita.'

'We have another greedy bugger outside –'

'Don't sound so superior.' But he grinned as he said it.

'Okay, lay off. This is another greedy bugger. Mr Vassily Todorov, Juanita's boyfriend. Asking have we found Mr Magee, so that he can sue him for what's owed to Juanita.'

'You're kidding.'

'No, mate, I'm not. I'm greedy – *was* greedy. But I have my standards. You want to see him?'

'Not particularly, not the way you describe him. But all right –' He got up from behind his desk, looked at his watch. 'If I were a superintendent I'd have been outa here half an hour ago.'

'You're not there yet.' Clements heaved himself off the couch. 'When you are, you won't meet too many like Vassily.'

Vassily Todorov was built as if chipped out of rock; all rough edges and a shard for a nose. He was a good six inches shorter than either of the two detectives, but as wide as Clements and none of it fat. Malone wondered if he was one of the Bulgarian wrestlers or weight-lifters who always seemed to be deserting their homeland. Juanita Marcos must have been desperate to choose him as a boyfriend. Or maybe Todorov was a good rock, in different ways, in bed. *What women see in a man, outside the obvious . . .*

He was surprisingly polite: Clements hadn't led Malone to

expect politeness. 'Good afternoon, Inspector. It is good of you to see me. Sergeant Clements has explained?'

'Yes, Mr Todorov. But we haven't found Mr Magee yet. You're a little prema— you're a little early.'

'Premature?' Todorov had flecked eyes, as if someone had thrown sand into them and he hadn't even blinked. 'I suppose we should have expected it.'

'You speak English very well. How long have you been out here?'

'Two years.' *So he could have been an absconding weight-lifter, from the Olympics.* 'I taught English at a Berlitz school in Sofia.'

Malone had been slow on the uptake: it was Clements who said, 'Why do you suppose you should have expected it? Expected what?'

'My girlfriend to be down-sized.'

Was that how they spoke, even at Berlitz in Sofia? Malone waited for him to say, *at the end of the day.*

'Why?'

Todorov's head was the smoothest part of him; he scratched the dark stubble that covered it. 'Her English was good, too. She understood what was being said.'

'Said where?' asked Malone. 'When?'

'When the Japanese would come to talk to Mr Magee. They said he was asking for trouble. She said she saw one of the men show Mr Magee a gun.'

'Which man?'

Todorov shrugged. 'She never told me, she didn't want to talk about it.'

'Did she tell you anything else?'

Todorov shrugged again; he could have been discussing the dangers of hernia from weight-lifting. There was no hint of any grief at his loss of Juanita Marcos; he was here strictly on business. 'One day down in the garage she saw two men – she went out that way, through the service entrance.'

'What were the two men doing? What did they look like – Japanese?'

'They were looking at Mr Magee's Porsche – she thought they were going to steal it. They ran away when she asked them what they wanted. No, they were not Japanese. Two young men, white. Australians, she thought. But you can never be sure these days, can you?' But he was sure of himself, right down to the redundancy pay and the sick leave and the loss of whatever Juanita had offered him in the way of conjugal rights. 'We all look Australian, don't we, unless we're black or Asian?'

Clements ignored that, looked at Malone. 'Is it easy to get into the garage?'

'The Rocks blokes had a look at it. One of the tenants or owners said they'd lost their parking card or it'd been stolen. The doors operate from a card machine. I didn't check, I took their word for it. The Porsche is still there and no cars were stolen. The kidnappers must've brought their own car into the garage. Or Errol was in on the act.'

The flecked eyes had been flicking from one detective to the other. 'Mr Magee kidnapped *himself*?'

'No, Mr Todorov, I was joking.' He had told Clements too much in front of the Bulgarian. 'Mr Magee has been kidnapped. Until we find him, alive or dead, I'm afraid you'll have to wait for any compensation for Miss Marcos' death.'

Todorov stood up. 'I am patient. When you are teaching English to stupid students, you learn to be patient.'

'What do you do here, Mr Todorov?'

'I am a courier, on a bicycle. Car drivers hate us. I am used to abuse.'

'Who's been abusing you?'

He looked from one to the other; the rock of his face cracked. 'I am also a mind-reader.'

Malone's tongue got away from him, as it so often did: 'Are you also greedy, Mr Todorov?'

'Of course.' He was so unoffended it was almost an insult.

83

'The greedy are the true romantics, Inspector, the dreamers. We make the world go round.'

'They teach that at Berlitz?'

The rock cracked in another smile. 'No. I learned it when communism collapsed. Good day, gentlemen.'

Clements had one of the junior detectives escort Todorov out of the building, then he came back into Malone's office. 'You really are shoving the needle in, aren't you?'

'The greedy bit? That slipped out, I just wanted to kick him in the balls. It wasn't meant as a slap at you –' But Clements looked unconvinced. 'Russ, I mean it. We're going to be talking a lot about greed in this case. Every time I mention it, it's not meant as a kick in the slats for you. Don't be so bloody touchy. Keep that for Romy.'

It was a long moment before Clements said, 'Okay . . . Well, what do you think of him?'

'He's not on my list. He's a smartarse, but he had nothing to do with Magee's disappearance. And I don't think Errol had anything to do with his own kidnapping. If he's as smart as everyone says, he wouldn't be asking the *yakuza* to ransom him. Someone else has got him, they took him instead of Miss Doolan. All those messages on the computers, they were a blind.'

'Then do you think Miss Doolan has got a hand in all this?'

Then Malone's phone rang: it was Paula Decker. 'Inspector, Miss Doolan has done a bunk –'

He sucked in his breath, held back his anger. 'How?'

'I went to the toilet, when I came out she was gone –'

2

'I'm sorry, sir, I've really stuffed things up . . . She gave me no hint she would leave as soon's I turned my back. She was relaxed, we talked, we read some magazines . . . I

84

was in the bathroom no more than a coupla minutes. When I came out –'

'Righto, take it easy –' Malone could see that Paula Decker was ready to belt herself over the head. 'It happens, Paula. Sergeant Clements and I have made mistakes, too.'

Clements came into the living room from the main bedroom. He and Malone had arrived here at the Magee apartment within twenty minutes of the call; Clements, driving, had used the siren and the blue lights in the peak-hour traffic. 'Doesn't look as if she's taken any clothing –'

'I checked that,' said Paula Decker. 'She had a light coat, she's taken that. And her handbag . . . She had a phone call about an hour ago. She took it, but she hung up before I could get to one of the extensions in the bedrooms.'

You've been a bit slow today, Paula. But Malone held on to his tongue on that thought. 'She say who it was?'

'Just a friend. Said she'd cut her off, she'd call back later. I know I sound damned stupid, sir – I've *been* stupid. But she took me in. Completely.'

'Maybe she's taken us all in. When did Sheryl Dallen leave?'

'Just over an hour ago. She said she was going home to Leichhardt to get some night gear – she was going to sleep here tonight. We thought we'd take turns keeping an eye on Kylie. She was going to report back to Homicide first thing in the morning. She was getting on as well with Kylie as I thought I was.' Paula Decker sounded bitter, as if she had never been let down before.

'What did you talk about? With Kylie? She give you any dope on Mr Magee, the boyfriend?'

Paula, now that she realized she was not going to be dressed down, was regaining her composure. 'I think she knew she was gunna be ditched. She said nothing specific, but Sheryl and I looked at each other on a coupla occasions.'

'Women's intuition?' Clements' grin was meant to be friendly.

'If you like,' she said, a little stiffly. Evidently feminism and male chauvinism clashed at The Rocks, as it did in most stations and divisions. 'Kylie will survive, though. She's a tough cookie, I think, under all that Little-Girl-Lost act she was putting on.'

'That was how she was acting?' said Malone. 'Little-Girl-Lost?'

'It wasn't a very good act. Sheryl and I didn't think so.'

'When did you exchange opinions?'

'We didn't. We just looked at each other.'

Malone looked at Clements. 'Don't you wish we had that silent communication?' Then his mobile rang: 'Malone.'

It was Sheryl Dallen: 'Boss, I caught Kylie Doolan coming out of her apartment building as I was coming back. She didn't see me, but went scooting up Macquarie Street. I followed her.'

'Where is she?'

'In the Aurora building. I'm in the lobby. She caught a lift to one of the upper floors. There were other people in the lift, but it stopped at five floors. She could of got off at any one of them.'

'I know where she's gone, she'll have got off at the Kunishima Bank. I've forgotten the floor. Russ and I'll be there in five minutes. Are you in your nightie?'

'What?'

He switched off, turned to Clements and Paula Decker. 'Sheryl is keeping an eye on Kylie, she's up the road at the Kunishima Bank, I'll bet. Stay here, Paula. We'll be bringing Kylie back.'

'Can I wring her neck?'

'Be my guest.'

Sheryl Dallen, overnight bag beside her, was waiting for Malone and Clements in the foyer of Aurora. The lobby was busy with office workers going home to their own problems, the lifts vomiting them as they hurried towards the outer doors. Malone and Clements fought their way upstream, going to work. Nine to five was a luxury every police officer dreamed of.

'No sign of her so far,' said Sheryl. 'She must still be up there.'

'I'm going up,' said Malone. 'You two keep an eye on the lifts, case she comes down while I'm going up. Call me if she does, so I don't barge into Kunishima and be met with a blank stare. They're very good at that.'

'Watch the *yakuza* guy,' said Clements with concern.

'*Yakuza*?' said Sheryl.

'Tell her about it,' said Malone and rode up to the bank's floor in an empty lift, wondering if Mr Tajiri, the *yakuza* man, would greet him with a blank stare or something else. He eased his .40 Glock pistol further round on his hip, just in case.

He had no plan of action other than to get Kylie Doolan back into protective custody. He had long ago begun to rely on his instinct; not the most reliable of spurs, but it beat having no plan at all. He could be analytical with the best, but only after facts had been registered. And so far he had very few facts on Okada and the men who ran Kunishima Bank.

There was no one in the reception area of the bank's office. He had remarked that Kunishima had two floors; the floor below this one was probably still inhabited by computer slaves. In banks these days there were no dead periods; the computers and their slaves worked round the clock; anywhere in the world, at any given time, money was tumbling in the lottery barrel called dealing. But here on the executive floor, it seemed, everyone had gone home.

Malone hesitated, then he moved towards the door of Okada's office where he and Clements had entered a couple of hours ago. The door opened in his face; Okada stood there, a surprised smile on his face. 'Why, Inspector Malone! Back so soon? You have found Mr Magee?'

'Not yet, Mr Okada. I'm here looking for Miss Doolan.'

'Who?' Okada looked genuinely puzzled.

But Malone was still trying to read a Japanese face, especially one as controlled as Mr Okada's. 'Errol Magee's girlfriend.'

Okada shook his head, smiled. 'I never had the pleasure. Why are you here looking for her?'

She came up here . . . But had she? Had she gone to the other floor of the bank? Or some office here in the building totally unconnected with Kunishima? He felt suddenly uncomfortable, but he had felt that way before; it came with the job. So he lied: 'We understand you called her at the Magee apartment.'

'She told you that? She must have been joking, Inspector. I have never met the lady and have no interest in her. We are interested only in Mr Magee.'

'Do you mind if I look around?' Malone nodded at the room behind the banker.

'Yes, I do mind, Inspector. But also yes, you may look around.' He stood aside, almost theatrically; Malone waited for him to bow. 'Should you not have a warrant?'

'Yes, I should. Do you want me to get one? We could be standing here for a couple of hours while they find a judge. Judges tend to go home early.'

'A most relaxing profession. No, go ahead, Inspector. Mr Magee's lady friend is not here, never has been.'

Malone stepped into the room, glanced around. He could barge into the other rooms, but already he could feel Okada smiling at him behind his back and the impassive face. Then he said, 'Why aren't you interested in Miss Doolan? She was the one who was supposed to be kidnapped, not Mr Magee.'

'Really? We didn't know that.'

I'm not sure, either. 'And you're still not interested in her?'

'No, Inspector. Our only interest is Mr Magee. Back home in Osaka our shareholders will be asking questions about the shortfall in our profits. I hope when you find Mr Magee you will allow us a few minutes with him. Our forty million dollars,' he explained, as if Malone might have forgotten *that*. 'Now will you excuse me?'

Malone couldn't resist it, even though it was juvenile: he bowed and backed out. Okada looked after him with a smile as empty as a flash of light on porcelain. Malone turned quickly and headed for the lifts before his temper got the better of him.

Down in the lobby he told Clements and Sheryl Dallen, 'He denies he ever heard of her. I think he was bullshitting. Go down to the garage, Sheryl, till I get someone over from The Rocks. There's probably three or four floors of garage – no, wait a minute.' His anger was clouding his thinking. 'There'll only be one exit ramp. Stand there and check every car comes out till I get The Rocks people over. They can cover it for the next coupla hours. If Okada and company have kidnapped Kylie –' He looked at Clements. 'You remember The Rocks number?'

'Why would I remember it? I'm not supposed to be on this case –'

'Jesus wept!'

It was Sheryl, looking a little puzzled at the two men, who gave him the number. 'I'm the junior around here and it seems to me I'm the least frustrated. Frankly, if Kylie's in trouble, it's her own fault, not ours.'

'Let's simmer down,' said Clements.

Malone took the advice, called The Rocks on his mobile, gave instructions, then closed the phone. 'Righto, Sheryl, down to the exit ramp. Russ will be with you in a few minutes.' Sheryl went to walk off, leaving her bag. 'You've forgot your nightie.'

'I'll use it to strangle Kylie if I find her coming out of the garage.'

When she had gone Malone turned to Clements. 'This is getting out of hand. What's holding up setting up a strike force?'

'The bulletin board is full, Headquarters told me. We've got more strike forces than they had in World War Two. While you were out today, they tried to hand us three more homicides. I told 'em the locals had to handle 'em themselves. The point is, the dead maid, Juanita, has become unimportant. But if we get two more murders on our hands, Mr Magee and his girlfriend . . .

Okay, I'll try again. I'll ring Greg Random and see what he can do.'

'That superintendent's job can't come soon enough.'

'Bullshit,' said Clements and went off.

Malone stood alone in the suddenly deserted lobby, wondering what life would be like out there in the comfort zone, wondering if that was what he really wanted.

3

'Phoenix Briskin?' said the woman from Centrelink; she was new and had not interviewed him before. 'Phoenix? You made that up yourself?'

'No, me mother give it to me. It was her favourite song.' He hummed a bar or two. 'By the time I get to Phoenix –' He broke off, gave her his cowboy's smile. 'She liked "Wichita Lineman", too. All them Glen Campbell songs.'

'Why didn't she call you Phoenix Wichita then?'

He knew the bitch was taking the piss out of him. All these fucking people who worked for the government were the same. He'd show 'em when he got his share of the Magee ransom.

'You're going to have to pull your socks up, son,' she said, looking at his papers. 'Two jobs in three weeks. We don't run a place where you takes your choice. What happened?'

He hadn't even turned up at the first job. 'The manager, he was gay. He kept wanting to feel me up.'

'Why didn't you come back and complain?'

'How could I? You know, that whatdotheycallit? That Anti-Discrimination thing.'

She sighed, not believing him; it was written all over her face. 'Okay, what about the second job? The brickie's labourer? That should've suited you. You're built like – like –' She wasn't supposed to insult those who came here, but sometimes it was difficult not to.

He helped her out: 'Like a brick shithouse? Yeah, that's what me brother says. I stayed three days, that job, but I hadda leave.'

'Why?' She sounded as if she had asked this question a thousand times.

'Sun cancers. I was out in the open air alla time, I get sun cancers.'

'Where'd you get that tan, then?'

'It's natural. Me father's half-Tongan.' Clyde had come from a long line of Yorkshiremen. 'He's related to Jonah Lomu.'

'Who?' She knew nothing about football, of any code. She had her own sporting problems, she was a dysfunctional synchronized swimmer, she always put up one foot too many when she was under water. She sighed, wondering why she hadn't taken a job down a coal mine. 'I don't believe a word of it, Phoenix. Here. You walk out on this job and we cut off your welfare cheque.' She sorted through papers on her desk, extracted one and handed it to him. 'You can start today.'

He looked at the piece of paper. 'Lavatory attendant?'

'You've got the build for it,' she said and looked out at the other hopefuls. 'Next!'

Phoenix Briskin was blind with fury when he walked out of the Centrelink office. He stepped on to a pedestrian crossing right in front of a Range Rover driven by a woman with six kids in the vehicle.

4

'Mum, for Crissakes, there's a police car coming up the road!'

Corey had been sitting out on the cottage's narrow front verandah, wondering if he would retire to the bush, on a bigger spread than this, if and when he got his share of the five million bucks. He liked the peace and quiet, he had come to recognize the different types of trees, he even knew some of the bird calls.

If he could find a decent bird, of the human kind, to settle down with, there would be worse ways of living.

But at the same time he was despondent, wondering what they would do if nobody came up with the ransom money. Then he looked down the distant road and saw the police car creeping up towards them like a stalking blue-and-white dog.

Shirlee came to the screen door, but didn't come out on to the verandah. 'Go down to the gate and see what they want. I'll take care of His Nibs.'

She went back into the kitchen, donned one of the blue hoods, took a long carving knife and went into the bedroom where Errol Magee, half-asleep, sat slumped in his chair. He blinked and looked up as she came in, holding the knife in front of her as if about to use it.

'You open your mouth and I'll cut your throat.' She said it matter-of-factly, as if suggesting she might give him a slice of roast beef.

He was so tired and despairing he was almost beyond fear. 'You would, too, wouldn't you?'

'Try me. Now shut up!'

Outside Corey had gone down from the verandah and, forcing himself not to hurry, walked the fifty-yard path down to the battered front gate where the police car had just come to a stop. Two cops got out, a stout, grey-haired sergeant and a tall young constable who looked uncomfortable. The Briskins had never had any dealings with the local police and Corey had never seen these two before.

'Mr Briskin?'

Corey nodded, keeping himself together. If they wanted to search the house, he was not going to fight them; while their backs were turned he would make for the timber and Mum could look after herself. He would not be deserting her, he knew she would tell him to run.

'I'm afraid we've got some bad news. Not tragic news, but bad news.'

'My sister?' He had always been protective of Darlene.

'No, your – brother?' The sergeant looked at his notebook, then looked again. 'Phoenix? That his name?'

'Yeah. We call him Pheeny or Nix. What's happened to him?'

'He stepped off the footpath, far's we can gather, right in front of a four-wheel drive. He's in St George's Hospital in intensive care.'

'How'd you find us here?' Had Pheeny been babbling while unconscious?

'The Hurstville police went to your home. The next-door neighbour said you hadn't been there for a coupla days, you were probably down here at your weekender. They phoned us and Constable Haywood here, he remembered seeing your car when he drove past here this morning.'

Corey wondered why Constable Haywood would have driven up this deserted road this morning, but he wasn't going to ask him. 'I'll go up straight away, see my brother. Anyone else hurt?'

The sergeant looked at his notebook again. 'Everybody but the woman driver of the vehicle. Evidently after she hit your brother, she went up on to the footpath and hit a pole. There were –' he checked his notebook again, 'there were six kids in the vehicle, none of 'em wearing a seat-belt. All six are in hospital with broken noses, smashed teeth, concussion. Quite a mess, evidently.'

Just like you, Pheeny, We want things fucked up, leave it to you. 'Okay, I'll go up. Thanks for the info.'

'You got someone here with you? Constable Haywood said he saw a woman out the back when he drove past this morning.'

Bloody Hawkeye Haywood. 'My mother. She's laying down right now. I'll tell her.'

'You want any help? Case she, you know, collapses or something. It's pretty shattering news for a mother.'

You dunno my mum. 'No, she'll be okay. We'll go up straight away. Thanks.'

'We'll wait and give you an escort out as far as the main road. Take your time.'

All at once Corey, irrationally, wished Pheeny was here so that he could kick his dumb arse. Jesus, you couldn't trust him to cross the road . . . Then he saw his mother coming down from the house, minus the hood and the knife.

'Some problems?' She was wiping her hands on her apron, ready to deal with any problems.

'Yeah, Mum –' He explained what had happened. 'Pheeny's in hospital, in intensive care.'

'And six children,' said the sergeant and looked at his notebook again. 'All under eight years old. In hospital. Not intensive care, fortunately.'

'Oh, the poor dears!' Shirlee sounded as if she had devoted her life to the care of children. 'Well, we better get up there, Corey.'

'The police are gunna escort us as far as the main road, Mum.'

If Shirlee was fazed by the complication, it didn't show. 'No, sergeant. I have to get things for Phoenix – pyjamas, things like that. I wouldn't think of holding you up. Thank you for bringing us the news. We'll let you know how my son is when we get back. Come on, Corey, I need some help.'

She turned and went back up the path; the general had despatched the troops. Corey looked at the police and shrugged. 'That's Mum. She'll run the hospital when we get there.'

The sergeant looked after the disappearing Shirlee. 'Yeah, well –' Then he, too, shrugged. 'Okay, give us a call when you get back, let's know how things are. Drive carefully.'

They got back into the police car, it swung round and went back down the road, raising a little dust as if that was what all police visits did. Corey looked after it, cursing, then he ran up the path and into the house.

'You stay here –' Shirlee had a suitcase on the kitchen table, was folding a pair of Phoenix's pyjamas. 'If they pull me up down the road, the police, I'll tell 'em you stayed behind to tell Darlene what happened.'

'How's she gunna get back from the station? When I dropped her off this morning I said I'd be there to meet the train. Four o'clock, I dunno, something like that.'

'She's got her mobile. Call her, tell her to meet me at the hospital. I wish Pheeny'd listen to me. I told him to buy a dressing-gown. How's he gunna look, walking around the hospital in this?' She held up a plastic mac.

'Mum, for Crissakes, stop worrying about how he's gunna look! He's in intensive care, he's not gunna be wandering around the fucking hospital!'

'Wash your mouth out.'

She closed the suitcase, pulled on a light coat. She was neat and professional, a hospital visitor. She would have Pheeny out of his coma in no time.

'Look after His Nibs.'

'You look after yourself, Mum.'

'I always do.'

She picked up the suitcase. Brisk now as a regimental sergeant-major, a breed more practical than generals; they are close, not to the big picture but the small picture of war, which is where you are wounded or die. She went out by the screen door and down to their car, a light-grey Toyota ('if you're gunna hold up a service station,' Clyde had advised, 'you always wanna have a car that's hard to identify, no fancy colours'). A minute later Corey heard the car drive away.

He put on one of the hoods and went into the bedroom. Errol Magee looked up at him, shifted uncomfortably in his straps. 'What's going on? You heard from anyone about the ransom?'

'No luck, sport. I'm beginning to think you're expendable. They've got to the bottom line and you don't add up. At the end of the day.' He had taken to reading the financial pages once they had planned the kidnapping.

Magee slumped in his chair. After a while he looked across at Corey, who had sat down in a chair. The blue hood faced him impassively.

'You ever give up hope?'

'I dunno,' said Corey. 'I was never the hopeful sort. I just took things as they come.'

'I read something once. Hope is the prayer of fools.'

'I dunno nothing about prayers. You must of been pretty hopeful when you first started out. You weren't a fool, were you?'

'Do you care what I was?'

'I dunno. Maybe I do. You must of had a life like I never dreamed of. *Hoped* for. What happened, sport? You got greedy?'

'I guess so.' He would never have talked like this to Kylie or Caroline or any of the other women in his life. But they had never been threatening . . . 'Are you going to kill me?'

'I dunno. I'd keep hoping, sport. Or praying.' Corey stood up. 'You wanna a leak or something?'

5

The police car was parked on the main road, just south of where the dirt road entered. Constable Haywood nudged his sergeant as the Toyota came out of the side road. 'The mother's on her own. Why isn't her son going up to see how his brother is? I would.'

'Jack, never interfere in a family, 'less you have to. He might hate his brother's guts, for all we know.'

'I still think I might go up there later, after I've dropped you off back at the station. Just a social call.'

'Please yourself. In the meantime we're supposed to be looking at semi-trailers doing more than eighty along this stretch. Here comes one now. He looks a sucker for a ticket.' He raised the speed camera, aimed it at the truck came towards them. 'How about that! Ninety-seven. Let's go and give him an Easter card.'

Chapter Five

1

'You had lunch with Romy today,' said Malone. 'What did you talk about?'

'World politics,' said Lisa. 'Women's rights. Public transport.'

'Neither of you ever travel by public transport.'

They were in the kitchen, she at the stove, he sitting at the table sipping a light beer. It was a very modern kitchen, refurbished a year ago at what was, by Malone's standards, great expense; but it was a workplace, not a sterile display of kitchen furniture. Lisa's touch, that of *home*, was in every room in the Federation house. The house was a hundred years old and year after year it had survived, under various owners, as a *home*.

'Did Russ ask you to ask me what we talked about?'

'No. I left him at the Aurora building – they've got a stake-out there. What *did* you talk about?'

'Stupidity. Men's. Open the wine, give it some time to breathe. Why on earth did Russ risk all that money?'

'He's admitted it. Greed. What are we having?'

'Chicken stroganoff. The whites are in the fridge. Sixty thousand dollars. Romy said she wanted to cut his balls off.'

'She said that in a restaurant? Out loud? Where were you, at Machiavelli?' A restaurant for suits, where balls, metaphorically, were cut every day. 'We'll have the Semillon. I'll give Con Junior a sip or two, start him young as a wine connoisseur. He's already got as much sense as some of them.'

Tonight was family night. Claire and her husband Jason were coming, bringing six-month-old Cornelius Junior with them. Maureen would be bringing her favourite of the moment, an

ABC reporter named Eddie or Freddie or Teddy. And Tom might or might not be bringing a girl: his whims were below his navel, an unreliable region. It was a weekly ritual that Scobie and Lisa looked forward to, a small reward for all the effort of bringing up Claire and Maureen and Tom. Malone, an Old Testament sceptic, sometimes wondered how much Adam and Eve had missed out on. Family night in the suburbs of Eden couldn't have been a ball of fun.

'Is Russ on the I-Saw case? The murder?'

'Yes and no. I kicked him off to start with, then I needed him.'

'How's it going?'

'Nowhere, so far. The murder of the maid seems to be getting lost in the kidnapping. Everybody's talking ransom so much, or how much money has gone down the gurgler at I-Saw, the maid's on the back burner. If they have back burners in morgues. Do we have to talk about this?'

'You brought it up.' She turned from the stove, pressed herself against him and kissed him. 'Resign tonight and let's fly.'

Then Tom came in the back door. 'Oh hell, you're not at it again!'

'You're just frustrated,' said Malone. 'You didn't bring a woman?'

'She'll be here in time for dinner. She's having drinks with a guy about a job. She worked for I-Saw till yesterday. You told me to look into I-Saw, remember?'

'How do you know her?'

'I dealt with her on the internet.'

'You've never met her?' Lisa was back at the stove.

'I took her out once or twice.' Tom turned a blank face towards his father; and Malone knew he had taken Whoever-She-Was to bed once or twice. 'Her name's Daniela. Daniela Bonicelli. She's half-Italian.'

'Which half? Bottom or top half?'

'All right, cut out the juvenile jokes,' said Lisa. 'We don't talk police business at the table, understand?'

'How long's she been with I-Saw?' said Malone.

'Almost since it started, I think.'

'Is anyone listening to me?' asked Lisa. 'Police business is out. O-U-T. If you want to grill Miss – what? – Bonicelli, if you want to question her, you can drive her home.'

'What's she like?' asked Malone. 'Attractive?'

'A dish. Sexy as all get out,' said Tom.

'Then I'll drive her home,' said Lisa.

'That's a drag. She lives out at Hurstville.' For Tom, like most of the young from the eastern suburbs, anything south or west of Central Station was a suburb of Jakarta ('there are so many, y'know, *Asians* out there').

'There's the doorbell,' said Lisa. 'Answer it.'

'How do you stand her?' asked Tom, grinning.

'A cop's patience,' said Malone and went through to admit Claire, Jason and baby Con.

Claire had matured into a younger version of Lisa: blondly beautiful, serene and in calm control of her husband. Malone kissed his daughter, shook hands with his son-in-law and tickled his grandson's two chins.

'You want to hold him?' Claire proffered the baby.

'No, thanks.' He was not an infant-loving grandfather; they were too often wet and smelly, they had no conversation and they were all autocrats. 'Send him along to me when he's twelve. I'll tell him about the birds and the bees.'

'They learn that at day care,' said Jason.

He was a very tall beanpole of a young man, but moved without awkwardness, almost gracefully. One had to look twice at his face to discover he was good-looking; it was almost as if he had chosen anonymity as a look. He was relaxed, but still cautious. His mother and her lesbian lover had murdered his father; he had a dichotomy of feeling towards her, he still loved her, yet hated her for what she had done. How he would explain his feelings to his own son in later years was something that Malone often wondered about.

'How's work?'

'Round and round,' said Malone. 'How's it with you?'

Jason was a civil engineer. 'Enough to keep us going. Just.'

'Just as well I'm going back to work,' said Claire. After nine months off, she was starting as an associate with the biggest law firm in the State. Malone, a cop, wondered at the future: not only too many lawyers, but too many *women* lawyers. 'I've never learned to spell *budget*.'

'She didn't inherit any of your tight-fistedness, Scobie,' said Jason.

'I think we adopted her.'

It was banter, the sort of lightweight glue that holds families together when nothing serious is threatening.

Then Maureen arrived with her man of the moment; or the nano-second. Her tastes changed too quickly for her parents to keep up with her; they just prayed that these playthings never hurt her. She referred to them as her toy-boys, but never in front of them. This latest one was Neddy: Neddy Brown. Malone recognized him. He was an ABC reporter, one of the new breed who referred to the *de-bree* left by floods and bushfires and thought *fantastic* a cover-all adjective for everything from delight to disaster. Tertiary education, Malone often thought, taught them not to waste words.

He was short and compact and amongst Malone, at six-one, Tom six-three and Jason six-four he looked like a rugby scrum-half waiting to be thrown the ball by the big men in the line-out.

'This is a fantastic coincidence, Mr Malone. Only today I was assigned to the Errol Magee kidnapping, so I guess our paths will be crossing –'

Malone decided to cut him off at the pass: 'I'm not on the kidnapping. I'm just handling the murder of Magee's maid –'

'They're connected, though, aren't they?'

'Drinks, anyone?' said Lisa, doing her own cutting off at the pass. 'Get that, will you, darl?'

The front doorbell had rung. Malone escaped, went down the hallway and opened the door. Daniela Bonicelli had arrived; a dish, sexy as all get-out. She had dark, appraising eyes, a short straight nose and lips like a baby's teething ring. Malone marvelled at his son's luck, at all the bon-bons that just seemed to fall into bed with his son. *Fantastic!*

'Daniela? I'm Tom's father.'

'I can see the resemblance. The eyes, the widow's peak –' Without moving she was all over him, like a silk rug.

'Come in. Did you get the job? Tom told me –'

'It's mine if I want it. I'll decide tomorrow –'

She turned her back for him to take off her jacket, looked back at him over her shoulder. All of a sudden he wanted to laugh: she was a Late Late Movie fan, she had seen Lana Turner and Lauren Bacall do this. He had always told Tom to find a woman with some mystery to her. Daniela Bonicelli was as mysterious as Marge Simpson. She would be no help at all on the I-Saw case.

Then Lisa, cruising like a destroyer escort, was in the hallway. 'Oh, you must be Daniela. Has my husband –' Malone could count the space between the letters – 'has he made you welcome? He's gauche around women. Come in and meet the younger men.'

'I'll get some more drinks,' said Malone and went down to the kitchen. A minute or two, then Lisa came in. 'What were you expecting? Me to rape her in the hallway?'

'She wouldn't know what rape is. How does Tom get himself involved with girls like her?'

'He's not *involved*. He's like Maureen – she's one of his toys. I think.'

'How did we raise such libertines? Will you be driving Miss Bonicelli home?'

'Not unless you hold a gun at my head.'

'Fat chance. Kiss me.'

He did and Maureen, in the kitchen doorway, said, 'Don't you two ever stop?'

'Only when we're interrupted. Did you bring Neddy here to interrogate me?'

'Come off it, Dad. You know I wouldn't do that. He's a nice guy, he understands *family*. He's got four brothers and four sisters, his mother was a nun.'

'She must be wishing she'd stayed one. How are Neddy and Jason getting on with Daniela?'

'Boy, she's a bundle, isn't she? Did Tom win her in a raffle? She worked at I-Saw, did she? How well did she know Errol Magee?'

'Why?'

'We had a *Four Corners* meeting this morning. We're going to do an investigative piece on I-Saw. Who lost money and how much. I might talk to Daniela.'

'Not tonight, you won't,' said Lisa. 'Get everyone seated. I'm bringing in the first course.'

'Where do I put everyone?'

'Put all the men in Daniela's lap. That should please her.'

But dinner, as it happened, went off beautifully. When Lisa brought in the dessert Daniela rolled her dark eyes. 'Diplomat pudding! My favourite – my mother makes it.'

Lisa warmed to her; or anyway turned off the refrigeration. 'Do you like to cook?'

'Love to. I alternate between the kitchen and the gym – it's the only way I can keep my weight down. Errol used to laugh at me –'

'Errol?' Malone couldn't help himself.

'Errol Magee. We lived together for six months.' Then she looked around at the silent watchers. 'Have I said something wrong?'

Malone looked down the table at Tom, whose smile was almost a smirk. As if to say, *This is why I brought her.*

'Not at all,' said Claire. 'We're always interested in the rich and famous.'

'Errol?' Daniela had a nice laugh; it shook every rounded inch of her. 'He was rich, sure – once. But he was never famous, never wanted to be, he said. He hated being photographed.'

'When did you – er – live with him?' asked Malone, avoiding Lisa's stare from the far end of the table.

'Oh, three years ago, maybe a bit more. Just when things were starting to click for him. Oh, this dessert is fantastic!' She swallowed a mouthful. 'Then we sort of broke up –'

'But you stayed on at I-Saw?' Tom, also avoiding looking at his mother, put the question.

'Of course. The pay was fabulous and I was worth it.'

Malone had to bite his tongue not to ask what her worth was. He looked along the table at Lisa, who just smiled: *she* knew what Daniela was worth.

'Those of us who were there early got stock options.' Daniela grimaced; then saw the look on Lisa's face. 'Oh no, it's not the dessert! It's fantastic – I'm loving every mouthful. I'll tell my mother about this . . . No, the stock options. One week they were worth eighteen dollars, a month later –' With her spoon she made a sharp downard motion. 'That's the story of life in IT, isn't it? Never knowing when to sell.'

'And you fell no resentment at the way things have gone?' It was Claire, the lawyer, who asked the question in Malone's mind.

Daniela put her spoon down on her plate, as if her appetite had suddenly been spoiled. 'Yes, we all do. We'd wring Errol's neck if we could find him.'

'Did he have any other girlfriends at I-Saw?' asked Malone, risking his own neck as he avoided Lisa's look. 'He had a wife, you know.'

'Did he?' Daniela looked genuinely surprised. 'Well, how about him! Yes, he had other girlfriends from I-Saw, but they were just, you know, one-night stands.'

'What an exciting life you modern girls live,' said Lisa and closed the subject; one could almost see her slamming the door on it. 'More pudding? Mo, when is *Four Corners* going to do an investigative piece on TV cookery shows? There were thirty-seven, last time I counted. Cooks are taking over TV, not Murdoch and Packer.'

Malone smiled in resignation at her. She could run a UN peace conference and get peace, even bring order to an Italian or Japanese parliament. He would have to talk to Daniela Bonicelli tomorrow morning.

The phone rang in the hallway and he got up and went out to answer it. It was Clements, sounding dispirited: 'I've just got home. We had no luck – Miss Doolan's disappeared. We kept surveillance on the garage for two hours, but there was no sign of her. Okada came down at six-thirty and drove out in a Lexus 400. No sign of the other two Japs. I went upstairs and checked on Kunishima's trading floor. Nobody had seen Nakasone or Tajiri. I think we might have another kidnapping on our hands, mate.'

'So long as it's no worse than that.'

'Who'll pay ransom for her?'

'Maybe they'll be ransom for each other, her and Errol. At the moment, mate, I don't really care. Have you sent everybody home?'

'Everybody but Sheryl and The Rocks girl – Paula? They're spending the night at Magee's apartment, case Kylie decides to come home. But it doesn't look good . . .'

'How's it with Romy?'

'Still chilly. See you tomorrow.'

Malone hung up, checked his notebook, then rang Sheryl Dallen at the Magee apartment. 'She come back yet? No? Righto, Sheryl, call her sister, tell – Monica? – to call you if Kylie shows up. Tell her not to panic, that Kylie may have her own plans.'

'Do you think she does?' said Sheryl.

'No,' he said and hung up, suddenly tired. It was not physical weariness, but exhaustion of the spirit. Like Whoever-it-was, he had 'seen the future – and it stinks!' Or was it not the future, but the past? He remembered a toy from his childhood, a glass globe with a landscape inside it, that changed from sunlight to darkness as one turned the globe, as if one held in one's hand the prism of life. His seven-year-old mind had grasped none of the message, it was a toy for wonderment, not enlightenment. Only now did he read the message.

The Magee case, in terms of the murder in it, was not a major one. He had experienced much worse and much more dangerous. A strike force was to be set up to handle the Magee kidnapping; Homicide would be a player in it because of the Marcos murder. Yet suddenly he felt weary of it all. Of twenty-five years of other people's crimes, of hatred and cruelty and prejudice and, yes, greed, for power and money. All at once he thought not just of promotion but even of retirement.

Then Claire, on her way to a bedroom to check that Cornelius Junior was still asleep, paused beside him. 'You okay, Dad?'

'Does the, y'know, human condition ever get you down?'

She took her time, reading him well. 'Sometimes, yes. Jay's mother is coming out of jail in six months, maybe a bit more. She'll want to come and see the baby, her grandson. I'll look at her and remember what she did to Jay's father . . . And yet –' She paused, then went on, 'I have to give her another chance. For Jay's sake and maybe young Con's.'

He looked at her with love. She and Maureen and Tom, even Lisa, had not been in the toy globe; the landscape therein had been unpeopled. Shadows would come and go in the future, just as they had in the globe he had held in his hand all those years ago. 'Take care of young Con.'

She looked at him, understanding. 'I'll do that. You take care, too.'

2

Darlene Briskin had been waiting outside the hospital when her mother arrived. 'God, I was afraid I'd miss you! There are cops inside –' She nodded at the police car and the paddy-wagon parked in the nearby ambulance area. 'God, Mum, what else can go wrong? It's been a bloody disaster from the start –'

'How's Pheeny?'

'He's still unconscious, but he'll live, they say. There are six kids in there –'

'Relax, everything's gunna be all right.' Generals need a certain heartlessness; Shirlee had to put a bit of spine into the backs of her troops. 'We'll just go in there and talk to the police as if nothing's happened –'

'For Crissake, Mum, everything's happened!'

But Shirlee was already on her way into the hospital. Darlene shrugged, then followed her.

Phoenix was still in intensive care, tubes coming out of him like tentacles feeding on him. His face had not been injured and Darlene, looking at him, thought he looked more innocent and, yes, intelligent than the brother who had irritated her all her life. If only he would stay like that . . . Then the big-shouldered, blunt-faced sergeant approached them. Shirlee was ready for him.

'I understand he was hit while on a pedestrian crossing. Are you charging the driver?'

The sergeant was patient. He had spent thirty-five years dealing with voters who never looked at anything from the other side. 'The driver of the vehicle will be charged with having children in the vehicle without seat-belts. But the accident was not her fault. Your son –' He looked at his notebook, blinked as if there was an entry there in Sanskrit – 'Phoenix? That his name?'

'Yes. Phoenix Glen Campbell Briskin.'

His face was a mixture of unspoken comment; but he said, 'We have witnesses who say the accident was his fault. He stepped off right in front of the Range Rover –'

'He was on a pedestrian crossing.'

'Mum,' said Darlene, 'let it lay. Till later –'

'I believe in the law being the law.'

Darlene felt a faint swooning fit and the unconscious Phoenix seemed to wobble his tubes. The sergeant said, 'We'll discuss it in a day or two, Mrs Briskin. In the meantime –'

'In the meantime?' said Darlene, getting in ahead of her mother.

'The parents of the children may sue. The driver of the vehicle and your brother. Everybody's for litigation these days. Don't quote me.' He folded his notebook, put it away. 'We'll be in touch. At your residential address or your place down the South Coast? Where?'

'At home,' said Darlene, silently telling her mother to keep her mouth shut. 'Hurstville. You've got the address?'

'Oh yes,' said the sergeant. 'We're organized.'

When they were alone beside the silent Phoenix, Shirlee said, 'You didn't have to take over like that. I'm not a heart-broken mother.'

Darlene tried for the image in her mind, but gave up. 'Mum, you were rubbing that sergeant with sandpaper. He was doing his best to be sympathetic –'

'Sympathetic?' Shirlee grunted in disgust. 'He was blaming Pheeny for what happened –'

'Mum –' Darlene wanted to belt her mother. 'Maybe Pheeny *was* to blame –'

Shirlee wasn't paying attention. She was going through the plastic bag containing Phoenix's belongings. 'What's this? From Centrelink – lavatory attendant? They were sending him to clean out toilets?'

'Mum . . .' Darlene was holding in her temper and frustration. 'Mum, we're gunna have to move that guy Magee. If the cops come down there –'

'They've already been.' Shirlee put Phoenix's belongings into a drawer of the table beside his bed. Neatly. 'They come to tell us Pheeny was in hospital. We headed 'em off down at the gate. Did you talk to Chantelle today?'

'Yeah. She said to be patient. But that was before this happened –' She gestured at her inert brother, for once keeping his mouth shut. 'I think we oughta call her again, see what she advises.'

'I think she oughta come and see us. We might have to change our plans,' said Shirlee, tucking in the sheet around

108

her son, shaking her head at how un-neat nurses were these days.

'I don't think that would be a good idea. When I talked to her this morning she said she thought everyone at I-Saw was being watched by the cops. She said she'd heard something else. That the bank – Kunishima? – they'd never pay up for Mr Magee. They're saying he syphoned off a load of cash before the roof fell in.'

Shirlee found an unbandaged section of Phoenix that could be stroked. 'Will Medicare pay for all this?'

'Mum, are you listening to me?' Darlene was going to blow her top any minute now. 'I think it's close to time we unloaded Mr Magee and put it down to experience. I don't believe in omens, but we've had so many things go wrong – *Mum*!'

Shirlee looked at her across the still form of Phoenix. 'I'm listening. If Mr Magee's the one with the money, wherever he's got it hidden away, then he's the one gunna pay for himself. We start cutting bits off of him, a finger or something, till he tells us where the money is. It's the only way.' She sounded now like a surgeon, one in a field casualty hospital in World War One. 'He'll talk, leave it to me.'

'Mum, I'm not gunna be in anything like that –' She shuddered at the thought.

Then a nurse came in, young, pretty and brisk. 'You're not expecting the worst, are you? He's going to be fine. He looks as if he was as strong as – as a horse. What did he do?'

'He was a gym instructor,' said Shirlee. 'Black belt.'

Darlene waited for the impersonator on the bed, the gym instructor with the black belt (in what?), to twitch. Phoenix remained still. 'When he comes out of the coma, will he know where he is? I mean, will he be incoherent or anything? You know, *babble*?'

'Possibly,' said the nurse, re-arranging Shirlee's neat bed-straightening. 'He'll be disoriented. He might think he's in the gym, that he's been knocked or something.'

'Then I'd better stay here,' said Shirlee, planning once again. 'Just in case –'

'Good idea, Mum,' said Darlene, trying to avoid being at any dismemberment. 'I'll go back to the cottage, see that Corey is okay. My other brother,' she explained to the nurse.

'Are they close?'

Like Cain and Abel. 'Bosom buddies.'

'Maybe you should tell him to come up here. It often helps, I mean if the patient is disoriented, if they have close family around when they come to.'

'I'll do that,' said Darlene.

'Take the car,' said Shirlee and passed her the keys. 'I'll hold Pheeny's hand while you're gone.'

'Pheeny?' said the nurse.

'Short for Phoenix.'

'Oh yeah. That was the bird that rose from the ashes, wasn't it?'

'I dunno,' said Shirlee. 'Glen Campbell never sang that verse.'

Darlene rolled her eyes at the bird on the bed, which didn't stir, let alone rise.

The nurse left and immediately was replaced by a man in the doorway. 'Relatives?'

'Yes,' said Shirlee.

'Fantastic! Mother and girlfriend?'

'No,' said Darlene. 'Sister.'

'Fantastic! Close family, that's what we want. Allow me to introduce myself. George Bomaker, solicitor.'

He was short and round, and his clothes looked as if they had been pressed while on him; he had a glazed look, like toffee on an apple. He had a rapid-fire delivery, at least 165 words a minute, and apparently only one adjective, *fantastic*. He was a natural-born sports commentator, but somehow had become an ambulance chaser.

'I'm rounding up the families of the six poor little dears who were in the accident – a class action, that's what I'm suggesting.

In your case, a separate action. I've checked on the lady who drove the Range Rover – her husband's a property developer. We'll sue –'

'How much?' said Shirlee.

'Too early to tell,' said Bomaker, looking at the dead-to-the-world Phoenix. 'If there's brain damage or paraplegic damage –'

Darlene felt faint, leant against the bed. She hadn't even considered those possibilities. Shirlee, a true commander, kept a stiff upper lip. 'He's got a broken leg and a broken arm and smashed ribs. We dunno if he'll be worse –'

'Let's pray he won't be,' said Bomaker and looked towards the ceiling; God was on the side of litigation. 'First things first. I can represent you, I and my two partners?'

'You're experienced at this?' said Shirlee. 'I mean, I've read about these cases, they're all the go, aren't they?'

Bomaker tried hard to look offended. 'I wouldn't put it like that, not exactly. But yes, careless people and corporations are being made to pay.'

'And how do we pay you?' said Darlene.

Bomaker spread a generous hand. 'No win, no pay.'

Then Darlene's mobile rang.

'I'll take it outside,' she said and left, wondering at the risk of leaving her mother and Mr Bomaker together. But then, she told herself with resignation that was new to her, things couldn't get worse.

3

Errol Magee, depressed in his straps, having exhausted all other subjects to keep his mind alive, had been summarizing his sexual encounters with women. At school in the eastern suburbs the girls at Ascham and Kambala had written him off after single encounters; he had been a nerd not only in class but in bed. It was Caroline, in London, who had educated him; but she had been a clinical lover, like a therapist. On his return to Sydney there had been one or two brief flings before Daniela; she had been completely different from Caroline, basing her bed technique on World Championship Wrestling. Then there had been Louise, who was dreamily romantic in bed, but spoiled matters by murmuring *Oh Bruce!* (who the hell was Bruce?). Finally there had been Kylie, whose favourite position was *soixante-neuf*, which was okay up to a point but had its dark moments and rather muffled any love talk. He had never been completely successful in love and in the end he had put it down to the influence of his mother, that squash-playing, tennis-playing, golf-playing bungee-jumper who had wanted him to be nothing but a sporting hero.

It was then that he had let out the scream of anguish that had no meaning but the sound of the emptiness into which he had fallen.

Corey Briskin, wrench in hand, was down at the road, tightening the bolts that held the sagging gate to its upright. He was a natural handyman, something his father had never been, and he was always looking for things to be fixed. He had seen the state of the gate when he had been down here earlier and now he was doing something about it.

Then he saw the police car coming at a steady pace up the road. He stiffened, the wrench tight on a bolt; but all his strength had drained out of him. The car drew in at the gate and Constable Haywood got out. He was a handsome young man, the sort featured on posters; but they were all bastards underneath, Corey knew for a fact. Haywood bent to reach in for his cap, then decided against it and left it on the front seat. He came round the car bare-headed, smiling warmly. This was an informal visit, police public relations, as the Commissioner kept advising.

'You come down here often? I haven't seen you before.'

'We don't use the place much.' Corey straightened up, satisfied all the bolts had been tightened; his stomach, too, was tight. He wasn't going to offer the bastard a cup of tea or a beer. 'We're thinking of putting it up for sale.'

Haywood looked up towards the house. 'Yeah? I might be interested. I'm renting at the moment.'

Don't ask to look over the place. 'Yeah, well, you'd have to talk to me mum about that.'

'You heard yet from her? How your brother is?'

'Not yet. She'd of only just got to the hospital, I think.'

Then there was the terrible yell, scream or whatever it was from up in the house. It seemed to Corey that everything around them had fallen silent, so that the yell was amplified. Constable Haywood's chin shot up.

'What was that? It sounded like a yell for help! Who's up there?'

Without thinking Corey hit him on the side of the head with the wrench. Constable Haywood, a tall man, went down like a falling tree, slowly at first, then crashing into the dirt. Corey looked down at him, then at the wrench as if it were something that had suddenly and uninvited appeared in his hand.

'Oh Jesus Christ!' He cursed himself, as if he were twins. His father, the fucking hothead, had come out in him; his mother would never have lifted the wrench, would have *planned* how to distract and get rid of Constable Haywood. He knelt down and felt the pulse in the policeman's neck: he was still alive, but absolutely dead to the world. A case for intensive care . . .

So am I, he thought with a brain that was a stew. He looked wildly around him; but only the timber stared back at him. Then his mother, the planner, abruptly took over in him. He opened the second gate, the one on to the track that led up to the house. He picked up Constable Haywood, staggering a little under the bigger man's weight, carried him to the police car and dumped him on the back seat. Then he got into the car and drove it up to the house. His mind, his mother's mind, was beginning to work.

He got out of the car, went up into the house and put on a

hood. He picked up a second hood and went into the bedroom where Errol Magee, exhausted by his thoughts and his scream, lolled in the chair.

'You should of kept your mouth shut, sport. What the bloody hell was all the yelling about?'

'I'm fed up,' said Magee. 'Kill me.'

'Don't be fucking stupid. What would you be worth dead? Here, put this on. Back to front, sport. I don't want you to see where we're going.'

He slipped the hood over Magee's head and instantly there was a protest inside it. He lifted the hood. 'What's the matter?'

'I'm going to smother in that –'

'Jesus, you're a whinger!' He slipped the hood back over Magee's head. 'Shut up and save your breath.' There was another murmur from inside the hood. Corey put his ear against it. 'What'd you say?'

It was smothered but it was distinct: 'I said, fuck you.'

'Yeah,' said Corey but to himself, 'I'm doing that without any help from you. What now, for Crissake?'

He put his ear close to the hood again: 'Where're we going?'

'I dunno. I'll let you know when we get there.' The planning, so far, didn't extend to a destination. Where did you dump an unconscious cop you'd just clouted?

He undid the straps, but bound Magee's hands together behind his back. Then he led him out to the police car, guiding him down the front steps, opened the boot and pushed him in.

'Just lay still, mate, and you'll be okay.'

He closed the boot, went round and checked on Constable Haywood. The big young copper was still, but he didn't look too hot. Corey stared at him a long moment; shook his head at how things today had suddenly started to go wrong. Then he stripped off Haywood's shirt, with some difficulty, and slipped it on over his own.

Then he walked away from the car, so that Magee wouldn't

hear him, and called Darlene on his mobile. It seemed forever before she answered: 'Yes? Who's that?'

'It's me, Sis. We got a problem –'

'What sort of problem?'

'Listen. Are you with Mum?'

'Yes, we're at the hospital. Pheeny looks as if he's going to be okay, but only just. Corey, what's the problem?'

'I'll tell you when I see you. Get the car from Mum and head south. Just after you pass Heathcote –' He paused, closing his eyes, seeing the main road in his mind. 'Just after you pass Heathcote, maybe less, there's a road goes off to the right into the bush. Take it and keep going up till you see a police car –'

'Till I see a WHAT?'

'I'll be in it – I'll explain when I see you. Leave now.' He clicked off the mobile, closed his eyes and lifted his face to the sun. But there was no sun. Just low dark clouds that had crept up on him like everyfuckingthing else. Then it began to rain.

Only then, his mind working again like his mum's, did he recognize that the rain might be his one piece of luck. It would wipe out the tyre-marks of the police car if anyone should come up here looking for Constable Haywood.

Ten minutes later, behind the wheel of the police car, capless but wearing Haywood's shirt with the insignia on the shoulders, he turned out of the side road into the main road and headed north. The rain was heavy, flooding gutters, smearing his view of the road ahead. His inclination was to put his foot down hard, but he restrained himself and kept the car going at a steady seventy. He went through Dapto, circled Wollongong and began the long climb up the Bulli Pass. He had just reached the crest when, through the rain, he saw the other police car coming towards him. It flashed its lights and, without panicking, he flashed his own lights in return. Then in his rear-vision mirror he saw the other car do a U-turn and come after him.

Oh Christ, he was done for! His first reaction was to run for it, to put the foot down and try to lose them. But the foot and the leg were paralysed. And then the white Subaru Impreza, trailing a comet's-tail of water, went by as if his own car were standing still. A moment, then the police car behind him drew out and, siren wailing, lights flashing on the roof, fanning a blue-and-red kaleidoscope of water, went after the disappearing Subaru. Corey hadn't realized he had stopped breathing; suddenly the air spat out of him in a long gasp. Saved by an idiot revhead!

He drove on through the rain, passed the Subaru and the other police car by the side of the road several kilometres further on, flashed his lights at them and continued north. Twenty minutes later, now out of the rain and into thin sunlight, he came to the turn-off into the bush. He swung off and drove up the narrow tarred road, which he knew led nowhere. He turned into a cleared patch surrounded on three sides by thick bush that was like a rough wall. He had come here with girls, parked in this clearing at night and done them in the back seat where their cries of ecstasy had got puzzled replies from the wakened birds in the trees. The good old days, or nights, the last time only a week ago . . . But he had forgotten her name. He was going senile at twenty-two.

Darlene arrived ten minutes later. She came cautiously up the road in the grey Toyota, pulled in behind the police car and got out as if expecting to be arrested. There had been no traffic on the narrow road while Corey had been waiting, but with their luck breaking the way it had been he would not be surprised if a gay Mardi Gras procession suddenly appeared.

'Corey, what's going on?'

He led Darlene away from the police car so that Magee, in the boot, would not hear what he had to say. He explained as quickly as he could, trying to stay calm but the words spewing out of him as if they were choking him.

'Jesus!' Darlene threw up her hands. 'Christ Almighty, how did I ever cop you two as brothers? Corey, do you know the shit we're in?'

He nodded. 'You think I haven't thought about it?'

'How's the cop?' Darlene walked back to the police car,

opened the rear door and looked in. Then she bent forward and put her finger against Haywood's neck pulse. She stayed like that, as if she couldn't straighten, as if her back had suddenly locked. Then she came up slowly, turned and said:

'He's dead, Corey.'

Chapter Six

1

Strike Force RLS had been formed.

'Why RLS, sir?' asked a young detective.

'Robert Louis Stevenson,' said Chief Superintendent Random. 'He wrote *Kidnapped*.'

'Ah yes,' said the young officer, a postmodernist graduate who hadn't a clue who Robert (*Louie*?) Stevenson was. Probably some FBI guy who'd written a thesis on abduction. They were always writing something on something or other.

Random, dry and unruffled as usual, who sailed always on an even keel through rough seas of crime, took Malone aside in the big room at Police Central. On a wall near them the map of the latest crime had been laid out: pictures of the murder victim, of the two kidnappees, plans of the Magee apartment, a potted history of I-Saw. Malone stood with his back to the wall, wanting no reminders.

'You're in this, Scobie, but the maid's murder isn't the major event.'

'That's interesting. Murder is now just a misdemeanour?'

'None of your Irish wit. You know what I'm getting at. Magee and his girlfriend may already be dead – in which case you take over. But while there's a possibility they're both still alive, finding them is the prime objective. We've got two experienced negotiators on hand to deal with the kidnappers, if and when they get in touch with us again. One'll be at I-Saw and the other at the Kunishima Bank.'

'Kunishima won't like that.'

'Tough titty.'

Kylie Doolan's kidnapping had been the major item on this morning's radio and TV news; tomorrow morning's press editorials were right now being written with whip-handles. Talk-back hosts were asking what the police were doing to protect the citizens of this great city; the great city's citizens, Gert and Sid and Larry and Aunty Kate, were responding with advice on how much better they could run things than the mug coppers. Random had advised the strike force to read no newspapers, listen to no radio, look at no television. The public could always run things better: politics, crime prevention, the economy, everything. All it was waiting for was a leader to organize the anarchy.

'The Commissioner would like all this cleared up by yesterday.'

'No problem. Nothing is impossible.'

'Ever tried to snap one finger?' Random illustrated.

'Tell me about one hand clapping. You can get the sound of applause by slapping one hand on your bare bum. How come you Welsh are so bloody philosophical?'

'We're melancholy. Like you Irish.'

'Not any more. The Irish are laughing all the way to the bank. We're now the rich cousins of Europe. My old man, who's been a socialist, almost a communist, all his life, is now talking like Kerry Packer.'

'Seduced. You tossed off the Catholic Church and you're in the grip of Mammon.'

'And enjoying every dollar or punt or whatever they're spending. Like the bastards in this case, till the bottom fell out of the bucket. How's my promotion coming?'

'It's on hold till we wrap this up. Find out who murdered the maid, bring back Magee and his girlfriend alive and you can go straight to Assistant Commissioner.' Then he said seriously, 'Do you think the *yakuza* have taken the girl?'

'Yes.'

'Do the media know who are behind Kunishima?'

'I don't know. Maybe some of the financial columnists do. But libel is another game for the greedy guts and they're not going to mention it in their columns. There are blokes out on the street who'll tell you all the banks are run by *yakuza* of some sort.'

'Does *Four Corners* know? About Kunishima?'

'You mean does my daughter Mo know? If she does, she hasn't told me. And I haven't told her.'

'Don't get shirty. I had to ask.' Random changed the subject: 'Keep a couple of your people standing by – Wollongong command may call them. They were on to me at Crime Agency this morning.'

'That murdered officer? They got any leads?'

'They're working on a couple, pretty slim ones, they said.'

'Who found the body?'

'Some woman phoned in, said she'd been bird-watching in some bush near Heathcote and she came across his body.'

'They interviewing her?'

'They don't know who she is, she hung up on them. Said she didn't want to be involved in the killing of a cop. Whoever did it might come looking for her. You can see her viewpoint, but that's no help.'

'Are we going to be involved, as the lady describes it?'

'Us? They probably won't need us, it's none of our business. But tell Russ to have someone on hand if they call.'

'I might take it myself, just to get away from this.'

'No, you won't. Where are you heading now?'

'Over to I-Saw offices. I have a date with a sexpot my son brought home last night. She's meeting me there.'

'You'll have none of those thrills when you get to Superintendent. You meet only old boilers.'

'Lisa will be glad to hear that.'

Malone debated whether to take someone with him, decided to go alone. Now that he was leaving the job, heading for a desk, he wanted more time with his thoughts, not with a colleague. He was wrapping up a large part of his life and he preferred to do it alone.

He drove over to Milson's Point. Last night's rain had cleared the air; the day was polished for new uses. The buildings, too, looked as if they had been scrubbed for new uses. Bankruptcy maybe, he cynically wondered. He rode up in an empty lift that seemed surrounded by emptiness, as if the building were only a shell. Yet on other floors but those of I-Saw other companies, still solvent, were at work.

The executive floor looked deserted when he stepped out of the lift. Then at the far end of the room he saw the four people around Jared Cragg's desk. He was halfway towards them before he recognized the three women with Cragg: Caroline Magee, Daniela Bonicelli and Louise Cobcroft.

'We were going to call you, Inspector,' said Caroline Magee while he was still approaching them. 'The news about Miss Doolan being kidnapped.'

The three women all looked too friendly, like witches with a common stew in the cauldron. Poor Errol Magee, he thought, but said, 'We don't know she's been kidnapped. She's missing, that's all.'

'That's all?' said Cragg.

Is he the witch-master here? But then Magee thought, I'm not on top of this. He had been thrown off-balance to find the three Magee women, wife and ex-girlfriends, together. 'That's what we're telling the media. You think we should tell 'em more?'

'The whole bloody thing's getting out of hand!'

'I'm scared,' said Daniela Bonicelli, but didn't look it.

'So am I,' said Louise Cobcroft, who did look very scared. Or was a very good actress. 'Can we ask for police protection?'

'Miss Doolan had it,' said Caroline. 'It apparently didn't help.'

Malone smiled at her; or grimaced. 'Miss Doolan was a smartarse, Mrs Magee. Most people, when we're protecting them, try to co-operate with us. She slipped away while our backs were turned. If we give you protection, I hope *you'll* co-operate.'

'Me, too?' said Cragg.

'You feel you're in danger, Mr Cragg?'

Today he was more formally dressed than yesterday: a collar-and-tie job, suit trousers instead of jeans. Maybe, Malone thought, one dressed formally for the final rites of receivership. He wondered where Joe Smith, of Ballantine, Ballantine and Kowinsky was. Downstairs laying out the corpse?

'No,' said Cragg, tightening the yellow tie that lay like spilled egg against his blue shirt. 'No, I'll be okay. I'm walking out of here today and Errol can take care of himself.'

'And Miss Doolan, too?'

'She was never part of I-Saw. She's his responsibility.'

'And what about these three ladies?'

'I've just told them, they look after themselves.'

He didn't look at the three women and they ignored him. Malone had read about the mass sackings in the IT game over the past year and he wondered if they had all been as heartless as Cragg made it sound. There was one thing about the public service: when it came to sacking, downsizing, whatever one called it, you never met the real axeman. He was somewhere out there in the fog of bureaucracy.

'We'll look after ourselves,' said Daniela. 'You'd better believe it, Jared.'

'What does Errol owe you three ladies?' asked Malone.

'Worthless stock options,' said Daniela, as if reading from a list. This morning there was no sign of last night's amateur coquette; she was all business. 'Superannuation, sick leave, last month's pay.'

'The same,' said Louise, when Malone looked at her.

Then he turned to Caroline, who stood apart from the other two women. That's how she would be, he thought, always standing apart. Daniela and Louise were in casual clothes this morning, slacks and shirts; but Caroline was in a suit, ear-rings and necklace in place, handbag at the ready. It suddenly occurred to him that she was the only one of the four here around the desk who showed no sign of wreckage. It was there in the faces of the other three but not in hers.

'Errol owes me nothing,' she said, 'except my wasted time.'

'Lucky you,' said Daniela, but Caroline ignored her.

Malone changed tack, said to Cragg, 'The woman didn't ring back yesterday at five as she promised. The woman asking for the ransom.'

'No-o. How did you know that?'

'We got a warrant to have I-Saw's phones tapped. I must've forgotten to tell you,' he said with no hint of apology. He was becoming tired of these people. 'She called the Kunishima Bank, asked them for the *five* million.'

'What did the bank say?' It was Daniela who asked the question. She was the one who was doing most of the talking. Louise stood silent, as if she were no more than an office junior. Caroline still stood apart. Like a partner in Ballantine, Ballantine and Kowinsky? Malone wondered. But she had already declared she was no longer interested in I-Saw or Errol Magee.

'They told her, whoever she was, to get lost,' said Malone. 'But politely – they're Japanese. Errol's name stinks with them, Daniela. He's stolen forty million dollars from them and salted it away somewhere overseas.'

'Holy shit!' said Cragg; and Daniela and Louise looked as if they were silently echoing him. 'Jesus, that could've saved us!'

'You hadn't told them?' Malone looked at Caroline Magee.

'No.' Her tone was flat.

'What a bastard!' Daniela at last found her voice again. 'Why can't he pay his own ransom? And pay us?'

'I could cut his throat,' said Louise and for a moment looked a different, dangerous woman.

Malone's worst feelings were getting the better of him. Malice is there in everyone; even St Francis, when people weren't looking, had thrown stones at the birds of Assisi that shat on him. 'Maybe we should turn him over to you when we find him.'

Cragg, Daniela and Louise nodded; but Caroline Magee shook her head. 'You can have him. I'm going back to London.'

'When?' said Malone.

'I'm booked out on Friday.'

'What if we find him and he's dead?'

It was brutal, but Caroline didn't flinch. 'Then I'll say a prayer for him. In London.'

Malone felt he was getting nowhere. He had come over here to talk to Daniela, to get more background on Errol Magee and who else might be involved with him. But the three women, together, even if unwillingly, were behind a barricade. He would have to take them away separately, subject them to hard interrogation. And he couldn't do that without having lawyers brought in and he was in no mood for that sort of obstruction.

He changed tack again: 'Mr Cragg, may I see you alone? Excuse us, ladies.'

The three ladies were impassive; it was as if two territories of gender had been staked out. Malone took Cragg back through the desert of work-stations to the front desk. 'Jared –' Be matey: first rule of police interrogation. 'That woman who rang the other day – did you recognize her voice?'

'You had a bloody hide tapping our phones without telling me!'

'I wasn't the one who authorized it. Take it up with our strike force commander . . . Did you recognize the voice? You didn't seem surprised when you got the call.'

'You don't miss much, do you?'

'I try not to. How d'you reckon I'd go in IT?'

Cragg shook his head. 'The game's full of fucking blind men – you'd eat 'em.'

'But not you? Weren't you blind to Errol and what he was up to?'

Cragg nodded, glum at his own blindness. 'Yeah . . . About that girl. Yeah, I thought the voice was familiar, but I couldn't place it. Still can't – I'm not an expert on women's voices.' He would never listen to them, Malone thought; Cragg would make some of the chauvinists in Homicide look like handmaidens to feminism. 'It might've been one of Errol's girlfriends. Yes?' He was looking over Malone's shoulder.

Malone turned. Vassily Todorov stood there, dressed for battle in the city streets. He wore black training shoes, black socks, tight black shorts, a green polo shirt with FOLEY'S FLYERS across the front of it in white, and a green-and-white cyclist's helmet shaped like a plume. He wore black gloves and there was a green haversack on his back. He looks bloody ridiculous, thought Malone.

'Mr Todorov! You delivering something for Mr Cragg?'

'Who's he?' asked Cragg. 'A police courier?'

'Mr Todorov's girlfriend worked for Mr Magee. She was the maid who was murdered.'

'Terrible,' said Todorov and the plumed helmet shook from side to side. 'In the prime of her life.'

'Do you have something for me?' said Cragg.

'Only a question, sir.' Todorov was not aggressive, but with every muscle exposed in his tight gear, the plumed helmet on the rock of his head, there was a suggestion he was ready for aggression. 'Miss Marcos, God rest her soul – she was a Catholic,' he explained; communism still clung to him, like another polo shirt. 'She was employed by I-Saw. Her pay cheques were drawn on I-Saw. Signed by Mr Magee. I think I-Saw owes her superannuation, sick pay and holiday pay. I have added it up. Three thousand, seven hundred and twenty dollars. I am her next-of-kin.'

'Mr Todorov, you are just her boyfriend,' said Malone.

'Inspector, I am her *de facto*. I have studied the law. I-Saw owes me three thousand, seven hundred and twenty dollars. I will take a cheque.'

'Mr – Todorov?' said Cragg. 'Go down to the floor below and ask for Mr Smith. He's in charge of I-Saw now. Tell him what you want and he will put you on his list of creditors. I wouldn't build my hopes, if I were you.'

Todorov looked at Malone, who said, 'They're bankrupt,

Vassily. I think you'll be lucky if you get five cents. I wouldn't leave Foley's Flyers if I were you.'

'I am no fool, Inspector.' Todorov seemed to grow another inch or two; Malone looked to see if he was standing on his toes. He wasn't. 'Bulgarians are born looking four ways at once – history is our godfather. I did not come to Australia to be a bicycle courier for the rest of my life. I am pedalling for higher things.'

This bloke's having me on. But perhaps he wasn't. Multi-culturism had been in this country for fifty years, but the weave was still as loose as a shark net. Understanding slipped through every day. He knew he would have trouble placing Bulgaria on the map. Somewhere at the arse-end of Europe, bum-wiped by history.

'He's all yours,' said Cragg bluntly and walked away towards a door that led to stairs, going down to the laying out of the corpse of I-Saw.

'They don't care, do they?' said Todorov, looking after him.

'He has things on his mind.' *Why am I defending Cragg? Of course he doesn't care*. But then Todorov himself had given the impression that he didn't care, not about Juanita; only about what was owed to her, down to the last dollar.

'I saw the news – Mr Magee's girlfriend has been kidnapped. It is like Moscow.'

Malone had to smile. 'Not quite, Vassily.'

'I hate the Russians. They ruined communism.'

Malone wasn't going to defend Russians or communism. 'How did Miss Doolan and Juanita get on?'

'Not very well.' Todorov was not hesitant about his opinion. 'Miss Doolan was rude. Australian women are not good with servants. They are either rude or too friendly.'

Ask a Bulgarian communist, a Foley's Flyer, for a considered opinion on Australian women as domestic bosses and don't complain if you get a considered answer. He would have to ask Lisa's opnion tonight. 'How did Mr Magee get on with Juanita?'

'He hardly spoke to her. Except once.'

Maybe Australian men were just as bad with domestic help. Had Errol put the hard word on the maid, as happened in Britain and Europe, according to the movies he saw on SBS? 'When did he speak to her? About what?'

'Two weeks ago. Juanita told me about it, she was so surprised.'

'Why?'

'Mr Magee asked her to keep a secret.'

'What secret?'

Todorov took off his plumed helmet; he looked more human. 'A woman came to see him. They seemed to know each other – Juanita thought it might be someone who worked here.' He gestured about him: a little scornfully, as if they stood in the middle of a rubbish dump. Which I-Saw might soon prove to be. 'They talked to each other, Juanita thought for about an hour. She was out in the kitchen most of the time. When the woman left, Mr Magee kissed her.'

'That doesn't prove anything. Mr Magee seems to have kissed a lot of women. What did he say to Juanita?'

'He came out to the kitchen, she said, and asked her not to tell Miss Doolan the woman had been there. He said he was planning a business surprise for Miss Doolan.'

Mr Magee had done that, all right. 'Did Juanita say what the woman looked like? Describe her? Blonde, brunette, redhead?'

'Women never describe other women's hair.' He was an expert on women, too. Foley's Flyers should be paying him a bonus. 'Juanita just said she was smart, in the way she was dressed. But so many of them are these days, aren't they? Power women. Even in Bulgaria.'

'Did Juanita mention the woman to Miss Doolan?'

Todorov shrugged. 'Who knows what women mention to each other? I don't think so. Juanita and Miss Doolan were never friendly.'

The question came without thought, the tongue finding its

own way: 'Do you ever deliver anything to the Kunishima Bank?'

Todorov raised an eyebrow. 'Yes. Why do you ask?'

'What do you hear about them?'

'What does one ever hear about banks, except complaints? But not the Kunishima. One never hears anything about them – even the Aussies who work there never gossip. So I'm told.'

'So you're told?'

'Bicycle couriers gossip. You see them sitting around together, what do you think they talk about? Places they have to deliver to, little managers who are rude. Where the good women are on the reception desks.'

'Good women?' Virginal receptionists?

Berlitz had let him down. 'Good – sorts? Yes, good sorts.'

Then Caroline Magee came down the long room, moving gracefully, calm as a nun on a sea of charity. 'Goodbye, Inspector,' she said as she went by. 'Good luck.'

'You'll still be at the Ritz-Carlton?'

'Till Friday,' she said over her shoulder and was gone.

'Who was that?' asked Todorov.

'Mrs Magee. His wife. Or used to be.'

'His wife?' Todorov's mind slipped back into gear on the bicycle of his greed: 'Perhaps she would pay Juanita's superannuation?'

'Mrs Magee wouldn't pay the Virgin Mary's superannuation.'

Todorov strapped on the plumed helmet again. 'I shall not give up.'

'Nor I, Vassily,' said Malone, but felt he was on a treadmill.

2

Briskin brother and sister had walked away from the police car. 'God, Corey, what else can go wrong?'

'I dunno.' He leaned against a tree for support; he felt sick, but hollow sick, nothing to come up. 'How we gunna tell Mum? How's she taking what happened to Pheeny?'

'Okay. She's making a deal with an ambulance-chaser. We're going to sue the woman who knocked Pheeny over.'

Corey was unimpressed. 'Big deal . . . I wanna call it a day, Sis, turn our mate loose and call off the whole fucking thing. I'll go up to Queensland –'

'Where is he?'

Corey nodded across at the police car. 'In the boot. I put one of the hoods on him, so he wouldn't know where he is.'

'He could be smothered – Jesus, that's all we want! Three bloody corpses! Get him outa there. Put a hood on – I'll get outa sight till you've got him in the boot of the Toyota. Go on, move!'

'What we gunna do with him?'

'I dunno. Get him outa there and into our boot.'

Errol Magee was only semi-conscious; another half-hour and he would have expired. Corey, wearing a blue hood, carried him over to the Toyota and put him in its boot, taking off Magee's hood at the last moment. Then he slammed the lid down and leaned on the car, his legs hollow again.

Darlene observed the scene with sick wonderment. A man in a blue hood carrying another man in a hood from the boot of a police car to that of another private car. She wished that it was a nightmare and not reality.

She walked across to Corey, drew him away from the car, out of earshot of Magee in the boot. 'I've wiped everything in the cop's car that you might of touched, including the boot. Take that shirt off and we'll throw it away somewhere. And this –' She held up the wrench, looked at the bloodstain on its head and grimaced. Then, with a visible effort she gathered herself and him together. 'Okay, let's go and see Mum.'

'What use will she be?' All he wanted was to get away from this whole business. 'She talked us into all this. Her and Chantelle.'

'You got any other suggestions?'

He looked across at the police car. From where he stood it looked empty; but he knew it was full of total bloody disaster. He sighed, from the bottom of his belly, and said, 'No, let's see what they have to say. They're the brains.'

Darlene looked at him at that, but said nothing.

They drove out of the bush and five kilometres up the main road Darlene pulled the car off the tarmac. Corey went into some scrub and buried Constable Haywood's shirt and the wrench. He came back to the car and, not talking to each other, they drove on to St George's Hospital.

Darlene went in and brought out Shirlee. Phoenix was still in a coma, the only one unworried. He lay under his nest of tubes, more innocent than he had ever been or ever would be, if he lived.

Shirlee was already planning, even as Darlene told her what had happened: 'Corey will have to go back to the cottage, pretend he never left there. He'll –'

'Bugger that.' Corey got out of the car. The car park was almost full and he had had trouble finding a space. 'That's the first place they'll come looking –'

'Exactly,' said his mum. 'We'll drop His Nibs off at our house and Darlene can stay with him. You and me'll go down to the cottage and when the coppers come we'll say you never saw Constable What'shisname –'

'Mum,' said Darlene, another planner but still learning, 'who stays with Pheeny? It'll look suspicious, nobody with him while he's still in intensive care. They'll think we're bloody heartless –'

'Yeah, you're right – Didn't your mother tell you not to stare?'

She was looking across the roof of the car at three children, two boys and a girl, all aged about eight or ten, sitting in a Toyota Nimbus with the windows down, staring intently at the Briskins as if watching a TV soap. 'We're not staring,' said the girl, more cheek than a bare backside, 'we're just looking.'

Then there was a faint yell from the boot of the Briskins' car. Shirlee looked sharply at Darlene. 'What's that?'

'It's Errol,' said Darlene, keeping her voice low, seeing the ears on the three heads in the Nimbus standing out like antennae. 'We better get outa here.'

So the three of them got back into the Toyota, drove out of the car park; the three kids in the Nimbus waved them goodbye, then thumbed their noses. Corey took the car on a leisurely tour of the nearby streets while they discussed their plans.

'We can't take him back home, not in daylight. Old Mrs Charlton, she's always at her window watching what's going on. She'd be out, hanging over the fence, before we'd got His Nibs into the house. No, we gotta take him back down to the cottage. We'll keep him there till midnight, then we'll bring him back up here to home, smuggle him in while Mrs C's asleep. Darlene, you stay with Pheeny, keep in touch with us.'

'On the mobile?'

'Yeah, sure. Just don't mention Mr Magee, that's all.' Then she looked at Corey, silent behind the wheel. 'What got into you? You turning out to have something of your father in you?'

'Dad never done in anybody –'

'Only by accident, he didn't. He always carried a gun . . .' She arranged her thoughts, and theirs, neatly: 'All right, it's all arranged. We get on to Chantelle, tell her there's been a hiccup –'

'A hiccup?' said Darlene in the back seat.

'Don't quibble. There's been a hiccup, but His Nibs is still alive and we want the ransom for him. By five o'clock tomorrow at the latest.'

'I was supposed to call the Kunishima Bank today –'

'It don't matter. They're not gunna run away.'

'What happens if I-Saw or the Kunishima Bank don't come good? I was supposed to call I-Saw –'

'Don't be pessmistic,' said the general.

'Holy Jesus!' said Corey, blind with pessimism and despair,

131

and had to brake sharply to avoid running down a small girl on a pedestrian crossing. The little darling stopped, stared at him, then gave him the middle finger salute and walked on.

In the back seat Darlene lay back, laughing a little hysterically.

Corey and Shirlee dropped Darlene back at the hospital and drove south again, back to the cottage. When they took Magee out of the boot of the Toyota, he was once again only semi-conscious. Corey slung him over his shoulder, carried him up into the cottage and into the third bedroom and strapped him in the chair again. Magee opened his eyes, dull as smoked glass, and gazed at Corey as if he didn't recognize him.

Corey slapped him gently on the cheek, shook him. 'Come on, sport, snap outa it!'

Magee twitched in his bonds, as if trying to stir up the blood in himself.

Corey was wearing his blue hood. 'Sorry we been carting you around like this, but blame your mates. We thought we had a deal on the ransom, but they reneged on it.'

'I don't fucking care any more.' Magee found his voice, a growl that sounded as if it had been buried for a long time.

'Come on!' Corey tried to sound jovial; but didn't feel that way. 'Where's your fucking capitalist spirit?'

Magee was slowly coming back to normal; or near normal. 'What do you think you are? You're out to make money. Five million. That's not pension stuff.'

For the first time in several hours Corey grinned, behind the hood. 'It is for me, sport. You want a leak or anything?'

'Not yet. I'd like a beer, a light one.'

Corey laughed this time; the hood fluttered like a mask about to crumble. 'You're on your own, Errol. I'll get you a beer, but it's a VB, not a light one. That okay, sir?'

'Up yours,' said Magee. 'Yeah, a VB.'

Out in the kitchen Corey said, 'What do we do with him if the cops come?'

'You better gag him,' said Shirlee. 'Case he hears 'em and starts yelling. What're you doing?'

'Getting him a beer.'

'You're spoiling him.'

'Yeah. Fucking ridiculous, aint it?'

'Wash your mouth out.'

The police sergeant and another constable arrived at seven-thirty in the last light of the day. The sun had gone down beyond the escarpment and there were no shadows, just the diminishing light. The timber back beyond the house was losing its shape, the trees merging into each other, a dark grey wall. Down in front of the house, beyond the road, the timber there had some pale-trunked eucalyptus that still reflected a little light, like thin ghosts waiting for the nights.

Corey, at his mother's instructions, had been waiting out on the front verandah for the police that he and she knew would come. As soon as he saw the police car coming up the road, its headlights already on, he got up and walked unhurriedly, but like a gaited two-legged horse, down to the front gate. Shirlee had come out on to the front verandah, but stayed there, wiping her hands on a dish towel.

'You got some word on my brother?' Corey tried to sound natural. He stepped carefully round a mud patch, noting out of the corner of his eyes that the wallow of mud across the other, wider gate showed only the tracks of one car, the Toyota. 'I mean, we ain't heard anything –'

'No,' said the sergeant, 'it's another matter. Did Constable Haywood come up here this afternoon?'

'Constable Hay – Oh, the young guy with you this morning? No. Was he supposed to?'

'He said he might.' The two policemen, the younger man standing behind the sergeant, were almost po-faced in their seriousness. 'You been here all afternoon?'

'All the time. Me mum come back about an hour ago. When she left, me brother was okay, still unconscious but okay. Me sister's staying with him.' Every word made the Briskins sound like a tightly-knit family, battlers to the core. 'When I seen you coming . . . Why are you looking for your mate?'

'We're not looking for him,' said the sergeant. 'He's been found. Dead, from a wound in the head.'

'Jesus!' Corey shook his own head, as if it had been clouted. 'How'd it happen? Where?'

'We dunno where it happened or how. We thought you might of seen him up here and he'd told you where he was going next.'

'I'm sorry, mate, I can't help you. This is gunna upset me mum when I tell her – she's got a lotta time for you guys.' Feeling more confident, he was letting his tongue get away from him. He pulled back: 'I dunno I oughta tell her. Not while she's worrying about me brother.'

The sergeant looked up towards Shirlee on the verandah, now barely discernible in the gloom. 'No, don't mention it. Tell her, I dunno, tell her I was introducing Constable Gilchrist here, he's new to our station. Case you wanted any help. Tell her that. Thanks, anyway, for your help.'

'I didn't help at all, Sarge. And I'm sorry about your mate.'

'Yeah,' said the sergeant, getting back into the car. 'So are we.'

The junior officer swung the car round and they drove away, disappearing round a bend in the road. Corey stood staring after them, feeling no lift in his spirits. He felt like a swimmer in the surf who knew the waves would keep coming, getting bigger and bigger. The moon came up above the timber and a flying-fox scratched a line across it, defacing it for the moment. He turned and walked back up towards the house while a night-bird called from the timber, up where his father lay buried.

'What did they want?' asked Shirlee.

'Nothing to worry about, Mum.'

The rest of the night dragged till midnight. Then they woke the dozing Magee, put him in the boot of the Toyota.

134

'Where the fuck are we going now?'

'Wash your mouth out,' Shirlee told him from inside her hood.

They drove up to Hurstville and the three bedroomed house in a quiet street. They smuggled Magee, who had been gagged again, into the house and tied him to a bed in what was Darlene's room. Darlene was at home, waiting for them.

'Pheeny's still unconscious, but they say he's improving. They'll call if there's any change. What do we do now?'

'Go to bed,' said Shirlee, all of a sudden looking tired and (Darlene thought with shock) old. 'Tomorrow's the last day.'

'The last day for what?'

'We'll see,' said Shirlee and said nothing more.

In the morning they heard the news on the radio that Errol Magee's girlfriend, Kylie Doolan, was also missing.

3

Malone waited in the foyer of the I-Saw building for Daniela Bonicelli. He had to wait longer than he had expected, but he was a patient man. She stepped out of the lift after twenty minutes, pulled up sharply when she saw him.

'Waiting for me?'

'Who else, Daniela?'

Again there was no coquetry. 'I saw you eyeing Mrs Magee.'

'No more than I was eyeing you and Louise.'

'Are you going to offer me protection?'

'Against possible kidnapping? No, Daniela. I'm with Homicide, we come in after the event.' He was using the big club this morning. *Pull your head in, Malone.* 'I don't think you're in any danger, Daniela. Not unless there's something you haven't told me about?'

'Such as?'

'Did you go and see Mr Magee at his apartment a coupla weeks ago?'

She looked at him, then looked away. She was carrying a bottle of spring water; she unscrewed the cap and took a swig. Behind her Malone saw four other women, all with the statutory accoutrement of mobile phone and bottle of spring water. No one under the age of thirty, apparently, drank tap water any more. Ecstasy tablets were washed down with spring water; intestines had to be cleaned, though minds might be fogged. He waited till Daniela had capped the bottle again. But his patience was now beginning to wear thin; perhaps he should ask for a swig of spring water to cool him down. At last Daniela looked back at him.

'Yes, I did. I forget which day, I went there one morning when the place was clear. When Kylie wasn't there.'

'What for? I thought you and he had finished that sort of thing.'

'I didn't go there for *that*. I wouldn't have gone to bed with Errol again for – how much is the ransom supposed to be? Not for any money. I went there because I'd heard a whisper that things were much worse than we'd been told.'

'And what did he tell you?'

'Not to worry. The bastard!' He waited for her to take another swig at the bottle, but evidently she needed something stronger than water. 'He said they were negotiating for a Japanese company to come in and bail them out.'

'You believed him?'

'Well, yes and no. I believed him because I *wanted* to. Errol could be very convincing . . . But when I got back here to the office –' She nodded over her shoulder – 'I knew we were finished.'

'And what did you think of doing then?' *Like arranging a kidnapping*?

'I started looking for another job.' She uncapped the bottle, took another swig, capped the bottle again. Could someone go downhill from non-alcoholism? In the background the other four

136

women, all unconnected, it seemed, had their bottles to their lips, like a silent back-up group. 'Which I've decided to take.'

'Who with?'

She looked at him, still with no coquetry. 'Inspector, am I under suspicion or something?'

'Why would you think that, Daniela? I never suspect my son's girlfriends.'

'You should,' she said enigmatically; and Malone wondered what Tom got up to, or down to, in bed. 'I'm not Tom's girlfriend. We're just – friends. The job? I'm going to work for Kunishima Bank.'

'From IT to banking? The New Economy to the Old Economy?'

'They're connected these days. Don't you bank electronically?'

'No, I have it all in a jar under my bed. Take care, Daniela. And good luck at Kunishima. Especially take care there.'

He left her on that. When he looked back she had the bottle of spring water to her mouth again. Behind her the four women, bottles in one hand, had their mobiles to their ears.

He left Daniela with doubts about her still troubling him. Why had a job at Kunishima suddenly become available? Who had offered it to her? Okada? Tajiri?

He was halfway to his car when his own mobile rang. He stepped into a doorway, as if the call he was about to receive was from a sex worker. Instead, it was Paula Decker, not breathing heavily: 'Sir, I took time out from the Magee apartment – someone else is on duty there now. I went up to the Aurora building garage and had a word with Mr Okada's driver, from the Kunishima Bank.'

'Is he Japanese? You wouldn't have got far.'

'No, sir, he's Italian. I lifted my skirt a couple of inches and he was ready to talk.' Malone said nothing and after a pause she said, 'Sir, am I being too facetious?'

'No, Paula. I'm just sorry we don't have those male advantages. I'm also wondering why he wasn't interviewed before this.'

'Today is his first day back at work. Mr Okada told him to take a coupla days off.'

'That usual with Mr Okada?'

'The driver says no. I asked him about Mr Tajiri and Mr Nakasone. Seems the three of 'em aren't close mates. The driver says he's never driven Mr Okada to Tajiri's place. He also said that Mr Tajiri was not in the office today.'

'Does the driver know Miss Doolan?'

'No, he's never seen her.'

'Did he ever take Okada to the Magee apartment?'

'Never.'

'Where does Tajiri live?'

'I've checked that. He has an unlisted phone number, but Telstra turned it over to me. He lives at Kirribilli, just along the street from Kirribilli House and Admiralty House. He's a neighbour to the Prime Minister and the Governor-General. As respectable as you could ask. It must impress his *yakuza* mates back home.'

'Paula, don't forget – the *yakuza* connection is still not on the record. We don't want the media playing around with that, not on our say-so. What's the address?' She gave it to him. 'Have you got wheels?'

'No, sir.' She sounded disappointed.

'Go down to the Quay, catch the ferry to Kirribilli – I'll wait for you there at the wharf.' This was not, strictly, Homicide business; but he *was* part of Strike Force RLS. Greg Random would understand. 'Good work, Paula.'

'Thank you, sir.' She sounded as if she had curtsied.

He drove over to Kirribilli, two minutes away, parked the car and went down to the ferry wharf. Years ago he had caught the ferry from here to go to work; the skyline across the water, even life itself, had been much simpler then. The area had climbed up-market, bedsits had given way to million-dollar apartments. Breezes blew across from the city, carrying the scent of money.

When Paula Decker stepped off the ferry twenty minutes later he looked at her before he went to meet her. She was wearing a blue skirt and white shirt today and he saw that she had long slim legs that would have enhanced a stockings advertisement. He could understand why the Italian had responded.

'Are you armed?'

She patted the large handbag slung over one shoulder. 'My Glock and also a capsicum spray. Are you expecting trouble?'

'I hope not. But just in case –'

Back in his car he drove it along Kirribilli Avenue, past the two official residences, and parked it at a bus stop. They got out and walked along to the waterfront block of apartments. Malone stood a moment, appraising them like an estate agent looking for business. Even the smallest apartment in the block would have cost a million and a half; the penthouse would probably bring three or four million. Tajiri was doing well for a *yakuza*.

Paula Decker pressed the buzzer under Tajiri's name. A moment, then a voice said, 'Yes?'

'Police. We'd like to talk to Mr Tajiri.'

'What about?'

'We'll tell him that when we meet him. Let us in.'

'Just a moment, please.'

They waited, and three cars went past, one of them flying a standard on its wings. The Governor-General was on his way to a function, while two detectives waited to interview his neighbour, a *yakuza* gangster-banker. Only in Sydney, Malone thought.

Then the voice said, 'Please come in. First floor,' and the security lock on the front door clicked open. Malone and Paula Decker walked in, found that the first floor was at street level. A slim young man in white shirt, striped waistcoat and black trousers stood waiting for them at an open door.

'I am Teagarden,' said the young man. 'Mr Tajiri's butler.'

'Jack Teagarden?' said Malone.

'No, sir.' Slightly puzzled. 'Jocelyn Teagarden.'

'But you play trombone?'

'No, sir.' Still puzzled. 'Soccer.'

Malone gave up being a smartarse; he was getting old, the jokes were going downhill. In his mind's ear he could hear the needle screeching to a halt on his old vinyl of Jack Teagarden playing 'Lazy River'. 'Is Mr Tajiri in?'

'No, sir.'

'Do you speak Japanese?'

'No, sir.' Jocelyn Teagarden spoke *No, sir* fluently. Butlers were a rare breed in Australia, but he, apparently, was a well-bred one.

'Then how do you and Mr Tajiri communicate? I understand he doesn't speak English. Whom did you speak to before you decided to let us come in?'

Teagarden suddenly looked flustered, like a trombone player who had hit a flat note. They had come in through the small entrance lobby and now were standing in the big living room. Behind the butler sliding glass doors led out to a wide terrace; the city skyline was like a mural on a wall of the room, the Opera House shells hiding the lower face like a fan. Doors led off the living room, two on either side, all closed.

'I think you had better tell Mr Tajiri we're not leaving till he comes out to talk to us.'

The butler hesitated, but before he could turn one of the doors opened; out stepped Nakasone. 'Mr Tajiri is not here, Inspector.'

Malone looked at him, then turned his head towards Paula Decker, who up till now had been still and silent: 'This is Mr Nakasone, Detective Decker.'

Paula gave him a polite nod and he gave a small bow in return.

'He's from the Kunishima Bank. Yesterday I was told he didn't speak English.' He looked back at Nakasone. 'A quick course at Berlitz, Mr Nakasone? I know a Berlitz teacher who might help you.'

'No jokes, please, Inspector. Yesterday Mr Okada was our spokesman. In Japan we do not all try to be vocal at once.'

'Not like here, eh? We're a very vocal lot. But today you're the spokesman?'

'Yes, today, Inspector. How can I help you?'

Malone looked around. The apartment was apparently rented furnished. There was nothing Japanese in the room except a print of a chrysanthemum against the outline of a snow-capped mountain, a picture as delicate as the flower's petals. Everything else in the room was solidly Ikea. Whoever owned the apartment hadn't splashed money around.

'Do you live here, Mr Nakasone?'

'No.'

'Then you're just visiting Mr Tajiri?'

'Yes.'

'Even though he's not here? Is that a Japanese custom?'

Nakasone said nothing; then Paula Decker spoke for the first time: 'But you're visiting a woman?'

Up till now Nakasone had ignored her except for his small bow to her; he looked at her sharply, as if to admonish her for having spoken. 'What woman?'

'The one who owns that handbag on that chair there.'

Malone hadn't noticed the brown leather handbag tucked into the curve of a club chair. He mentally patted Paula Decker on the back. He let her continue the questioning:

'You're not entertaining the Australian version of a geisha, are you?'

Nice one, Paula. But Nakasone said, 'An insulting question.'

Paula went on: 'Or would it be Miss Doolan? She's been missing since yesterday afternoon and we know she paid a visit to Kunishima just before she disappeared.'

It was a moment before Nakasone replied: 'I know nothing about Miss Doolan. I heard the news this morning that she had disappeared, that she was Mr Magee's girlfriend. But I have never met her.'

'So whose handbag is that?' said Malone. 'There's no Mrs Nakasone or Mrs Tajiri, is there? If it's an Aussie geisha you're entertaining, we'll understand, we're broadminded. But just so's we'll know . . . Teagarden, open that door there and ask the lady to come out. We shan't hurt her.'

The butler hesitated, waited on his cue from Nakasone. The latter looked as if he might suddenly erupt in a burst of temper; one could almost see the effort at control. He drew a deep breath, then nodded. Teagarden moved to the door and opened it.

Malone would not have been surprised if Kylie Doolan had come through the doorway. Instead Louise Cobcroft appeared in it.

Malone sighed; this case was turning into a revolving door circus. 'Hello, Louise. Holding hands again?' *I'm getting to be as sour as that middle-aged cop in* NYPD Blue, *the one who never smiles.* 'Or are you like Daniela, taking a job with Kunishima?'

'Yes. And I'm not holding hands, nor am I an Aussie geisha.' She gave Paula Decker a look meant to slice her; but Paula just smiled. 'And I don't think it's any of your business.'

She was not flustered, she was cold and defiant. In the company of Caroline Magee and Daniela Bonicelli she had been quiet, just background to their defiance. Now she was throwing up her own barricades. She was smartly dressed today, in a black slimline dress with a silver belt and high-heeled shoes. Her hair was loose but neat and she was remarkably attractive. Errol Magee knew how to pick his women.

'Oh, you're wrong there, Louise,' said Malone. 'You'd be surprised just how wide police business can spread. The civil rights know-alls will give you chapter and verse.' He wondered how he sounded to Paula Decker, but she showed no expression. 'You're all deserting Mr Cragg?'

'He's already deserted us. You're okay in the police service, but out in the real world we have to look after ourselves.'

'So we're being told, all the time.' Malone turned to Nakasone, who had been almost rigid since Louise Cobcroft had come through the bedroom doorway. 'Is Kunishima taking over I-Saw from the receivers?'

Nakasone hesitated, then nodded. 'If the price is right, yes.'

'Five cents on the dollar?' Clements might get back a few bucks.

Nakasone unexpectedly smiled; he had good teeth, expensive ones. 'More than that, Inspector. We would hope to get all the money that Mr Magee has stolen.'

'And where is Mr Tajiri now? Out looking for it?'

'No. He is away on business.'

'Bank business or *yakuza* business?' Malone knew he was being reckless, but recklessness sometimes paid off. Be a samurai, he told himself as he stared at the Japanese, wield the sword or whatever it was they used.

Nakasone was unimpressed: 'You are very foolish with those sort of remarks.'

But Malone had seen Louise Cobcroft raise her chin and frown, as if she knew what the *yakuza* was. It was time to leave, now the pot had been stirred, if by a sword instead of a spoon.

'I'd think twice about taking the job, Louise. Goodbye, Mr Nakasone. Tell Mr Tajiri that we still want to talk to him.'

Teagarden showed them out. He, too, was frowning, as if suddenly wondering what extra duties a butler might be called upon to do.

Out in the street Paula Decker said, 'You put the wind up Miss Cobcroft.'

'I think we put the wind up Mr Nakasone, too. But we still have to find Miss Doolan.'

As they went to get into their car Paula said, 'Who is Jack Teagarden?'

'Was, not is,' said Malone. 'One of the best jazz trombonists ever, if not the best.'

She opened the car door and got in. He slid in beside her, anticipating her next remark: 'Never heard of him.'

Ah, he thought, lyrical and Celtic all at once, the small horizons of the young. 'You disappoint me, Paula. Your generation thinks that the Big Bang of Creation was in the 1960s, that Woodstock was the Garden of Eden. Back in prehistoric times we had music and movies and sex, all the things your generation thinks it invented. Some day I'll bring in my LPs of Bix Beiderbecke and Benny Goodman –'

'LPs?' She was all innocence. 'What are they?'

'Pull your head in,' he said, put the car in *Drive* and drove back through the present: clogged traffic, road rage, middle-finger salutes and some girl on the car radio screaming (not singing, like Doris Day or Kay Starr) lyrics that sounded like *Yah, yah, yah.* He was getting old, no samurai mob would take a second look at him.

4

Kylie Doolan was being held prisoner in a deserted warehouse in Chippendale. The warehouse had been taken over by Kunishima Bank as part of a failed mortgage, that of another IT company that had disappeared into the outer space of cyberspace. The building, one-storied and the lone commercial property on the block, was empty while the bank decided whether it should be sold or leased. With the economy going downhill banks, for the first time in a long time, were having to entertain second thoughts.

Chippendale is an old working-class area that is now becoming gentrified, like so many of the inner-city quarters. The old-time residents never went in for up-market crime such as kidnapping; thuggery was more in their line when they decided to break the law. There had been brothels catering to randy students from Sydney University up the road; there was still a brothel close to the university which, with its higher prices and wider variety of service, was only affordable by graduates. For the most part the area was now respectable, if not genteel, with just a few remaining warehouses and small businesses. It

144

would not have condoned Kylie Doolan's kidnapping if it had known of it.

Kylie knew who her kidnapper was. Tajiri had been waiting for her in the lobby of Kunishima. He had introduced himself as Chojoro Ikura, head of security for Kunishima and she had accepted him without query; she liked men's attention and he had been very attentive. He had told her they had got word where Errol Magee was and he was taking her to him. She had never met Tajiri, but he was Japanese and gentlemanly and an executive of the Kunishima Bank and she was delighted that Errol had been located and she was being taken to him. Only when they got down to the garage and the two men, coming out from behind a black van, put a pad over her face did she realize how dumb and stupid she had been. Errol had told her that, several times, and she had just laughed and told him he didn't understand women . . .

When she had woken last night, sick from the chloroform, she had found herself in a small glass-walled office that looked out on a dark, empty floor. The office had a cheap table, on which she lay, and four canvas-backed chairs; it was lit by a standard lamp almost at floor level. Two men, both wearing ski-masks, sat watching her.

As soon as she sat up she wanted to be sick. One of the men, gruff but solicitous, took her out to a toilet and she threw up in the bowl. He produced a paper napkin from somewhere and she wiped her mouth; he was awkward, as if not used to kidnapping women. He took her back to the office, sat her down in a chair and from one of two portable ice-boxes took a bottle of spring water and handed it to her.

'Unless you'd like a beer?'

She gagged at the thought. 'I don't drink beer. Why am I here? Where's Mr What'shisname? Ikura?'

Both men were burly with beer-belly profiles; they had rough Australian accents. The man who had given her the drink looked at the other, who said, 'Just relax, love. You'll get all the info you want tomorrow morning. We're just your minders. Like politicians have.' Both men laughed inside their masks.

'Who'll give me information? Mr Ikura?'

'Yeah, him. He's the boss. You want a sandwich?' The first man produced a plastic-wrapped sandwich from the ice-box. 'Ham salad? Or –' He ferreted around in the ice-box. 'Or some *sushi*?'

'No, thanks.' She was afraid, but she had the feeling that these two men would not hurt her unless she was – *dumb and stupid*. All at once she knew she was here because of bloody Errol and all at once she began hating him. He was a jerk, a rat . . . 'Do you know where my boyfriend, Mr Magee, is?'

'Save the questions till the morning, love. We're gunna have to tie you up in that chair, so you're gunna be a bit uncomfortable. If you promise not to be silly and yell, we won't gag you. But you try yelling and we gunna have to belt you, y'know what I mean? So okay, no yelling or screaming and we don't gag you, okay?'

She nodded. 'Okay.'

'You wanna go to the toilet? A bedtime pee?'

'I'd better. You're not going to rape me or anything?'

'Us? We're gay.' Both bellies shook with laughter. 'No, love, you're safe. Me and me mate don't go in for rape. Only mongrels do that.'

She went to the toilet, came back and sat down in the chair while they tied her up. 'Why are you doing this?'

'For the money, love,' said the second man. 'What else?'

She had never spent a more uncomfortable night; nor a more fearful one. She fell asleep after a long time and dreamed, not of the life she had led for the past four years but of Minto, which, for some strange reason, was vague in a golden light.

In the morning when Tajiri (or Ikura, as she knew him) came she felt like a limp doll, everything drained out of her. He stood facing her, bare-faced, no mask.

'You have been treated well, Miss Doolan?' She nodded, her mouth dry, and he jerked a hand at the two men: 'Untie her.'

She massaged her wrists and her ankles; he waited patiently. At last he said, 'This room is stuffy. We'll go outside.'

The two masked men carried two chairs out into the wide empty floor. Tajiri gestured to Kylie to take a seat and he sat down opposite her. The two men went back into the office, began breakfasting from the ice-box.

'Miss Doolan,' said Tajiri, 'we want to know where Mr Magee is.'

Sitting still and stiff in her chair she looked at him blankly, as if he had spoken Japanese. 'What?'

'We know you and Mr Magee planned his kidnapping. The five-million dollar ransom was just to put us off the scent. You and he planned to disappear with the forty million dollars he has stolen and we were supposed to believe that the kidnappers, whoever they were, had killed him. That, as they say, would be the end of the story. But it isn't . . .' He stopped and waited.

She had difficulty keeping her voice steady. 'Mr Ikura, you are out of your head. No, really. I have no idea where Errol is – I know nothing about the kidnapping –'

He held up a hand for her to be quiet; then he gestured to the two masked men to come out of the office. 'Would you gentlemen go for a walk, please? Without your masks.' He said it with a smile, a genial boss.

'Sure,' they said. 'Ten minutes enough?'

'Enough,' said Tajiri. He waited till the two men had gone, then he turned back to Kylie. 'I don't like hurting women, Miss Doolan, but I do it if it's necessary.'

Kylie looked around her. The windows of the warehouse were high in the walls, all of them barred. In one corner of the big space she saw a computer, its window smashed, on a small table. She was suddenly very afraid; but still she managed not to show it. She was fearful of physical abuse; Errol had never hit her nor had any of her previous boyfriends. She would have retaliated, anger overcoming her fear; but she knew she would not do that with Mr Ikura. There was a menace to him that she had never met before.

147

'Is that how you Japanese men treat your women?' She was working for time.

'Not necessarily.' He seemed prepared to talk with her, as if putting her at her ease; but the threat was still there: 'A long time ago one of our scholars, who had studied Confucius, said a woman's duty is obedience. He said the five worst things about a woman are for her not to be docile, to be discontented, to slander, to be jealous and to be silly. Seven out of ten women have all those faults. I hope you haven't, Miss Doolan.'

'I'm telling you, Mr Ikura, I know nothing about the kidnapping of Errol.' Her voice was shaky, but she managed to get the words out without stumbling. 'I was the one who called the police, for God's sake! Why would I have done that?'

'Because Mr Magee made a mistake and killed your maid.' Tajiri was drawing on a black leather glove, just the one. 'You knew her body would be discovered eventually. You had to change your plans. That was why you had to stay behind.'

'He killed no one! Jesus, he couldn't even kick a dog or throw a stone at a cat! He hated violence –' Then she stopped and looked at his gloved hand. 'Are you going to hit me?'

'I think so. Unless you stop telling lies.'

Then she found courage, or bravado: something found at the bottom of a barrel that she had never searched before: 'Then you'll have to kill me, too.'

'I can do that,' he said, but all at once sounded less sure of himself and what he intended to do.

'That's your job as head of security for the bank, to kill women?' The bravado, or whatever it was, was increasing; she had noticed his hesitancy. 'Does the bank know that?'

He was unsure of himself with women. Kaibara Ekken had been writing of women's faults in the seventeenth century; he might be confounded with Japanese women in the twenty-first century. For himself, Australian women, the ones in the offices of Kunishima, puzzled him with their independence; the younger women back in Tokyo and Osaka were going the same way. His

148

father, a garbage collector in Osaka, had picked up bits of wisdom besides garbage: never trust a woman was part of his collection. But that had been because Tajiri's own mother had been a woman of independent mind. Here in Sydney it sometimes seemed that he was surrounded by independent women, chewing away at their men as at a meal.

He put the gloved hand in his lap, as if laying away a tool for a moment. 'Let's be reasonable, Miss Doolan. The bank is never going to pay the ransom you are asking –'

She shook her head, growing confident by the moment: 'Mr Ikura, I had nothing to do with that ransom. Why would Errol bother about a lousy five million –' She paused, not believing her own tongue. 'Why would he bother when you say he has forty million salted away somewhere? Don't you think I'd be over there now, wherever it is, trying to get at it instead of hanging around in Sydney? You don't understand women, Mr Ikura, not practical women. And I'm practical.'

He was almost convinced she was telling the truth; and hated himself for his weakness. 'Then he arranged his own kidnapping and you had nothing to do with it?'

'Yes,' she said flatly. 'Errol could be a real bastard. Always looking out only for himself. I dunno what I saw in him,' she said, but Tajiri was unimpressed.

He had taken a risk in meeting Miss Doolan yesterday and coming here this morning. But he was returning to Osaka in two days' time and Nakasone would deny that a Mr Ikura had ever worked for Kunishima. Okada might prove a problem, but then honest bankers could never be relied upon. His father, the collector of wisdom, had told him that. Only the gods and garbage collectors knew what secrets were found in the waste bins of banks.

'Can you tell us where we might find him? A hideaway, some place in the country?'

She knew she was on top of him now. 'If I knew, don't you think I'd have already found him? I think you and the police

149

have all made a mistake, Mr Ikura. Someone else arranged the kidnapping. I don't know whether Errol had anything to do with it, but I'm sure there's someone else in on it.'

'Who?'

Sometimes she wondered at the intelligence of men, though she had not worked her way through too many nationalities. An American, an Italian, a Brazilian; but no Asians. 'Mr Ikura, if I knew who, I'd have been on their back as soon as I saw those stupid bloody messages on the computers.'

He didn't ask what computers. He had seen them two nights ago when he had gone to the apartment to kill, or torture, Magee.

He said nothing and she knew now she had him by the balls, a woman's cruellest hold: 'Take the glove off, Mr Ikura. You may not appreciate it, but we're on the same side.'

Tajiri stared at her. He was not accustomed to decision-making; the comfort of the *yakuza* was its committee-like resolutions. Yamamoto Jocho had taught that it was wrong to have personal convictions. Kunishima Bank should be here making this decision.

He was taking off the glove when the two men, pulling their ski-masks back on, appeared at the far door of the warehouse. 'Finished, mate?'

These two men wouldn't have lasted a day in the *yakuza*. They had their own discipline, take it or leave it, mate.

'Just a moment,' said Tajiri, putting up the ungloved hand and holding them at room's length. Then he turned to Kylie: 'If Mr Magee came back to you, would you kill him?'

She had lost her grip on him. 'What? No – no, of course not!'

Tajiri put the glove in his pocket, stood up. 'I would – after he'd told us where he has the forty million dollars. He's caused far too much trouble.'

Chapter Seven

1

Malone dropped Paula Decker off at the Magee apartment to resume her watch.

'I looked through some of Mr Magee's and Miss Doolan's tapes,' she said. 'Great stuff. The Doors and Pink Floyd.'

'Never heard of 'em.'

He drove on up Macquarie Street. There was a demonstration outside Parliament House and traffic was being let through at a crawl. The sergeant in charge of the police detail recognized him and saluted. The demonstrators, not recognizing him, booed him: he must be the enemy. He saluted them and, changing mood, they cheered him. It was a demonstration without fire in its belly, a march in the sun. Democracy at work, he thought; or at play. He drove on. He passed St Mary's Cathedral; a bishop was out on the front steps, feeding the pigeons. An ordinary day, too good for murder and chasing greedy bastards.

He saw a bicycle courier who looked like Vassily Todorov. He tooted his horn, but the cyclist, if it was Todorov, was too intent on delivery. Head down and arse up he disappeared into the traffic ahead like a fish into a current.

When Malone got back to Homicide, Sheryl Dallen was waiting for him. 'You look pleased with yourself,' she told him.

'I've just had fifteen minutes of looking at a normal world. What's new?'

'That South Coast murder – Constable Haywood. They've been on to us, asking us to make a few enquiries.'

'Where's Russ?'

'He said to tell you he was taking his wife to lunch at Leichhardt. The chill has lessened, he said.'

'And that didn't intrigue you? What he said?'

'I've learned to mind my own business about married men.'

'We're no different from single men, only tamer.'

'Yeah,' she said, unimpressed. 'The enquiries. Seems there's a family down that way –' She looked at the note in her hand: 'The Briskin family. Constable Haywood said he was gunna look in on them, they have a weekender on a back road just past Minnamurra. The local cops went out to see them, they said they hadn't seen Haywood. The locals accepted that. Then someone remembered the name, got on the computer and it turns out the father of the family had form as long as your arm.'

'They go back and talk to the family? To Dad?'

'They went back, but no one was there. One of the sons is in St George's Hospital in intensive care, he was bowled over by some woman driver – Don't say it!'

'Never crossed my mind. Go on.'

'They could of left to go up to the hospital. Or back to where they live, in Hurstville. South Coast would like us to pay them a visit. It may be nothing, but just in case. I thought I'd go out there with Andy or John.'

He looked at his desk. He had over the past few days begun a desultory cleaning-out of his drawers, a reluctant leave-taking, though he would not have described it that way to anyone, except perhaps Clements. There were notes, some even yellowed round the edges: a reminder, *Check the Hardstaffs*, from a case of ten or twelve years ago. There was a calculator that he couldn't remember ever using. A photo, found right at the bottom of a drawer, of Lisa with a baby, Tom, in her arms. Detritus and memory mixed together. What, he guessed, you gathered as you went downhill from the middle of your life.

He stood up. 'No, I'll come with you. I need a breath of fresh air.'

She looked at him curiously, but made no comment. She wasn't theatrical-minded, but John Kagal had remarked that the second act of the boss' career was coming to an end. So far she hadn't bothered to look towards the end of the first act of her own professional life. For women in the Police Service second and third acts were still just hopes.

'We'll go in my car,' he said. 'You drive. Carefully.'

'When you were young, didn't you ever put your foot to the floor?'

'Only in fear. Never on the pedal. Drive carefully.'

She did, but only because of the traffic. It was thick and slow; heavy semi-trailers rode like elephants through it.

'Shall I put the blue light on, start the siren?' she asked.

'What'd be the point? What are we going to use – the footpath? Relax. Drive carefully.'

Hurstville lies about fifteen kilometres south of the harbour city. Once a suburb it is now called a city; the rest of Sydney still calls it a suburb. It covers a ridge that slopes away down to Botany Bay and, to the south, the Georges River. Originally the whole area was covered by thick forest; indeed, the main thoroughfare is still called Forest Road. The original settlers, other than the Aborigines, were timber-getters and charcoal-burners. The timber men could drive their axes into ironbark, blackbutt, blue and red gums and other eucalypts that made a great canopy over the ridge. The main settler was an army officer, John Townson, who was given a major land grant; in the early days of the colony of New South Wales land grants were given away as freely as luncheon vouchers in later times. As the world turned, speculators and developers moved in, the forests and their workers disappeared, and proper civilization, with its rules and regulations and back-of-the-hand bribes, had arrived.

The Briskin house was a blue-brick from the 1920s, a Californian bungalow, as it used to be called. As with most things Californian, that was a loose term. Very few of the voters in the 1920s knew what came out of California other than Mary Pickford and Charlie Chaplin. The street was lined with large tallow-wood trees that did their best to hide the ugly hodge-podge of houses on either side of the street. There were weatherboard cottages from before World War I; Californian bungalows; Italianate mansions on fifty-foot blocks looking vainly for an estate; and an in-your-face cubist house that looked ready to take off for another location, maybe Silicon Valley. The tree in front of the Briskin house was a solitary crepe myrtle in full bloom. It was trimmed, neatly, the branches clustered together pointing upwards, the blooms like rosy fists.

The house had a driveway leading up to a fibro garage at the rear. The lawn and the garden at the front of the house were neat; they could not have been otherwise with Shirlee living in the house. A polished copper sign beside the front door was also from the 1920s: *Emoh Ruo*: the supposed Maori, Malone remembered, for *Our Home*. Darlene and her brothers joked about it, but Shirlee never let it be removed. She had forgotten that it was Clyde who had brought it home, lifting it after he had burgled a house.

The grey Toyota was in the driveway, the bonnet up, when the unmarked police car drew up outside. Corey, cleaning the spark plugs, came out from under the bonnet to look at the big man and the woman getting out of the unmarked car. He smelled *police* at once: he didn't need the blue word on the side of their car.

'I'm Detective-Inspector Malone and this is Detective-Constable Dallen. You are –?'

'Corey Briskin.' He was suddenly all caution, wiping grease from his hands as if it were some giveaway. Like blood. His mother was inside the house, tidying up an always-tidy house. Errol Magee, strapped to a chair, gagged now, was in the middle bedroom on the side of the house away from Mrs Charlton's. 'Something wrong? Me brother's not –?'

'The brother who was hurt in an accident? No, we're not here because of him. We're just following up enquiries about Constable Haywood. We understand you were contacted about him last night. His murder.'

Even Sheryl Dallen thought the approach had a sledgehammer in it. But she left it to the boss, he was the opening bowler. In the meantime she studied Corey, who looked more than a little nervous. Young guys, these days, never seemed to trust cops . . .

'The murder?' Corey batted that one on the back foot. 'Yeah. We told the sergeant, the one who come to see us, we told him we hadn't seen him. The dead guy.'

Then Shirlee, who could see through brick walls, who would have been aware at once of the two detectives even if they had been no more than silent ghosts, came out the front door, down the steps and across the lawn to where Malone and Sheryl stood by the grey Toyota.

'Mum,' said Corey, jumping the gun, 'these are two detectives –'

'From Homicide,' said Malone, still with the heavy approach.

'They're asking about the young cop who was murdered –' Corey was sending semaphore, Morse code, anything to stop Mum putting her foot in it.

'Dreadful.' Shirlee shook her head, looked mournful, as if she had lost a close relative. *For Crissakes, Mum, don't wipe your eyes with your pinny!* 'It's getting worse every week. Crime, I mean. Murder, things like that. I don't mean it's the police's fault –'

'Thanks,' said Malone and only a 747 going overhead silenced his sigh. He waited till the plane had gone, then said, 'We'd like a word with your husband, Mrs Briskin. Is he home or at work?'

Shirlee looked after the disappearing plane. 'Bloody planes! They oughta move the airport.'

'Mrs Briskin. Your husband – we'd like a word with him.'

'Clyde?' Corey had to admire his mother; they didn't come any better as an actress. 'I'd like a word with him, too. He walked out on me, on us – when was it, Corey?'

'Four years ago,' said Corey, falling into step. 'Don't mention him, Inspector. He ain't too popular around here.'

'What made him walk out?' asked Sheryl. 'You don't mind us asking?'

'A woman,' said Shirlee, and made it sound like a witch or Madame Dracula. 'It wasn't the first time. He was always a skirt-chaser. I dunno who she was, he just said he'd met someone else, packed his bags and he was gone. I haven't seen hide or hair of him ever since.'

Don't pile it on, Mum. Corey stepped in before they fell into soap opera: 'Why'd you wanna see Dad?'

'They thought he might've known Constable Haywood,' said Malone. 'Your dad had been in trouble a coupla times.'

'He was never in trouble down the South Coast,' said Shirlee, who knew Clyde's record like an oft-sung anthem. 'He wouldn't of know-en the officer.'

'You haven't heard from him since – since he walked out?' said Sheryl.

'Not a word.'

Then Mrs Charlton, from next door, appeared at the side fence. She was an angular-faced woman with thin shoulders and big breasts, so that she looked like a pinnace under full sail, especially since her blouse was white. She sailed into other people's business, regardless of wreckage. 'Something wrong, Shirl? Pheeny's all right, I hope? I heard about it on the news. You haven't lost him, I hope?' She was already donning black for the funeral.

'No, he's okay, Daph.' In Shirlee's best mind-your-own-business voice.

'They interviewed that lawyer, he's gunna start a first-class or second-class action, something like that. Alan Jones is on your side. For Pheeny and them little kids in the accident. You from the lawyers?' she asked Malone.

'No,' said Malone, 'we're from the Hurstville council. We were looking for Mr Briskin, but Mrs Briskin says he's no longer here.'

'No, he's been gone – I dunno. How long, Shirl? Don't matter, he's gone and good riddance, wasn't that what you said? I told you I wasn't surprised when he took off, remember?'

'I remember, Daph.'

'What did you want him for? The council? He was always very good with the trees, I'll say that for him. That crepe myrtle, he planted that, didn't he, Shirl?'

'It's council business,' said Malone. 'Now would you mind leaving us alone with Mrs Briskin?'

Mrs Charlton was evidently accustomed to rebuffs; she just sniffed, turned and was gone: sailing. Malone grinned at Shirlee.

'Have I ruined neighbourly relations?'

'You kidding?' Shirlee gave him a neighbourly smile: that is, one with reservations. 'She'll be back soon's you're gone.'

'Why'd you say you were from the council?' asked Corey.

'If I'd said we were from the police, you think she'd have left us?'

'Good thinking,' said Corey and nodded appreciatively.

'So you didn't see Constable Haywood, not after his first visit:' said Sheryl.

'No, I come up here yesterday afternoon. My mum was already up here.'

'How'd you come? By car?'

'No, by train. We've only got the one car, this –' He patted the Toyota. 'Mum had come up in it.'

Then Malone's phone rang. 'Excuse me,' he said and moved away out to the footpath, stood beside the bunched fists of the crepe myrtle.

It was Clements ringing from the office. 'Our girl Miss Doolan is back at her apartment. Constable Decker is down there, she just called.'

'How's Kylie? Knocked around?'

'Decker didn't say so.'

'Righto, I'll go straight there. We've got nowhere out here with this family, the Briskins. I think they're clean. They haven't seen our man, the father, in four years. It was a wasted trip.'

'You win some, you lose some.'

'That how it is with stocks and shares?'

'Don't rub it in,' said Clements and hung up.

Malone went back to the three by the grey Toyota. He had noticed that, though it wasn't new, maybe five or six years old, it was polished and – *neat*. 'Righto, Mrs Briskin. Maybe the detectives down south will want another word with you, but I'll tell 'em what you told us. That you didn't see Constable Haywood yesterday.'

'Give 'em our condolences,' said Shirlee. 'Good cops oughtn't be lost like that.'

Neither Malone nor Sheryl Dallen saw Corey roll his eyes.

2

'His – Nibs –' Shirlee was making an upside-down cake, a family favourite. She pushed a can of pineapple rings towards Corey. 'Open that . . . We've gotta get rid of him.'

'Mum –' Corey ran an electric can-opener round the rim. 'I'm in enough shit – okay, okay, I'll wash me mouth out. But I'm in it up to here –' He ran his finger across his throat. 'I've done in two people, I didn't mean to, it just happened. I'm not lining up for something deliberate, not on him –'

'I didn't mean *that*.' She opened a packet of shredded coconut; she had her own recipes, always had had. She looked at all the cookery shows on TV, but went her own way, adding bits and pieces. 'He's no good to us dead. But we'll have to move him from here. Them cops might come back again. Then there's that old stickybeak next door . . . No, we gotta move him.'

'Where?' He had the practical sense of the hopeless.

'I dunno. For the moment,' she added; she would think of somewhere. 'We gotta talk to Chantelle.'

'Mum, bloody Chantelle's left all the dirty work for us. We're in the shit, not her.' She didn't tell him to wash his mouth out; she continued mixing the cake. 'If it hadn't been for her, we wouldn't of got into this.'

'We done it for the money, not to please her.'

'Yeah. If we let Errol go, what's she gunna do? Get another job in IT, make a mint? While Darlene and me've been losing money, taking time off?'

'We'll talk to her.'

'Yeah,' he said flatly and pushed the open can of pineapple rings towards her. 'What we gunna have on it? Cream or ice-cream?'

'Whatever you like.'

'I'll ask our mate what he likes. He doesn't think much of your cooking.'

'He's lucky we're feeding him.'

Corey stood up, pulled on a blue hood, went out of the kitchen and down the hallway to the third bedroom. 'How you feeling, sport?'

Errol Magee was strapped to a rocking-chair, one of Darlene's scarves wrapped round his mouth and tied at the back of his neck, gagging him. Corey took off the gag and Magee said, 'You bastard. I fucking near swallowed my tongue.'

'That would have solved our problem,' Corey said to himself.

'What?'

'Sorry, sport. But we couldn't trust you to keep your mouth shut, you might of started yelling your head off and then I'd of had to clock you. Tonight for tea we're having upside-down cake, pineapple. You want cream or ice-cream on it?'

'Why? You going to send me out for it?'

Corey grinned inside the hood, shook his head. 'You're on your own, sport. You're not shit-scared any more, are you?'

'No, I'm just pissed off. You getting anywhere with the ransom?'

'Not so far.'

'What were you going to do with it? I mean your share?'

'I dunno.' He sat down on Darlene's bed. 'I used to be a

159

dreamer, when I was a kid. I got outa the habit, I guess. Probably bought a bike, a BMW or a Honda, gone travelling. You ever seen the rest of Australia?'

'Only from the air.'

Corey stopped dreaming before it had begun, got serious. 'Things are getting complicated, sport. They've kidnapped your girlfriend Kylie.'

'They've what?' Magee tried to sit up straight, just set the chair rocking.

Corey leaned forward and steadied the chair. 'Or she's done a bunk. It was on the news this morning. Alan Jones and John Laws are making stars of you, you're right up there with Tom and Nicole. You're the only news on talk-back radio.'

Magee was frowning, deeply troubled. 'Something's happened to Kylie. She wouldn't just *disappear*, not of her own accord.' He looked across at Corey. 'You're having me on.'

'Mate, have I lied to you yet? But you lied to us. Where's that forty million you've salted away?'

'That's bullshit. Propaganda. You dunno what banks and receivers are like. They're always talking about missing funds, loot that's been salted away somewhere. It's easy, it covers up their own mistakes. I'm telling you, there are more liars and rumour-mongers in business than there ever are in sport or the entertainment game. I didn't know it till I started to move up the ladder, it was a real eye-opener. Forty million!' He coughed a sneer, almost believing what he was saying. 'You think I'd still be hanging around for the receivers to move in? I'd be outa sight, overseas, with a new name.'

'You sound disappointed you're not.'

'Wouldn't you be?'

'Sport, you think that's where your girlfriend is? She's found out where the money is and she's over there trying her luck. She bright enough for that?'

The thought horrified Magee for a moment; then he knew it was an impossibility. Kylie couldn't add up a grocery account. If

American Express didn't send her a bill every month she would think the world was a giveaway.

'No, no way. She wouldn't have a clue –' He had said too much.

'She wouldn't have a clue where you've put the money? Sport, you've just told me you do have forty million –'

'No, no! For Crissakes, will you stop harping on it? I meant she hasn't a clue about business – she thinks American Express runs the world. If she's missing, someone's grabbed her –'

'Who, for instance?'

Magee took his time. 'I'm guessing and you're not going to believe me –'

'Try me.'

'The *yakuza*.'

'Who?'

'The *yakuza*. Japanese gangsters, like the Mafia.'

The blue hood fluttered as if a wind had blown through it; Corey was laughing. 'Errol, I think you're going off your head –'

'You blame me? Cooped up like this, tied up like a fucking chicken? No, I'm telling you the truth. Or guessing at it. The *yakuza* own the Kunishima Bank. I only found out a week ago.'

Corey leaned back on his elbows on the bed. It was a neat room; Shirlee came in every morning after Darlene had left for work and made it neat. Darlene had never been the sort for posters on the walls, not even as a teenager; Mum would have removed the posters of pop stars and suggested she get neatly framed photos of INXS and Whitney Houston. Foulmouths like Eminem and other unwashed wouldn't have been allowed in the house, tacked to the wall or framed. A Hans Heysen print of gum trees in central Australia, a region as remote from Darlene's imagination as the Siberian tundra, hung on one wall. It had been chosen by Shirlee and it hung perfectly straight, the sidebars of its frame absolutely parallel to the junctions of the walls.

'You've got a problem, sport.'

Magee nodded. 'Yeah – with you and them. I think I might be safer with you.'

'Don't build your hopes . . . What about your wife? She's turned up, did you know?'

'Yeah.' Magee said nothing more.

'Did your girlfriend know about her?'

'No.'

'Did your wife know what you were up to? Siphoning off that forty million?'

'Jesus, will you drop that!'

'Then why are the, whatd'youcall'em, the *yakuza*? That it? Why are the *yakuza* after you? That how they usually play the game, kill off bankrupts?'

Magee ignored the question. 'What are you going to do with me?'

Corey sat up. 'We're still making up our minds, they don't come good with the ransom.'

'You'll top me?' Magee tried to sound casual, but he was suddenly deathly afraid.

The blue hood stared at him. 'It's on the cards.' Then: 'What's the matter?'

'I wanna go to the toilet! Quick!'

3

Tajiri, driving a Honda Legend, dropped Kylie off at the Macquarie Street entrance to the apartment block. By that time they had reached an air of affability, each certain of his and her judgement of the other. For Kylie, though he had threatened to kill her, he had an attitude of politeness about him that was a contrast to that of the men she was accustomed to. She would not trust him *not* to kill her, but over the past hour she had gathered together resources she hadn't realized she

162

had possessed. The selfish are often the last to realize their own core.

Tajiri, for his part, had come to accept that risks had to be taken. Miss Doolan, a woman he would hate to be married to, had convinced him that she had had nothing to do with the kidnapping of Errol Magee. He had left her in the warehouse and gone out to his car and phoned Kenji Nakasone, like his father, a collector of wisdom. The latter had told him of the visit by the crude detective, Malone, and for a few minutes they had discussed whether the police were a threat and decided they were not. Then Tajiri had suggested that they should let Miss Doolan go.

'Does she know who you are?' asked Nakasone.

'No. I shan't be coming back to the office and I am booked out on Qantas tomorrow afternoon for Tokyo. I'm going home, Kenji,' he said and sounded sentimental.

'I envy you, Tamezo. I'm tired of the crudeness here.'

There was crudeness back home, especially in politics; but Tajiri didn't mention that. He was also not without humour: 'Come on, Kenji, you enjoy it. Think of the time it saves in business, being crude. And with the women.'

'Were you crude with Miss Doolan?'

Only when I threatened to kill her. 'No, not at all. I think she can be trusted. She is only concerned for her own welfare.'

'Like most women,' said Nakasone, thinking that was wisdom. 'Let her go. Don't go back to your apartment, the police may be watching.'

'Where will I go?'

'Try Cabramatta, it's full of Asians, so I read. The police don't know one of us from another. Be Korean.'

'You're joking, Kenji,' said Tajiri and hung up.

So now they were drawing up outside the apartments at Circular Quay. Kylie looked at him, then smiled, empty as a salesgirl's smile. 'It's been an experience, Mr Ikura, that's all I can say.'

'For me, too, Miss Doolan. Let's put it down to that – experience. Do we keep it to ourselves?'

'Who are you going to tell? The bank?'

'That was a lie, Miss Doolan,' he said, lying with ease. 'I don't work for Kunishima. I work for an organization that won't forgive Mr Magee for stealing from it. When you see him again, tell him that. He'll understand. Be careful, Miss Doolan. It was a pleasure meeting you.'

She stared at him, suddenly chilled again. A couple of joggers went by, a man and a girl running through agony to be healthy; she had never been a jogger, just a treadmill walker at gym twice a week. She didn't know it, but her own face suddenly looked as strained as that of the girl jogger. She got out of the car, stumbling a little as she realized there was little strength in her legs. Somehow she crossed the pavement and went in through the revolving door of the apartment block, her mind spinning like the door. Mr Ikura drove away, out of her life, she hoped.

When she entered the apartment she was relieved to find it empty, though she was not sure who might be there. She dropped into a deep chair, kicked off her shoes, put her head back and closed her eyes. When she opened them Caroline Magee, the bitch, was standing in the doorway of one of the bedrooms. The main bedroom, where she and Errol slept, for God's sake!

'What the hell are you doing here?' She sat up straight, but didn't rise.

'Stocktaking. Supervised by Detective Decker –' She looked across the big living room to Paula Decker, who had come out of the kitchen. 'All above board, as they describe it. Right, Paula?'

'Right.' Paula was fed up with these bloody Magee women, but she managed to remain professionally calm. 'Where have you been?'

Kylie stayed in her chair, still unsure of her legs. She looked from one woman to the other as she marshalled her lies: 'Visiting friends.'

'Balls,' said Paula, who didn't mind using male terms. 'We tried all your friends, we found them in your address book. You went to see someone at Kunishima. They're not your friends. Nor Errol's, either.'

Kylie ignored her, looked instead at Caroline Magee. 'Stock-taking? Of what? Have you been going through my things?'

'I wouldn't bother,' said Caroline, suggesting Kylie's *things* weren't worth a garage sale. 'I don't think you understand the situation. I am *Mrs* Magee. Errol and I separated, but it was never a legal separation. We were never divorced. I'm entitled –'

Then there was the sound of a toilet being flushed in one of the bathrooms. Kylie started up from her chair. 'Who's that? Is Errol back?'

'No,' said Paula. 'It's your sister Monica.'

'What's she doing here?'

'She was concerned for you. Are you surprised?' said Paula with almost a sneer and went out to the kitchen, taking out her mobile to ring Clements at Homicide.

Then Monica came into the room. She wore a floral-print dress, a sleeveless white cardigan and carried a a white handbag on a long strap over her shoulder. She was the least well-dressed of the women, including Paula Decker; she was the one with her prospects behind her, but she wasn't defeated. She stopped abruptly, put her hand to her mouth, then rushed at Kylie and embraced her.

'Oh God, where have you been? I kept thinking the worst –'

'I'm okay, Monny. Really, I'm okay –'

'We were outa our minds, Clarrie and me –'

'Clarrie?'

'Yeah, Clarrie! Okay, he was concerned for me – but he was concerned for you, too!' Suddenly she let go of Kylie, stepped back and sat down as if certain there was a chair behind her; there was. She wiped her eyes, looked slowly around her, then back up at her sister. 'But you don't have to worry, do you? You've got it all –'

'No,' said Caroline Magee. 'She hasn't, Monica. There's an old saying I've heard men say – two-thirds of five-eights of fuck-all.

Excuse the language. But that's what she's got. What we've both got. Errol's got the lot, if he's still alive.'

'I never met him,' said Monica. 'I'm glad now that I didn't.'

'He's a bastard, but he's not a monster,' said Kylie and looked accusingly at Caroline. 'You *married* him. You must of seen *something* in him.'

Caroline was cool, unoffended. 'Of course I did. I think it was his ambition. It was a sort of – of aphrodisiac. What woman wants to marry a no-hoper?'

'Too many,' said Monica; then looked defensively at her sister: 'But not me.'

Then Paula Decker came back into the room. 'Inspector Malone will be here soon. You'd better get your story sorted out where you've been, Kylie. We've been buggered about on this case and I think Mr Malone will be running out of patience. Now, coffee, anyone?'

'I'll help you,' said Monica and headed for the kitchen, as if it were the only place she would feel comfortable.

Kylie and Caroline were left alone. Caroline remained standing, leaning her buttocks against a low sideboard; one might have gained the impression that she was the one who lived in the apartment. Kylie dropped back into her chair, still unsure of her legs. Caroline, the intruder, looked around her.

'Errol and I lived in two rooms in London, in Fulham. We went to work by bus, used to eat a couple of times a week at McDonalds. A big night out was at an Angus Steak House. You know London?'

'No.'

'He never took you away?'

Kylie was reluctant to answer; but she wasn't going to learn anything about this bitch if she kept her mouth shut. 'We had just the one trip. He took me to San Francisco and LA. He went to London two or three times, he never took me. Did he look you up?'

'Yes.'

166

'What happened?'

'You mean, did I go to bed with him? Relax, Kylie, I had someone better at the time.'

'But not now. Is that why you've come home?'

Caroline smiled. 'Don't start asking questions. You'd better get used to answering them. We all want to know where you've been.'

Out in the kitchen Monica was saying, 'Will you look at this! It's like those incredible kitchens you see in magazines, never a grease spot, nothing out of place! Oh, I'd love to show this to Clarrie! He'd be baking more cakes than Sara Lee.' Then she smiled at Paula. 'Do I sound bitchy? Envious?'

'Envious, yes. But not bitchy. What woman wouldn't be envious of a kitchen like this?'

'Not Kylie. She ever built a house of her own, that'd be the last bit added. From the time she was about ten she thought KFC and Pizza Hut made kitchens out of date. At school she thought cookery classes were a punishment. She thinks TV cookery shows should only be on at three o'clock in the morning.'

Paula watched as Monica set out cups and saucers on a tray, looked for biscuits. 'Monica, who's the happy one?'

Monica paused with a cupboard open, looked sideways at Paula. 'Me or Kylie? I am. Kylie will never be happy because she's never gunna get what she wants.'

'What's that?'

'I dunno. And I don't think she does, either. Trouble is, I've got two daughters who are starting to think like her. Nobody's satisfied any more.'

When they went back into the living room Caroline, oblivious of their entry, was saying, 'Did you love him?'

Kylie thought a while, then said, 'No-o. But I *liked* him.'

'Not enough,' said Monica. 'Coffee. And you could afford better biscuits, for God's sake. Iced Vo-Vos!'

'Heritage stuff,' said Paula and smiled round one of the biscuits.

Malone and Sheryl Dallen arrived twenty-five minutes later. Sheryl had driven with the blue light on the roof and the siren wailing, grinning at the look on Malone's face.

'Keep your eye on the road,' Malone had said, feet ankle-deep in the floor.

'You want me to slow down?'

'No, I just want to get there and belt Miss Doolan about the head.'

But he knew as soon as he entered the apartment that he was on ground as thin as a salt-pan crust. Some men: fashion designers, hairdressers, psychiatrists: some men flourish in female territory. Other more prosaic but wise men tread carefully. Malone looked around at the five women and decided, even though two of them were working for him, to take a light step, at least to begin with.

'Miss Doolan, you've been missing. Have you told anyone where you've been?' He looked at Paula Decker, who shook her head. 'Care to tell me?'

'I don't know it's any of your business,' said Kylie.

'Oh, I'm getting tired of that one. Till we find out who killed your maid Juanita, anything you and anyone connected with you, anything you do is our business. If you don't tell me where you've been, I think we'll take you in –' Sheryl Dallen and Paula Decker were standing behind Kylie; nothing showed on their faces, but they knew he was bluffing. 'It's called helping us with our enquiries. We might let the media know. Now would you like to pack a bag or be sensible and open up?'

'Be sensible, Kylie,' said Monica and put down the cup she had been holding. 'Don't be so bloody stubborn!'

'What would you advise her to do?' Malone looked at Caroline Magee.

'Miss Doolan would never accept advice from me,' said Caroline and sounded as if she wouldn't offer Miss Doolan a rope if she were drowning.

'Miss Doolan,' said Malone, 'did you spend the night with Mr Tajiri?'

She stared at him, puzzled. 'Who?'

'He works for Kunishima Bank. A medium-sized bloke, slim, with wavy hair – a bit unusual for a Japanese.'

She hesitated, then said, 'He said his name was Ikura.'

'And you spent the night with him?'

'Spent the night with him? What are you talking about?'

'Righto. Where did he take you?'

'I dunno.' Her voice was unsteady, flattened; she was suddenly unsettled again. She sat in a chair, her hands gripping the arms as if the chair was charged. 'Some warehouse – it was empty. There were two other guys – Australians. They wore ski-masks. But he didn't.'

Monica, about to tidy up cups on a tray, housekeeping to keep her nerves under control, stopped and looked at her. 'Why did you go with him, for Crissakes?'

'He told me Errol wanted to see me. Then they –' Her hands tightened their grip on the arms of the chair; the last eighteen hours were spilling out of her, weakening her. 'They put a pad over my face – I passed out –'

'You're lucky you're still with us,' Malone told her. 'Tajiri, or Ikura, whatever he called himself, he's *yakuza*. A Japanese gangster, like the Mafia. Did you know that, Kylie?'

'Of course not!' She shivered, her hands scratched at the chair-arms, then clutched each other in her lap. 'He threatened to kill me – he was going to bash me –'

Monica dropped the tray; a cup smashed. Malone said, 'And he would have, Kylie. Why didn't he?'

She put her hands back on the arms of the chair, as if she had to hold to something solid. She didn't look around her, but straight at Malone, who had sat down opposite her. She had suddenly changed, the police were here to help her: 'Somehow, I dunno how, somehow I convinced him I didn't know anything about Errol's kidnapping. It was almost as if – as if he decided

I wasn't worth killing. But he's gunna kill Errol when – when they find him.' She could hardly believe what she was saying. 'If they do –'

'Not if we find him first. When we pick up Mr Tajiri, will you testify against him?'

Kylie said nothing; it was Monica who said, 'For God's sake, Kylie, do something to help them! It's not always gunna go away because you're ignoring it!'

'It's easy for you to say –'

'I know it is and I know it isn't easy for you. But Jesus wept – for once in your life stop thinking about yourself!'

This was *family*. The others were just tableau: silent judgement. At last Kylie looked back at Malone: 'I think I could take you to where he held me.'

'Good!' Malone stood up, turned to Paula Decker: 'Get on to the strike force, tell 'em to pick up Tajiri, either at Kunishima or at his flat. You stay here, keep an eye on Kylie when Sheryl and I bring her back.'

'I'll stay, too,' said Monica, and all at once looked as at home as she might at Minto; she was big sister playing parent again. 'Don't argue, Kylie. I'll call Clarrie – he can bring pizza and one of his apple pies. I looked in your fridge – there's nothing there but milk and orange juice. All this –' she waved an arm about her '– and an empty fridge!'

Somehow Kylie managed a smile. 'You're on your own, Monny.'

Monica put out a hand, touched her sister's shoulder. Malone and the other women turned away. Paula Decker went into a bedroom to phone Police Central and the strike force. Caroline Magee picked up her handbag and followed Malone and Sheryl to the front door as Kylie, excusing herself, went into a bathroom.

'You're not staying, Mrs Magee?' said Malone.

'I don't think Miss Doolan and I will ever be mates. She's just lucky she has a sister like Monica.'

'You have no family?'

'I told you, I have a brother, but I've lost touch with him.' She smiled at him as Sheryl held open the front door for her. 'Why the interrogation, Inspector?'

'It's habit. Police work is all questions.'

'What about answers?'

'Oh, they come. But answers always start with questions. An old Welsh philosopher said that.'

'You read philosophy?'

'No, he's my boss. Why were you here?'

They were out on the landing opposite the lift. Sheryl had pressed the lift-button and they stood waiting. Caroline, in the green suit she had been wearing yesterday, leaned back against the dull gold wallpaper of the landing. It was as if she knew the right background for her: she looked elegant.

'I was looking for that forty million that is supposed to be missing.'

'Looking for it *here*?'

'Inspector, what do you know of money?'

'I know how to hold on to it, so my kids tell me. Go on, educate me.'

'When money was coin they used to take the loot away in sacks. When they invented paper money, there was still physical evidence, it was *there*. Then came cheques and then came electronics. I work in a stockbroker's in London, I *know*.'

'Go on.' The lift had arrived, but they ignored it.

'Errol has got that money of his salted away somewhere in a bank, the sort of bank that has secret accounts. I've been going through all Errol's computers, because he would have sent it electronically. Five out of every six dollars or pounds or whatever that go through the economy on any given day goes through computers. There's a clearing house in New York, it's called the Clearing House Inter-Bank Payments System, CHIPS for short. It pushes through just on two trillion, *trillion*, dollars a day. Errol's forty million, say a million at a time, wouldn't be noticed.'

'So how do you hope to find it?' The lift doors had closed and the lift had gone.

'Somewhere in the computer world there's a hard disk with Errol's secret account name and number on it. IT made his fortune, but now it's going to bite him in the arse.'

'You have to find the password?' said Sheryl, who knew more about computers than her boss ever would.

'Yes,' said Caroline. 'That's all I have to find.'

'How about *Greed*?' said Malone.

She smiled, not letting him get away with it. 'The first word I tried.'

The lift doors opened again and Caroline leaned away from the wall and stepped into the lift. Malone said, 'We'll be in touch, Caroline. Take care.'

'I always do,' she said as the doors closed on her and her smile.

'I wish I had that sort of class,' said Sheryl.

'No, you don't. If you did, I'd have you transferred to Tibooburra.'

'A class place, if ever I've heard of one.'

'Have Immigration check when Mrs Magee arrived back in Sydney. Then bring Daniela Bonicelli and Louise Cobcroft to the office. I want to talk to them about computers . . . Ready, Kylie?'

'Yes.' She had come out of the apartment. 'I guess so.'

'Righto, let's go and see what we come up with.'

4

But they came up with nothing. Kylie, with some hesitation, at times not sure of direction, led them to the warehouse. A big sign said the place was for sale or lease; the agents were in Redfern, a bullet's flight away. Sheryl rang them, said she was looking at the warehouse for a client. The agent, with that hunting dog's nose for a sale that they have, arrived ten minutes later. Business must be slow: he arrived with a screech of tyres.

He was a gangly young man with a large mouth and teeth that would have brought a gasp of admiration from a horse. He displayed all the teeth, not in a smile, when Malone told him they were police.

'Police? What's going on? There been a break-in?'

'Who owns the place?'

The agent was fumbling with the locks on the main door.

'It's been repossessed. A bank has it now. The Kunishima Bank.'

'We've heard of it,' said Malone. 'What are they like to deal with?'

'Oh, fine. Very meticulous. But what's the problem here?'

'We got some information that some stolen goods might be stored here.'

The teeth came out again, still no smile. 'You got no idea what goes on, these empty warehouses. We had one place, they took it over for a rave party – no permission, how's about it, nothing. The local coppers came to us next morning wanting to charge us –' They were inside the building now. 'There. Empty.'

It was, indeed, empty; but for the two chairs still standing in the middle of the big expanse like props in an existentialist drama with no actors. On the floor there was a solitary paper cup.

Sheryl walked down to the office at the end of the building, while Kylie said, 'The two men who wore the ski-masks, they brought me a cup of water – I was pretty shaky –'

'Guys with ski-masks?' said the agent; he seemed unable to keep his teeth hidden, they were there like his words, 'What's going on?'

'You'll get a report,' said Malone in a tone that implied there would be no report. Then as Sheryl came back: 'What've you got?'

She held up a pizza carton and two paper cups. 'There'll be dabs on these –'

'Good,' said Malone. 'Thanks, Mr –?'

'Brown. Bill Brown.' He handed Malone a card. There it was: *Bill Brown*. Not even William. Malone felt kinder towards him. 'Let me know what's going on. I'll have to let our clients know.'

'Kunishima? Never mind, Mr Brown. We'll let 'em know. Thanks for your time and trouble.'

Once back in the police car Malone said, 'Kylie, I don't want you to move out of your flat –' He grinned; she looked wan and afraid. 'Apartment. I want someone there with you all the time. Your sister, if you like, but also a policewoman. Understand?'

'I'm still trying to get my mind around all this –'

Sheryl, at the wheel, said, 'You're safe now. That's all you've got to keep in mind. You're safe.'

'I hope so,' said Kylie, but didn't sound convinced. 'But what about Errol?'

5

Strike Force RLS didn't find Tajiri at the Kunishima Bank nor at his apartment in Kirribilli.

'I went with them to the bank,' Clements told Malone. 'That guy Okada, he never turned a hair. Sure, Mr Tajiri had worked at the bank, but they had terminated – that was the word he used, *terminated* – his contract only yesterday.'

'Why?'

'His work was unsatisfactory.'

'What did you say? Give it to me expurgated.'

'I was very restrained. But Mr Okada was even more restrained. I've met deaf-and-dumb crims who gave out more than he did.'

'Did you see Nakasone?'

'No. Okada was the only one to front. I asked if Tajiri had been terminated because he was *yakuza* and Okada didn't blink. He said, no, Mr Tajiri had been allowed to go because he was unsatisfactory. I asked what sort of work he'd done and he said Tajiri had been the director of human resources. I laughed when he said that – I always laugh when I hear it – and he gave me a nice smile. But that was all he gave.'

'They've recruited two of the girls from I-Saw. Did he tell you that?'

'No, he volunteered nothing. I did ask him if Kunishima would want their forty million back before the I-Saw shareholders got their cut, if any.'

'What did he say? You being a shareholder.'

'He said, unfortunately – that was the word he used, *unfortunately* – unfortunately that was not the way business worked. The bank had to look after *its* shareholders.'

'The *yakuza?*'

'He didn't say that and I didn't ask.'

'I admire your restraint.'

'Thank you,' said Clements, with his middle finger raised. 'Changing the subject, the morgue is releasing the Magee maid's body tomorrow. She's being buried tomorrow afternoon.'

'Who by?'

'A coupla sisters have arrived from the Philippines. And Mr Todorov has arranged everything. He's sending the bill to I-Saw.'

'It'll be put with all the other bills . . . How are things with Romy?'

'She's taking me to dinner tonight. Says I can't afford to take her.'

'They know how to twist the knife, don't they? Good luck.'

Clements went out to the big main room, Malone began gardening the paperwork on his desk and half an hour later Sheryl brought in Daniela Bonicelli and Louise Cobcroft.

'Ladies –' He rose from behind his desk, glad of the interruption. Lisa didn't need to know, but good-looking women were a better distraction than shoals of paper.

'We're not happy,' said Daniela, no longer the coquette

of the other night, 'bringing us in like this. What's going on?'

'Take a seat.' Malone gestured at the two seats opposite him. He had decided not to use the interview room with its accusing eye of the video recorder; these women were not suspects. Or he hoped not. He nodded to Sheryl to take her place on the couch under the window. 'We're only interested in your welfare.'

'I'm too ladylike to say it,' said Daniela, 'but you know what I think of that remark.'

'You ladylike, too, Louise?'

'I'll wait till I hear what you have to say.'

Both women today were in black, the business colour at the turn of the century. Daniela was in a suit with a pink shirt, Louise in a slacks suit with a cream shirt. Each had a shoulder-strap handbag that looked as if it could carry all the arsenal of business. Louise also carried a thin laptop. But no bottles of spring water and not a mobile in sight . . .

'You've already started at Kunishima?'

'No,' said Louise. 'Tomorrow.'

Malone leaned back in his chair, looked at Cheryl, then back at the two women. 'Daniela, Louise – have another think about what you're getting into. Kunishima aren't taking you on because they're short of staff or because they want your wizardry on computers. You're bait to get Errol, Mr Magee, to come out of hiding.'

The two women looked at each other, smiled, shook their heads. Then Daniela said, 'You're crazy. Errol doesn't have the slightest interest in us, he couldn't care less, the bastard. And if he's been kidnapped, why would his kidnappers, whoever they are, worry about Louise and me?'

'You know Kylie Doolan was kidnapped?'

'Yes –' Both women sat up a little straighter. Then Louise said, 'I thought it was her own stunt –'

'No, it was no stunt. She's back home, we've interviewed her. She was kidnapped by a man named Tajiri who, up till yesterday, so the bank says, was the director of human resources at Kunishima. Director of human resources, presumably, meant he was in charge of kidnapping.'

'You're a card, Inspector –'

'No, Daniela, I'm dead serious. A senior executive from Kunishima kidnapped her, threatened her, then eventually let her go when she convinced him she didn't know where Mr Magee was. Mr Tajiri, the director of human resources, is a *yakuza,* a gangster. We have an ASM out on him.'

'ASM?'

'All Stations Message. We'll pick him up. If he hadn't kidnapped Miss Doolan, he'd still be at Kunishima and you'd be working for him. You'd be willing to risk that?'

Daniela frowned, looked less confident now. 'The *yakuza*? You're sure?'

'You've heard about the *yakuza?*'

She nodded. 'One of our Japanese clients, a big firm of lawyers, we found out they did a lot of business for the *yakuza.*'

'What happened?'

'Jared, Mr Cragg, and I discussed it, then we took it to Errol.'

'And what did he say?'

'What we expected. He said I-Saw was in the IT business, not the morality business. We just went ahead supplying them.'

Malone looked at Sheryl. 'Wouldn't you like to have Mr Magee in here for a few minutes?' Then he looked back at Daniela and Louise. 'How much have Kunishima offered you to go to work for them?'

'Enough,' said Daniela after a glance at Louise. 'They asked what we got at I-Saw and they matched it.'

Malone looked back at Sheryl. 'We're in the wrong game.'

It was her turn to take up the bowling: that was what he was telling her: 'Louise, Daniela – when you were sleeping with Errol –'

Daniela's eyebrows went up in question of Louise: 'You, too?'

Louise nodded. 'Off and on. We all knew about you –'

'Thanks,' said Daniela and looked prim and insulted.

'Did he ever mention anything about retiring?' Sheryl said. 'Going overseas to live?'

'Daydreaming?' Louise shook her head. 'Errol never daydreamed, all he was ever thinking about was the next day. Why?'

'We're trying to trace the forty million he stole. Not us at Homicide – the strike force that's looking for him. He would have transferred the money electronically. To some secret account overseas – he could never hide that much money in this country. There would have been a password –' She glanced from one woman to the other. 'Did he ever have a secret word with either of you? The way some – some lovers do?'

Malone tried to remain impassive, as if heard this sort of talk every day. What secret words had Sheryl exchanged on a pillow?

Daniela looked at Louise again, as if *they* might have been lovers with secret words. Then she turned back to Malone, who kept his face straight. Then finally back to Sheryl.

'Yes, I guess there were some. But not words you'd put on a computer.'

'Like on a porno website? Errol and I never used that sort of stuff,' said Louise and tried to look virtuous.

Suddenly Malone laughed; he couldn't help himself. 'Righto, girls. Let's say Errol never gave you a hint of what he was doing or where he was sending the money. But was Kunishima going to have you playing code-breakers?'

'I don't know.' Louise was now beginning to look dubious. She had been holding the laptop on her knees, but now she put it down, as if it, too, might contain secrets she didn't want to know. Malone wondered what was on the hard disks in it, but he wasn't going to bother asking. 'I think they may just have wanted to keep an eye on us. Mr Nakasone told me he knew I'd had a – a relationship with Errol. I thought

178

we'd kept it pretty – well, discreet. Unlike you,' she told Daniela.

'I was never sneaky about it –'

'Ladies –' said Malone warningly. He wanted these two women on side; he didn't know when he might need them. 'Did either of you ever handle any money transfers for Errol? To overseas banks?'

'We were never in finance,' said Daniela as if that was a foreign country. 'I did programs for legal firms. Here and overseas.'

'I was the ideas programmer,' said Louise. 'Dreaming up new stuff. I worked with Jared Cragg most of the time.'

Malone took his time, then said, 'Don't go to work for Kunishima.'

Daniela gave him a hard stare. 'You're asking us to give up top money when jobs in our business are getting scarcer and scarcer.'

Malone waited for Louise to say her bit: 'Are you trying to scare us, Inspector?'

'Yes,' he said flatly.

'I'd listen to him,' said Sheryl, bowling from the other end.

'Unless you'd like to take the risk and work as a mole for us.' Malone saw Sheryl glance at him at that; but he wasn't trying to recruit Daniela and Louise, just frighten them. 'Would you?'

'No,' they said in the one voice.

'Good. Tell Kunishima you've decided not to take the jobs. Tell 'em you decided that on our advice.'

Both women looked dubious again; Daniela said, 'I don't know –'

'Daniela, we're not playing games.' But he was, of course: on Okada and Nakasone and Tajiri, if he was still around. 'Errol's maid was murdered, Miss Doolan was kidnapped, we have no idea where Errol himself is or if he's still alive –'

'We'll tell them,' said Louise, picked up her laptop and stood up.

Daniela hesitated, then stood up. 'Give my love to Tom. He's a nice guy, he'll go a long way.'

In bed or in business? 'I'll tell him. Take care, both of you.'

Sheryl escorted them out through the main security door and he watched them go, seeing them even after they had gone. Two women of the new millennium: emancipated, confident, well paid. Yet still vulnerable to the danger that had beset their mothers and their grandmothers. Men . . .

'What am I thinking?' he said aloud.

'I dunno,' said Sheryl back in his doorway. 'What are you thinking?'

He retreated behind a grin and a shake of his head.

Chapter Eight

1

'Chantelle –'

'Mum –' said Caroline Magee. 'My name is Caroline, not Chantelle. When I first started work at the stockbrokers in London and said my name was Chantelle they thought I was a stripper for the Christmas party. The women there had names like Philippa and Rosemary and Diana – there were three Dianas, all blondes. So I became Caroline and said Chantelle was a family joke.'

'I always liked Chantelle,' said Darlene.

'You can have it, then. If you and I had been twins she'd have called us Charlene and Darlene and asked Glen Campbell to write a song for us. "Rhinestone Cowgirls" or something.'

'I'd of sung you to sleep with it,' said Shirlee, glad to have her eldest back with her, even if she was not the girl who had left here eight, no, nine years ago.

The three of them were in a coffee lounge in the Westfield shopping mall in Hurstville. Store windows blazed with big signs: SALE! 50% OFF! EVERYTHING MUST GO! One or two store assistants stood glumly in doorways, like store dummies also for sale. The economy had slowed, everyone was caught in the sludge. But not Shirlee, Darlene and Caroline. The ordinary flowed around them, if sluggishly; they themselves looked ordinary. Three neatly dressed women, one a little smarter than the other two, finishing off a day out.

A young waitress, a Turk or Afghan, obviously new to her job and grateful for it, appeared beside them. Caroline said, 'A *café au lait*.'

'?'

'*Caffe latte*. Three,' said Shirlee and waited till the young girl had gone. 'Bloody foreigners. Why can't they all speak English?'

'Wash your mouth out,' said Darlene wearily. 'Bloody foreigners. You wanna get us run outa here?'

'Your father knew how to deal with 'em. He held up only Lebanese and Greek service stations –'

'You ever hear from him?' said Caroline.

Darlene looked at her. 'She never told you?'

'Told me what? Dad and I never got on, but I wrote him once. I don't know, maybe three or four years ago. He never answered.'

'He couldn't,' said Darlene. 'She'd poisoned him.'

'She'd *what*?'

'We don't have to bring it up now.' Shirlee had taken out her vanity mirror, was checking her hair was neat. 'We've got other things to talk about.'

Caroline leaned forward, kept her voice low. 'Mum – you poisoned Dad? By accident?'

'No. He had it coming to him.' Shirlee put away her mirror, snapped her handbag shut, waited till the young waitress brought their coffee and then went away. 'He was too much trouble, always *in* trouble –'

'And you don't think we're in trouble now?' Caroline sat back, all her poise suddenly gone. She looked at her sister. 'How did you let it happen? Jesus, *killing* him!'

'I didn't know about it till it was all over. Only Corey and Pheeny knew.'

Three Muslim women and three young children came in and with some fuss arranged themselves at a nearby table. The young waitress approached them, there were smiles all round and she took their orders in a tongue that brought a sniff from Shirlee. Darlene smiled and wriggled her fingers at the children, all of whom smiled back, one foot on the road to being true-blue Aussies.

'Where is he?' said Caroline. 'Dad?'

'They buried him in the timber up behind the house at Minnamurra.' Darlene sipped her coffee, added more sugar. 'Their coffee here isn't as good as that other place further down. I said we should of gone there.'

'I make better coffee myself,' said Shirlee.

Caroline hadn't even looked at her coffee. 'Do you realize what this family is embroiled in? Three fucking murders –'

Shirlee looked at her, totally shocked. 'I expected better from you. Is that how they talk in London stockbrokers? Wash your mouth out –'

'Mum, for Crissakes stop being so prissy and – and neat! Look worried, for God's sake!' The vowels had flattened, she was back at Coonabarabran when she was ten years old and the dreams had begun as London, Paris, New York had appeared on the jittery TV screen like mirages. 'I spent three months planning a neat job of kidnapping my own husband – What's the matter with you?'

Darlene was laughing softly. 'I thought that was funny when you first told us. Kidnapping your own husband!'

'It wasn't meant to be funny. And keep your voice down – those kids have got their ears wide open.' She looked at the three Muslim children, gave them a smile that cut their little throats. Then she turned back to her mother and sister: 'You didn't think the money was funny when I mentioned how much we'd ask for. A simple job, that was what it was supposed to be. Then, first, Corey buggered it up by killing the maid –'

'It was an accident,' said Darlene. 'He's not a killer.'

'The police don't think it was an accident. You haven't met this Inspector Malone –'

'I have,' said Shirlee, sipping the less-than-praised coffee. She explained the visit this afternoon. 'He seemed a nice bloke. Some of them are. He put Mrs Charlton next door in her place. Nicely.'

'Mum, he's on my back. I don't know whether he suspects me or not, but the whole thing's got out of hand. We're gunna have to let Errol go.'

'After all our trouble?' Shirlee put her cup down hard.

'That's it. Trouble. We're in it up to our necks. We let him go and we all go home. I'm going back to London.'

'I agree,' said Darlene. 'You want your coffee?'

'No,' said Caroline and pushed her cup towards her. 'I thought you didn't like it?'

'I'm trying to steady my nerves. I've tried not to think about the murders, but –' She put more sugar in the coffee.

'Your hubby,' said Shirlee, trying to keep to the subject, 'the one you wanna be kind to now, he's still got forty million dollars stashed away somewhere.'

'I'll ask him about it when we let him go.' Then as an afterthought: 'How's Pheeny?'

'He's conscious and out of intensive care,' said Darlene. 'Eating like a horse, the nurse said. He's gunna be okay.'

'We're still talking with the lawyer, Mr Bomaker,' said Shirlee. 'About the class action. We'll make some money outa that. Not five million,' she added sarcastically, 'but some. What do you want, dear?'

One of the Muslim children, a small girl with big dark eyes, said shyly, 'My mother asks could we borrow the sugar?'

'Of course,' said Darlene and gave the holder to the child. Then she said to Shirlee, 'Spoke English, didya notice?'

Shirlee ignored her. 'I don't like giving up –'

'Mum,' said Caroline, 'don't blame me because I'm calling the whole thing off. I didn't muck it up – Corey did.'

'I told you – he didn't *plan* to kill anyone. They just – they just *happened*. The stars weren't right or something.'

'She studies star charts now?' Caroline asked her sister. 'She's into astrology?'

'No, she listens to talk-back stars. Maybe we should ask Alan Jones or John Laws for advice.'

'All right, you two, finished with your sarcasm?' Shirlee was pulling herself, and them, together. Neatly. 'When do we let him go?'

'It'll have to be tonight, after dark,' said Darlene. 'Otherwise Mrs Charlton will be sticking her nose in. Where will we let him loose?'

'Somewhere where you won't be seen,' said Caroline. 'A station car park, after the last train. Give him some money so he can catch a cab back to his apartment. I'll be there.' Then she added: 'Whether Miss Doolan likes it or not.'

'A taxi?' said Shirlee. 'All the way from here to the Quay? That'll be – what? – thirty or forty dollars?'

'We owe it to him,' said Caroline.

'We don't owe him nothing. You pay, he's your husband.'

Caroline took out a fifty-dollar note. 'Here.'

'Who's paying for the coffee?' said Darlene.

'I am,' said Shirlee and laid out the exact cash.

'No tip?' said Caroline.

'Only if they speak English,' said Shirlee, defender of cultures.

They stood up and moved off. The three Muslim mothers looked after them.

'I'll never understand them,' said one of them in Turkish.

'They were talking about three fucking murders,' said the little girl who had asked for the sugar.

'Wash your mouth out,' said her mother in Turkish; then she turned to the other two women: 'Her kindergarten teacher says she has just the ear for English.'

2

Malone, having shaved, turned from looking in the mirror as Lisa stepped out of the shower. 'If there were no mirrors, everyone could think he was good-looking.'

'You think it's the mirror that tells you the truth?' She began to dry herself. Her figure was still good and she was proud of it in an unobvious way; she took care of it, rather than others taking stock of it. 'It's your enemies who tell you what you don't want to know. Dry my back.'

'Why is it I still get randy after all these years when I look at you?'

'I'll have to stop putting Viagra in your Milo. Keep your hands off.'

'I'm just trying to dry every nook in Granny.'

'I think your jokes could do with some Viagra. Kiss me.'

He did. 'Why did we have to invite the old folks here for dinner tonight? We could go to bed –'

'Forget it. Have your shower and don't try any *American Beauty* stuff.'

'You watch too many videos.'

He got under the shower, let the water wash the day out of him. He felt the old sense of retreat. *My castle, with hot and cold running water, with a good cook and an even better mistress.*

Con and Brigid Malone, Hans and Elisabeth Pretorius were coming to dinner, as they did every month. It was a duty call, Malone sometimes felt, but he always enjoyed the evening. Hans brought expensive wines from his cellar; Con brought vintage opinion from the cellars of another life. Brigid and Elisabeth, strangers to each other for the rest of the month, met as friends on these evenings. In-laws are the original immigration inspectors, ever watchful of what has crossed their borders. It gave Malone and Lisa a lot of pleasure that they were the anchors for these meetings.

Later, over dessert, blackbottom pie, Con's and Hans' favourite, Lisa was saying, 'With so little history, Australians have to invent myths –'

'Please explain,' said Brigid, almost merry on one glass of Hill of Grace shiraz. She was wearing a pink cashmere cardigan which, over her protests, Lisa and the girls had bought her for Christmas. She looked almost well-dressed till one got down to her lisle stockings and her comfortable Footrest shoes. Elisabeth, on the other hand and other foot, was all

Missoni and Ferragamo, at home amongst the double pay of Double Bay.

The discussions never got heated, they were part of the reasons for these monthly dinners.

'– look at rugby internationals,' said Lisa, 'all those players hugging each other like gays in a gale, all of them earning around half a million dollars a year, all of them singing about a suicidal, sheep-stealing drifter trying to evade the police. It's like Kerry Packer singing "Brother, Can You Spare a Dime?"'

'"Waltzing Matilda",' said Con. 'Beautiful song. We used to sing it at party meetings. After the *Internationale*" and the "Red Flag".' He grinned, a crack in a cracked face, and winked at Elisabeth, who winked back.

'But what's the connection on the rugby field? Another myth sought.' Lisa took a mouthful of the pie. 'A country needs to be old to have myths.'

'Ireland,' said Brigid, sipping her wine with reverence, as if the Pope himself had blessed it. She prayed regularly for her husband and her son and wondered sometimes why God gave her only half an ear. 'We have the melancholy for the myths.'

'Holland,' said Hans. 'We have our true myths. The little boy with his finger in the dike.'

Didn't she find it uncomfortable? But Malone saw Lisa's warning glare and he didn't unwind the old joke. Brigid didn't like dirty stories and would instantly lose her merry mood. He changed the subject: 'Hans, when you started out to make your money, were you greedy?'

'What sort of question is that?' But Elisabeth was not offended. 'Or are we still talking myths?'

'Greed isn't a myth,' said Malone, and Con nodded and raised the red shiraz in lieu of the Red Flag. 'Right now, at work, I'm dealing with some very greedy buggers.'

Hans had made a small fortune, since enlarged by wise

investment, out of rubber heels. For a few years half the population of the country bounced through life on Pretorius heels; then he had sold out to a conglomerate and the pedestrians had stopped treading on his name. It was his own private joke.

'No, I don't think I was greedy.' He had caught the point of Malone's question. 'In those days the aim was to make a living, not a fortune.'

'That was what us socialists believed,' said Con.

'You were a commo,' said his son.

'Only at work,' said Con and took another sip of the red.

He had been a boy during the 1930s Depression. A socialist at five, he had claimed, a communist at ten. He had told Malone lurid stories of deprivation and exploitation that had had Malone, living then in the affluence of the 1970s, laughing like a drunken oil baron.

'I'd have drowned him in holy water if he'd brought the *Daily Worker* home,' said Brigid and for a moment looked like a jovial Virgin Mary.

'Times have changed, Scobie. Everything these days is competition.' Hans, too, took a sip of his wine. He enjoyed his affluence, but never flaunted it. He was dressed all in grey, shirt, cashmere pullover, trousers: sleek as a seal, a good-humoured one who rarely barked. 'Look at the Russians. The ambitious and ruthless are as greedy now as the rest of us.'

'I never trusted the Russians,' said Con piously, conveniently shutting a door of memory.

'Neither did I,' said Elisabeth from the other end of the spectrum. She believed in monarchs, preferably female.

'You're involved in that kidnapping of Errol Magee, aren't you?' said Hans.

'Only indirectly,' said Malone. 'We're trying to find who murdered his maid.'

'I made a small investment in Mr Magee's company,' said Hans.

Oh crumbs, why did I mention greed? From the other end of the table Lisa sent another warning glare.

Hans went on, 'I'm not really interested in the New Economy, as they call it. But I-Saw, Mr Magee's company, seemed to me to be on to a good thing. I thought anything to do with lawyers couldn't miss, there are so many of them. Worldwide, hundreds of thousand of them, perhaps millions, studying their websites to see what Mr Magee had to tell them.'

Malone didn't ask how much Hans had lost. 'It's all down the drain now.'

'I wonder who has kidnapped Mr Magee? Lawyers?'

'It would be the first time they've asked for ransom. They usually ask for damages.'

At ten o'clock the Pretoriuses and the Malones rose to go; they left at this hour every visit, like draught horses out of a gate. Con shook hands with Lisa and Malone, told them to vote Labor. Hans, smiling, shook hands and told them to vote Coalition. Elisabeth hugged then both, told them to hug the children for her. Brigid, one and a half glasses into abandon, kissed Lisa and then, for the first time in almost forty years, kissed Malone on the cheek. He almost wept.

The in-laws drove off into the night in Hans' Jaguar. He would drop Con and Brigid in Erskineville, then drive himself and Elisabeth home to Vaucluse, another country. Duty had been done as parents, bonds linked as in-laws. They would not see each other nor communicate till next month's dinner.

Malone and Lisa had rinsed the dishes and stacked them in the dishwasher when he touched his cheek. 'Did you notice? Mum kissed me tonight.'

'Be grateful.'

'I am. I almost cried.'

She kissed him, on the cheek. 'She's always loved you, you know that. She was just always afraid to show it. Some of them, her generation, were like that. Let's go to bed.'

'I have a headache –'

She thumped him. 'I wasn't thinking of that –'

Then Tom came in the front door and down the hallway to the kitchen. 'How were the oldies tonight?'

'You're home early,' said Malone. 'You get a knock-back?'

'I've been down to the rugby club. I didn't fancy any of the guys, especially the front-row forwards.'

'You seen any more of Daniela?'

Tom shook his head. 'You scared her off. Anything left to eat?'

They left him with a slice of blackbottom pie and went along to their bedroom. Malone undressed and pulled on his K-Mart pyjamas. He never spent money on sleepwear, underwear or swimwear; Sulka, Derek Rose and Charvet would go bankrupt waiting for him. 'When we are old, you think our kids will hold duty dinners for us?'

'I hope so. Goodnight. Kiss me.'

'You're covered in Ella Baché.'

'Not on the lips.'

Malone was asleep when the phone rang. He reached for it without turning on the light, feeling the same old chill in the breast: something's wrong with Claire or Maureen! But it was Clements:

'He's back. Errol Magee. Sheryl's just called me. She's calling in someone from the strike force. They can talk to him first. You and I can see him in the morning.'

'Where is he?'

'At his apartment, he arrived there ten minutes ago. Sheryl says he appears to be okay. His girlfriend and his wife are there. And Sheryl and Paula Decker. He's got more company than I'd think he'd want. See you in the morning.'

Malone hung up and crawled back into bed. Lisa asked sleepily, 'What's happening?'

'I don't know,' he said. 'Errol Magee's just come back from the dead.'

Shirlee and Darlene had called in at the hospital on their way home. Phoenix had been moved out of intensive care and was now in a ward with three other men. He was still swathed in dressings and he had one leg in a cast held up on a pulley; he looked like a small white shark that had been hooked and landed. Shirlee and Darlene sat down on either side of the bed.

'It's all over,' said Shirlee in her softest voice, leaning towards Pheeny's only exposed ear.

'What's all over?' Pheeny had never had a soft voice, it had been given him for use in football crowds and in a steel foundry.

'S-sh,' said Darlene, shaking her head and moving her eyes from side to side to indicate the other patients. Two of them, old men, appeared to be asleep or dead, but the third, a young Mediterranean, was wide awake and looking at Darlene with bold interest that suggested he was not in hospital for impotency.

'The business,' said Shirlee. 'It's finished. All over.'

It was no effort for Pheeny to look puzzled; it came naturally. 'What the fuck – sorry, Mum. What you talking about?'

Darlene thought: do other kidnappers hold their conferences in coffee bars and hospital wards? 'Our mate Errol –'

Light dawned through the dressings; Pheeny's mouth fell open. 'Holy shit! Why?'

'Complications,' said Shirlee. 'But don't you worry, we'll handle it.'

As if he's going to get out of bed, broken leg and all, thought Darlene. She was fast becoming fed up. She had always been sensible about dreams. You took them out, enjoyed them for a while, then put them away again; they were never durable. 'Look, do we have to talk about it *here*?'

'We owe it to him,' said Shirlee, being motherly. 'Has Mr Bomaker been in to see you again? The lawyer?'

'No,' said Pheeny. 'Are we gunna ditch that, too? Not sue the bitch put me in here?'

'No,' said Shirlee, 'that's our Number Two priority.'

'Our Number One priority now,' said Darlene and stood up. 'Go back to sleep, Pheeny. Dream about Mr Bomaker and the class action.'

She waited while Shirlee found an exposed space to kiss Pheeny. 'Look after yourself, love.'

Even Pheeny looked puzzled by the advice.

As she passed the leering young man in the bed opposite, Darlene, sour as a lemon, paused. 'You're outa luck, mate. I'm a dyke.'

'What did you say to him?' asked Shirlee as they went out of the ward.

'I told him I was a lesbian.'

'You're not, are you? Oh migod!'

'Wash your mouth out,' said Darlene and smiled at two ambulance men as they wheeled in a woman in labour.

Shirlee stopped by the mother-to-be, patted her hand. 'Good luck, dear. It's always worth it.'

'Forget it,' said the woman. 'This is me ninth.'

Darlene went out of the hospital laughing.

Back home they gave Corey the bad news.

'Thank Christ,' he said to their surprise. 'It's been nothing but a fuck-up since we started.'

Shirlee was past washing out mouths; she was bitterly disappointed. She had had her secret plans for her share of the ransom money. She would sell this house, buy an apartment in a retirement village up on the Central Coast, join the lawn bowls club, meet up with a widower with a comfortable income, put the life of crime behind her, be neat and respectable. And put behind her, too, the ghost in the timber up behind the house at Minnamurra.

'It's getting too dicey,' said Darlene. 'There's something called the *yakuza*. Chantelle told us about it.'

'The *yakuza*? Jesus, I've read about them. They're after him?'

'They've gotta find him first. And us.'

'Okay, we get rid of him.' Corey sighed. 'I think I'll be glad to get back to work. I'll go in tomorrow, tell 'em me back trouble's over. When do we get rid of him?'

'We'll drop him somewhere tonight,' said Darlene.

'What about Chantelle?'

'She'll be at his flat waiting for him, to welcome him home. She's gotta do that, so's the police won't be suspicious. Then she's going back to London. Incidentally, she hates Chantelle as a name.'

'I always did, meself.'

Shirlee was sniffy. 'You think I should of waited till you'd all grown up before I named you? Got your own choice? What would you of called yourself?'

'Bert. Or Fred.' He grinned at her, felt for a moment like kissing her. He was so fucking relieved the kidnapping, the whole business, was over.

'I'm hungry,' she said, 'waddya you want for dinner?'

'It'll be His Nibs' last supper,' said Corey, who had once attended Sunday school. 'Let's give him a good send-off. He told me he liked French cooking.'

'He'll get what's in the fridge. You're getting too matey with him.'

Corey thought about it. 'Yeah, maybe. We could of picked worse to kidnap.'

'Like a rock star or one of them rap stars with the foul mouths?' Darlene grinned at her mother. 'You'd of loved cooking for one of them. She'd of fed soap to Eminem.'

Errol Magee got grilled sausages, mashed potatoes, green beans and what was left of the upside-down cake with whipped cream. He was appreciative. 'This isn't bad.'

'I'll tell the chef,' said Corey through his hood. 'Sport, we're letting you go, later on.'

Magee stopped eating. 'Why?'

'Things've got complicated.'

'The police on to you?'

'No, nothing like that. They haven't a clue who we are. Neither have you, right?'

'Is that a threat?'

'Errol, sport –' Corey studied the man whom he was still trying to understand. A successful man, a millionaire forty times over. 'How much were you worth when things were going well?'

'On paper? About two hundred and fifty million. But it's all gone.' The taste of the food for the moment turned sour in Magee's mouth. 'The world, the IT world, that was all it was for a while. Paper.'

Corey himself had never thought in terms of success; the word wasn't in his vocabulary. You battled from one day to the next and if today was better than yesterday, you were ahead. But ahead of what? He had never given any consideration to that.

'You've still got that forty million, though.'

Magee went back to eating. 'I told you, that's all bullshit. You let me go, I'm going back to bankruptcy. You're going to forget the ransom, all that shit?'

'All of it, sport. You go scot free.'

Magee stopped eating, suddenly relaxed. It was maybe a little premature; nonetheless he felt he could trust this guy. Trust had never been one of his weaknesses, but you had to use it occasionally. 'When?'

'Later.'

'Do you have to keep me trussed up like this till then?'

The smile was apparent even under the blue hood. 'Errol, did you ever trust the other guy till the deal was signed and delivered?'

Magee, too, smiled. 'What business are you in, other than kidnapping?'

Corey stood up. 'Ladies underwear.'

Magee laughed, totally relaxed now. 'You and I must have a drink when this is all over.'

'Yeah,' said Corey and went out of the room with the dinner tray.

At midnight Shirlee, Darlene and Corey, all hooded, came back into the bedroom. Corey gently woke Magee, who had dozed off. 'Time to go, sport.'

Magee blinked, came awake. 'Where are you going to let me go? Not out in the fucking bush, I hope.'

'Wash your mouth out,' said Shirlee, but it was automatic now, she no longer cared.

'You'll find that out when we dump you,' said Corey. 'I'm gunna have to strap your hands behind your back and gag you, too. We can't have you yelling your head off.'

'You don't have to do that. Trust me –'

Shirlee's laugh inside the hood was a cackle; she hated the thought of letting him go. 'Mr Magee, I'm not the trusting sort. I've had too much experience . . .'

She had continued to argue against letting him go. She could see her fortune going out the door, dreams disappearing as if Darlene and Corey had abruptly shaken her awake. They had been adamant. For the first time that she could remember, they had taken charge. Later, in bed, she would be surprised at her anger at them.

Corey was moving around Magee, pulling back the waist on his jeans, the collar of the football jumper.

'What're you doing?' Magee was now on edge, fearful of a change of plans at the last moment.

'Relax, Errol. I'm just checking there's no names on the jeans and the jersey. Laundry marks. When we say goodbye, sport, it's gunna be forever.'

'I never send anything to the laundry,' said Shirlee; she, too, was on edge. 'They never wash anything as well as I do.'

'Okay, I'm looking for dry-cleaning marks. No, you're clean, sport. You can make a comeback in a Souths' jersey. The only one they probably will make.'

The veteran rugby league club had been dropped from the local competition after decades of involvement and a court case was pending. A small war was going on; so far the UN had not been asked to intervene. Errol Magee had as much interest in it as he had in wars in the Congo or Chechnya.

'We should put him back in the blue dress he was wearing when you picked him up,' said Shirlee, still shirty.

'Don't put it like that,' said Corey, grinning inside the hood. He was feeling much better now things were under way to get out of this mess. He still had pangs of guilt about what had happened to Magee's maid and the cop Haywood, but eventually, he hoped, he would turn the back of his mind to them, too. 'I didn't pick you up, did I, sport?'

'I don't know how else you got me here,' said Magee. 'You –'

But Darlene was gagging him with some tape. 'When you peel it off, Mr Magee, rip it off quickly. It hurts less like that.'

Magee's eyes shone: it was hard to tell whether he was abusing her or thanking her for her concern. Corey hauled him to his feet.

'Behave yourself, sport, and in another twenty minutes you'll be free as a bird.'

'Free to spend all that money you have somewhere,' said Shirlee, getting in the last word.

All the lights were out in the house as Corey and Darlene took Magee, blindfolded and gagged, out the back door of *Emoh Ruo* and led him across to the Toyota in the garage. Shirlee took off her hood and stayed in the house, sitting down in the dark kitchen and suddenly, for the first time in years, bursting into tears. Dreams and greed are bedmates, of a sort.

Darlene got into the back seat with Magee. She felt a mixture of excitement and relief; but she knew she would walk away with less emotion than the rest of the family. Except, perhaps,

Chantelle, who, even when they were kids, had always been the cool one.

Corey gave the car a push, jumped in behind the wheel and they ran silently down the short driveway and out into the roadway. Corey swung to the right and they were halfway down the street before he switched on the engine. Mrs Charlton, sound asleep, missed the street gossip item of the new century.

Twenty minutes later Corey pulled the car in beside a deserted park. He turned round in the front seat. 'Good luck, sport.'

Magee felt something being pushed into his jeans' pocket. 'What's that?'

'Cab fare,' said Darlene. 'Fifty dollars. You've made more outa us than we made outa you.'

She laughed, kissed him on his blindfold, then pushed him gently out of the car. By the time he had freed his hands and pulled off the blindfold, the Toyota was just two red tail-lights disappearing into the distance like fireflies that had had their fun. He felt for the gag, hesitated, then ripped it off as the girl, whoever she was, had suggested. It hurt like buggery and he yelped.

Ten minutes later he was out on a road he didn't recognize and hailing a wandering cab. He fell into the back seat, a most un-Australian thing to do and which instantly aroused the suspicion of the driver, a Korean and still learning how to deal with the natives.

'Where are we?' asked Magee.

'Rocky Point Road.'

That meant nothing to Magee. 'Okay, take me to the Garden Apartment. East Circular Quay.'

The Korean was also still learning the geography of Sydney: 'Where's that?'

'Holy Christ!' said Magee, gave him instructions and lay back, all at once exhausted and wanting to cry with relief. He could hardly believe he was free, that the ordeal was over.

When the cab drew up outside the apartments in Macquarie Street, Magee handed the driver the fifty-dollar note and waited.

'No tip?' said the driver, who was also learning the necessary phrases of English. He was learning, too, that the average Australian, especially the women, had fists as tight as those of Kim Il-Sung.

'No tip,' said Magee. 'Give me my change.'

There was no night concierge and Magee only then realized he had no key. He pressed the buzzer against his name on the board beside the locked doors. He kept his finger on the buzzer till a sleepy voice said, 'Yes?'

'Kylie? Let me in!'

'This is Detective Dallen. Who's that?'

'Me, for Crissake! Errol Magee!'

When he got upstairs there were four women in night attire waiting for him. Kylie, Caroline and two women he had never seen before. One of them, Sheryl Dallen, as she introduced herself with Detective in front of her name, was holding a gun aimed at the front door, which had been opened by the other strange woman.

'What the hell –'

'I'm Detective Decker. Come in, Mr Magee.'

Kylie rushed at him as if expecting to have to race Caroline. She flung her arms round him and kissed him. Caroline, arms folded, watched the reunion with a smile. Detectives Dallen and Decker busied themselves putting on lightweight dressing-gowns, non-police issue. Sheryl put her gun in the pocket of her gown, where it sagged like a hidden growth.

Magee broke free of Kylie's possessive embrace, ignored the two policewomen and looked at Caroline. 'What are you doing here?'

Sheryl stepped forward. 'Before we get into the domestic scene, Mr Magee –'

'Who are you?' He was tired and belligerent.

'Detective Constable Dallen, of Homicide. This is Detective Constable Decker –'

'Homicide? You thought I was *dead*?'

'No, darling –' Kylie had her arm locked in his; she wasn't going to let him go. 'Juanita was murdered –'

Then Monica and her husband, Clarrie, appeared, both in pyjamas. The room looked like an adult slumber party. Magee was puzzled, bewildered. All at once the last two days caught up with him, swamping him like a huge surf dumper. He did something he had never done in his life before: he fainted.

4

At six the next morning Darlene, in her Spirit of Olympics T-shirt and shorts, went out for her usual daily jog. She carried with her a brown paper bag half-full of twenty-cent coins. Shirlee put all her spare coins into a large jam jar and each year, when the Salvation Army made its usual annual door-knock, she gave them the jar full of coins and, for an hour or two, felt like Mother Teresa.

Darlene jogged half a mile from home to a public phone box. From there she rang four television stations, three radio stations and two morning newspapers. Then she jogged back home, feeling healthier and in better humour than she had in the past two days.

Chapter Nine

1

At seven-thirty Malone, Clements and Chief Superintendent Random arrived simultaneously, as if on cue, outside the Garden Apartments. There were press cars and radio cars and TV vans and a horde of reporters; one might have thought a sporting hero had come back from the dead, instead of just another IT whiz. The three officers double-parked, gave their keys to one of the several uniformed men keeping the peace, and went into the lobby of the apartments.

A brown-uniformed concierge was already on duty, holding open a side door beside the revolving door through which the detectives had entered. A thin, prematurely grey-haired man in a track suit and trainers was pushing someone in a wheelchair out through the doorway. Malone had to look twice, discreetly, to tell whether the cerebral palsy victim in the wheelchair was a boy or a man. It was a boy, maybe twelve years old, who twisted his head and looked out at the packed pavement with fear. Then he and the man were gone, the crowd opening up to let them through, then closing behind them.

'They go out every morning,' said the concierge, recognizing Malone. 'For their constitutional.'

Malone could only nod, silently blessing himself and Lisa for their luck. Some people were born, he thought, while God was looking the other way.

'Fantastic news, eh?' said the concierge, holding open the lift doors for them. 'Mr Magee being back.'

'Fantastic,' said Malone; then added to Random and Clements as the doors closed: 'Basically, that is.'

Random looked at Clements. 'Is he usually as shitty as this early in the morning?'

'No, usually at the end of the day,' said Clements and he and Malone shook hands on the cliché.

'I hope by the end of *this* day,' said Random, 'all our troubles are over.'

'For you, maybe,' said Malone. 'We still have to find who killed the maid. She keeps being overlooked.'

They rode up to Magee's floor, got out of the lift to be greeted by a young uniformed officer standing outside the apartment's closed front door.

'Anyone in there?' asked Random. 'The strike force guys?'

'No, sir. They've come and gone. They were here at six. Mr Magee didn't exactly welcome them.'

'Neither would I,' said Random. 'But don't quote me.'

Magee, hair in a ponytail, dressed in pyjamas and a silk dressing-gown, was having breakfast with Kylie Doolan, Caroline Magee and Sheryl Dallen. The latter, fully dressed, rose as the senior detectives came into the apartment. She was in charge, but the other three were unaware of, or ignoring, the fact.

'Paula Decker has gone off, sir. Miss Doolan's sister and brother-in-law left half an hour ago.' She looked at Malone as if to tell him it was time she, too, left. She looked tired and fed up. 'The strike force officers questioned Mr Magee for almost an hour.'

'I've had questioning up to here,' said Magee without rising from the table.

'I'm sure you have,' said Random.

'Who are you, anyway?' Magee was making no effort to be polite. Malone felt Clements, beside him, stiffen and he waited for the big man to smear Magee's face with the poached eggs he was eating. Something he would have applauded.

'I'm Chief Superintendent Random, in charge of the force that's been trying to find you.'

'You weren't too successful, were you?'

'Pull your head in, Errol,' said Caroline.

On the surface Random looked unperturbed by Magee's rudeness. 'The men who were here earlier would have questioned you about the kidnapping. Inspector Malone and Sergeant Clements are here to question you about the murder of your maid.'

'I know nothing about that! I told those other guys –'

'Take it easy,' said Caroline.

'Mind your own business!' snapped Kylie and in the background Sheryl rolled her eyes at Clements, who grinned.

'Mr Magee,' said Random, 'could we talk to you in another room? It won't take long.'

Magee looked as if he were about to refuse; he had a piece of toast halfway to his mouth, his fork sliced into the poached egg. Then he put down the toast and the fork and stood up. Kylie, too, stood up. 'I'll come with you, darling –'

'No,' said Random and for the first time since coming into the apartment his voice had iron in it. 'Sergeant Clements will talk to you ladies out here. Mr Magee?'

Magee led them into a small study off the main bedroom. Through the open bedroom door Malone could see the rumpled bed and he wondered who had slept with Magee last night. Or maybe Magee, if he were sensible, had slept alone.

The room was too small; the three men were close together. Magee sat in a chair at the small desk against one wall; Random sat in the only other chair. Malone found a place for his bum on the desk, hard up against a computer. Which, he noted, now had a blank screen. Magee, it seemed, was not yet interested in the world he had once occupied, that cyberspace out there full of strangers you were asked to trust.

'Look, I was shocked when they told me last night about Juanita –'

'We accept that, Mr Magee. But the people who kidnapped you –'

'Jesus, do I have to go through it all again?' There was no mistaking his fatigue.

'Inspector Malone would prefer it. Were the kidnappers vicious towards you? Did they threaten to kill you?'

'I don't know if they were threats, I mean real threats. I got on pretty well with the guy I saw most. Well, I didn't exactly *see* him. He wore a hood all the time, a blue hood. So did the other two, the two women. Yeah, and there was a second guy, I think. He sorta disappeared.'

'Two women?' said Malone.

'Yeah. They seemed to be mother and daughter. They called the older one Mum.' Malone tried to hide his grin, but Magee caught it. 'Yeah, I know, that was what I thought. Kidnapped by a gang run by Mum.'

'There was a famous outlaw gang in America run by a mum, Ma Barker,' said Random. 'The worst Mafia gang in Naples is run by a mum. It happens, Mr Magee. Where did they hold you? You got any idea?'

Magee had had time to think about it; he was still tired, but his mind had begun to click like a computer. One that had a virus in it somewhere, but which still worked: 'The first night and the second day we were in the bush somewhere. I don't know where, it sounded as if it was pretty isolated. Then when they moved me, I was in the boot of a car, I dunno, we must've travelled for about an hour. We stopped somewhere along the way and pulled off what sounded like a main highway. I was pretty groggy, I couldn't breathe in the hood they'd pulled over my head. I dimly remember being pulled out of the boot of the car and being dumped in another one. I must've passed out, because the next thing I remember, I was in a bedroom in a house in the suburbs, I'd say. I could hear the occasional car and every so often a plane would go over. So I couldn't have been too far from the airport.'

Malone was listening intently. 'What happened last night?'

Magee was more co-operative now, his bad temper seemed to have evaporated. 'They said they were going to let me go, that things had become too complicated. The old lady, Mum, she didn't seem to think it was a good idea. Letting me go, I mean. They put me into a car, they blindfolded and gagged me.' He felt around his mouth, which was still sore. 'The guy who spent most of the time with me, he and the girl dropped me near some park, I think it could've been in Arncliffe, I dunno much about out there –'

Out there, thought Malone. Maybe ten kilometres from the heart of the city. He makes it sound like the Far West, out there where the rabbits and kangaroos roam. Just east of Tibooburra . . .

'I was in a main road when I got a cab – the driver said it was Rocky Point Road, I've never heard of it –'

Malone felt the computer against his back. Buried in its hard disk were roads and streets all over the world. But not Rocky Point Road . . .

'Did they ever mention the maid?' asked Random.

Magee shook his head. 'Look, I don't think they could've been the ones who did it. The guy spent most of the time with me, we got on well. I mean, after a while I began to *like* him. The girl, too. I don't think they were killers.'

'Mr Magee,' said Random, 'killers come in all shapes and sizes and temperaments. Inspector Malone and I have had too much experience of them. You said they wore hoods all the time. You saw only half of what they might truly be like.'

'No.' Magee shook his head again. 'I think – I'm *sure* I'm right about the guy and the girl. The other guy, the one who disappeared – I dunno about him. Or the mum. I just, y'know, I just don't believe they were killers.'

'*Someone* killed your maid,' said Malone.

'Yeah, I know.' He felt some guilt about that; or something. Juanita had been a stranger to him; not because of her, but because of *him*. The circle of which he was the centre had always been small; he had slept with women who had been strangers, even though they were on first-name terms. He would never have missed Juanita if she had suddenly departed, though he had not expected her to depart in the way she had. 'Look, your guys who were here earlier, they mentioned the *yakuza*. Kylie told me about 'em, too. Could they have killed Juanita?'

Random looked at Malone, who shrugged. 'Maybe. But my money's on the kidnappers. Errol, what was the woman like, the mother?'

'Christ, I dunno. How do you describe a woman who's got a bag over her head all the time?'

'Don't tempt me,' said Random, and the three men laughed, allies for the moment, all blokey.

'I'd say she was maybe in her forties – I'm not good at women's ages.'

'Join the club,' said Malone, keeping Magee at ease, seeing he was now more ready to co-operate.

'Slim and – and *brisk*, I guess is the word. *Organized*. She ran the show. I remember thinking she'd have made a good office manager.'

'There was no older man? A father?'

'Never saw one. The young guy gave me a jersey to wear, a Souths' one. It's outside somewhere. He said his old man played for Souths years ago, but he could've been bullshitting me.'

'Did they talk to you about Kunishima Bank?' asked Random.

'They said they'd called the bank and got nowhere.' Magee made no attempt to hide his bitterness.

'We've had a negotiator sitting with them and one at I-Saw, but there were no more calls after we put them in place. Just the original two calls, the one to I-Saw and the one to the bank. I think your kidnappers were rank amateurs, Mr Magee.'

Magee thought a moment, then nodded. 'You could be right.'

'When they stopped calling was when things must've started going arse-up,' said Malone. 'I wonder what went wrong and why?'

Magee shook his head. 'I can't tell you. The guy used to

talk to me, he, I dunno, he sounded depressed. I didn't think anything of it at the time –'

'I wonder,' said Random, 'if the kidnappers found out the *yakuza* were looking for you?'

Random's tone, as usual was dry and soft. He shovels dust, thought Malone, better than anyone I know. You could be gasping for breath . . .

Magee was gasping. 'Kylie told me – I thought the guy was, whoever he was –'

'Tajiri,' said Malone. 'He told her his name was Ikura, but we know it was Tajiri. He works for Kunishima.'

'Jesus, I know him! Well, no, not *know* him – but I met him! A coupla times, no more. He just sat in on a conference with Okada, the Kunishima boss, and some other guy –'

'Nakasone.'

'Yeah. Yeah, Nakasone –' He took another deep breath. 'They're really after me? To kill me?'

'I gather,' said Malone, soft and dry as Random. 'Unless you tell 'em where the forty million dollars are.'

'There's no forty million dollars missing! That's all bullshit –'

'Come on, Errol, we're not Fraud Squad or the Tax Office. We couldn't care less where the forty million is, could we, Superintendent?'

Random gave his dry smile, playing the friendly game. 'Speak for yourself. But we'll forget it for the moment, Mr Magee. Your main worry is the *yakuza* boys, with or without the missing money.'

'When your wife Caroline came out from London, did she know about the forty million?' asked Malone, still gentle.

'Of course she didn't!' Then he saw his mistake. He shrugged, no longer denying the missing dollars. 'I didn't know she was coming. She just turned up a coupla weeks ago.'

'Were you glad to see her?'

Again the shrug. 'I dunno. Yeah, I guess so. She understood

me better than any of the others. We were *married* . . . You married?'

'Very much,' said Malone. 'The Superintendent, too.'

'We separated, but I guess we always understood each other. You know what it's like.'

The other two married men nodded, then Malone said, 'She wasn't coming out to help you with your problems?'

'How could she?' He was no longer defiant on the money question. 'The shit was too deep. You know what it's been like. You pick up the papers every day and another two or three dotcoms have gone bust. I could've survived if the big overseas lawyers hadn't got smart. They saw all the IT companies going bust and they decided to set up their own service sites. I'm suing half a dozen of them, but whoever sued lawyers and won? Especially the American and European firms. I could cry,' he said, but didn't.

If he had, Malone might have belted him over the ear.

'What are you planning to do? Go back to I-Saw?'

'What's the point? It can't be saved. I'll look around for something else, another job. In the IT business they don't hold a failure against you. It's part of the game, like a knock-on in football.' He had chosen a sporting metaphor, but he didn't know why. 'You play rugby or rugby league?'

'The Superintendent is Welsh,' said Malone. 'Rugby is their religion. My son plays rugby.'

'Inspector Malone's game was cricket,' said Random. 'They're very tough on failure there.'

'Till you make up your mind, Errol,' said Malone, 'we're going to give you police protection. Free of charge.'

Magee looked as if he was about to protest; then he nodded. 'Okay, I guess that's sensible. But shit –'

'Out of the frying pan,' said Random, 'into the fire. An old Welsh cliché.'

'What's he on about?' Magee asked Malone.

'He's an old Welsh philosopher. The Welsh are good at that.'

'You should practise it, Mr Magee,' said Random. 'You may need it.'

Out in the living room Clements was at the table with the three women, drinking coffee poured for him by Sheryl. He was affability itself as he said, 'Mrs Magee, why did you tell us you had only just arrived back in Sydney? You've been back two weeks.'

Caroline was just as affable. 'I didn't tell anyone I'd just arrived back. No one asked me when I'd arrived.'

'You let us think –' said Kylie.

Caroline cut her off as if she had picked up one of the breakfast knives and slid it across her throat: 'Kylie dear –'

'I'm not your Kylie *dear* –'

'No. No, that's true. You're Kylie's dear, selfish as hell –'

'Ladies –' Clements held up a hand, looked at Sheryl for support.

The latter hid her disgust and her smile. She had found herself both liking and disliking Mrs Magee, but the girlfriend was just a pain in the butt.

'We checked with Immigration, Caroline. It's standard procedure.' It wasn't, but lies are one way to the truth: standard police procedure. 'It must of been our mistake, assuming you'd just arrived.'

'It was,' said Caroline, reaching to pour herself more coffee. 'Errol knew when I arrived.'

'You'd seen him before the other night? Last night?' Sheryl was exhausted, it seemed she had been here in this apartment a week or more.

'Yes, when he told me I'd arrived too late.' She stood up. She was in a green silk dressing-gown; green, Sheryl noted, seemed to be her colour. She looked around her, then down at Kylie. 'It's all over, Kylie dear. You'd better get used to it.'

Carrying the cup of coffee she turned to leave as Random, Malone and Magee came back into the room. Random said,

'We'll be giving Mr Magee police protection. Are both you ladies staying on here?'

'Not me,' said Caroline. 'I'm going back to my hotel now and I'll be flying out tomorrow, going back to London. I'll talk to you later, Errol.'

'No, you won't –' Kylie was throwing up barriers.

Magee looked at his two women; looked, thought Malone, as if he wanted neither of them. But he said nothing and Malone took over: 'It will be easier to give you protection if you are all in the one place. It would be better if you moved in here till tomorrow, Mrs Magee.'

'No!' Kylie was piling barricade upon barricade.

Magee said wearily, 'Cut it out, Kylie. I won't be sleeping with her –'

'Thanks,' said Caroline and put down her coffee. She smiled wryly at Sheryl. 'Isn't it nice to be wanted? . . . All right, Inspector. I'll stay here tonight. Will I need an escort to the airport tomorrow?'

'We'll see to that,' said Malone, then looked at Random: 'Anything more, sir?'

'I think there's a lot more,' said Random. 'We just have to see when it turns up.'

2

'You've heard the news,' said Nakasone. 'He's back!'

'I don't want to know!' Okada threw up his hands as if he had been told General MacArthur had sailed back into Tokyo Bay. His father had been one of the junior officers on board the USS *Missouri* that soul-destroying day; his father had kept the memory alive in the family like an inherited disease. His father was dead now, beyond the knowledge of his son's involuntary involvement with gangsters. 'The bank washes its hands of it!'

They were in Okada's office, the early-morning sun making the room more cheerful than the mood of its occupants. Nakasone sat down, not in the chair behind the big desk; but there was no doubt who was assuming charge. He, too, came of a family of tradition: his father and his grandfather before him had been *yakuza*. They had been rougher, but no tougher.

He looked at his nominal boss. Hauro Okada was that too-often impediment to progress, an honest man. 'Hauro, we have to be sensible. Our patrons back in Osaka –'

'Yours, not mine.' Okada sat down behind his desk, but he knew the position meant nothing. He might as well have been sitting on a toilet seat.

'*Ours*,' said Nakasone. 'Things are so bad back in Japan, we can't just turn a blind eye to what Magee has stolen. Our bank is like all the other banks – we were too trusting –'

Despite himself, Okada laughed. 'Kenji, Kunishima wasn't trusting. It was like all the other banks – greedy. And now it's in a hole. Not as big as some, but a hole nonetheless.'

'You approved the original investment in I-Saw –'

'Only after you and Osaka had supposedly done due diligence. I'm not going to commit *hara-kiri* over this –'

Nakasone looked out the window behind Okada; gulls climbed up towards them on shafts of sunlight. 'The means are behind you.'

'Don't talk to me about honour when it comes to money. Your bosses –'

'*Our* bosses.'

Okada continued as if there had been no interruption: '– are owed no *giri* by me. When we are this level –' He waved a hand behind him; a poor man's debts never flew at this height.

'Up here, money has no pride or shame. It's a commodity, Kenji, nothing more, nothing less. Mr Magee is your problem, not mine. If your bosses want him attended to, then you and Tajiri have to do it. I'll be looking the other way – for the bank's good name.'

He smiled inwardly at the hypocrisy of what he had said. The bank, unlike the *yakuza* who financed it, had no tradition; it was a mere ten years old, a sucker-fish amongst the sharks. He himself was more honourable than Kunishima; he had a *name*. Which Nakasone and Tajiri did not. Up till a hundred and fifty years ago only noble families and *samurai* families had surnames. The Okadas had been *samurai*, going back five centuries, coming forward to his father on the deck of the USS *Missouri* and the ignomy. Now there was only himself, no *samurai*, just a banker. But, he was desperately trying to prove, an honourable one. Working for a bank whose profit-and-loss columns were its only bow to *giri*.

'Where is Tajiri?' he asked.

'On his way home,' said Nakasone. 'He flew out yesterday to Perth, on a domestic flight. He is travelling on a second passport, under another name.' He didn't mention the name and Okada did not ask. 'He flies out of Perth tonight for Singapore, then home to Osaka.'

Okada was almost afraid to ask the question: 'What about Magee?'

Nakasone stood up. 'I'll attend to him. He trusts me, he knows I was the one who took him to Osaka. He will tell us where the forty million dollars are.'

'Good luck,' said Okada and turned to stare out the window, looking north to Osaka, Japan and home. Where corruption and cronyism prevailed in politics and business, but where some pockets of honour still remained.

3

Back at Homicide Clements said, 'What d'you reckon?'

'Let the strike force blokes look after Magee,' said Malone. 'We go looking for the kidnappers – they were the ones who did in Juanita.'

'So where do we look?'

Then the phone, as if Malone had willed it, rang. It was Sheryl Dallen: 'Boss, I've just talked to Immigration again. It didn't click with me the first time, I was checking when Mrs Caroline Magee had arrived. I've just checked again, they've read off their computer particulars on her. Mrs Caroline Magee, maiden name Briskin.'

Malone felt the lift in spirit that in him passed for excitement; nobody would have known. 'She still at the apartment? You still there?'

'Still here, both of us. Till the strike force guys arrive to relieve me.'

'We're on our way, Sheryl. I love you, but only platonically.'

'Good enough,' she said and hung up.

'What's the love-in all about?' asked Clements.

Malone told him: 'Caroline probably organized it. She bullshitted us about having only a brother, one she hadn't seen in years. She's got a mother and a sister and two brothers, all out at Hurstville.'

'So where do we go first – down to the Quay or out to Hurstville?'

'Get the locals to pick up the family – and the younger brother, he's in hospital, St George. Tell 'em they won't need the State Protection blokes – I don't think Mum Briskin is going to come out with guns blazing. But tell 'em to send more than a couple of men. Bring 'em back to Police Centre – we'll have Mrs Magee there to front them. Here's the Hurstville address.'

Clements went out to phone the Hurstville commander and Malone picked up his own phone to ring Greg Random. The latter, as usual, was as excited as a drowsy owl. 'Sooner or later things fall our way, Scobie.'

'It's a long way from over –'

'Don't sound so pessimistic –'

'I'm not,' said Malone and hung up, smiling, which is another expression of excitement.

He got up, pulled on his jacket, took his pork-pie hat and went out to Clements. Normally he would have taken a junior officer with him, but on this one, maybe his last Homicide case, he wanted Clements. It would be a ceremonial handing-over.

When Malone and Clements got to the bottom of Macquarie Street the media horde had thinned to a scribble. Mr Magee, the word had come out, would not be making any statement at this point in time nor at the end of the day. The two detectives got out of their car and the first person Malone saw was Vassily Todorov, helmeted and geared for action, his bicycle held at the ready like a skeletal horse. He plunged at Malone.

'Tell Mr Magee I must see him!'

'Mr Todorov, we're here on police business –'

Several of the reporters had gathered around, notebooks ready, tapes held out like tidbits to be munched on. 'What's going on, Inspector? Who's the guy on the bike? Is he the new Flying Squad?'

'Tell 'em who you are, Vassily,' said Clements and pushed Malone ahead of him through the revolving door. 'They might run your story.'

They went up to the Magee floor, knocked on the apartment door and it was opened by Caroline Magee, dressed in black slacks and cream shirt. She appeared unsurprised, unperturbed, to see them.

'Come in, Inspector. Good news?'

'It could be. Where's Mr Magee?'

'He's asleep,' said Kylie, watcher of the bedroom. She and Sheryl Dallen were in the living room behind Caroline. 'Why are you back again? Aren't you going to give him any rest?'

'I'd like a word with Detective Dallen,' said Malone and took Sheryl out on to the apartment's balcony. 'You're sure Immigration's got everything right? I don't want her making a fool of us.'

'I got them to repeat it,' said Sheryl. 'They don't have the maiden name of a woman on a passport any more – they said they stopped that back in 1984.'

'Germaine Greer arranged that?'

'None of your male chauvinism – *sir*. But today, when a passport is applied for, they put the lot, married name, maiden name, on the computer. Her passport was issued at Australia House in London in March 1993. Just after she married him, I guess.'

He looked out on the scene below them. The city, as always, was oblivious of its undercurrents. The ferries came into the wharves of the Quay without fuss, passengers ready to leap, running, towards whatever had brought them to town. On the other side of the water a cruise boat eased out towards the harbour to show tourists and day-trippers the better aspects of the city, the harbourside mansions of those who had made good, or bad, depending on how they had got their money. Over by the wharves a busker noiselessly tap-danced to the silent music of his banjo, like a puppet without strings. Immediately below, people meandered towards the Opera House, watched by diners in the cafés and restaurants along the colonnade, different levels of credit cards waving to each other. Errol Magee was yesterday's news and the public eye, seeking distraction, not disaster, was looking elsewhere. If Magee, or his wife Caroline, jumped off this balcony, then, ah then, they would stop to look, thankful that they had not been felled by a low-flying suicide.

'Righto, we take her in. Watch Miss Doolan's face when I tell Mrs Magee where we're going.'

Caroline just raised an eyebrow when Malone told her he wanted her to accompany him and Sergeant Clements back to Police Centre. 'You never let up, do you, Inspector?'

'We try not to,' he said amiably.

'Why are you taking her?' said Kylie, as if she had been excluded from something.

'Just for questioning.'

Kylie's expression changed: she had just won the lottery. 'You think *she* had something to do with Errol's kidnapping? Oh, wait till I tell him!'

'Let's get out of here,' said Caroline abruptly and picked up a jacket and handbag. 'She's going to have an orgasm.'

'Go home when the strike force fellers come back,' Malone told Sheryl. 'You look wrung out.'

Sheryl's voice was just a murmur: 'Wouldn't you be?'

As they went down in the lift Malone told Caroline, 'There are reporters still outside. You may be in the news from now on.'

He had to admire her composure: 'Any escape from Miss Doolan is welcome. Do I stop and give them a statement?'

'You do, and Sergeant Clements will knee-cap you.'

She smiled at both of them. 'Are you two married?'

'Not to each other,' said Clements as the lift reached the lobby. 'Okay, here we go. If I knock anyone over, don't stop to help him up.'

As they got out into the street Vassily Todorov led the charge, plumed head thrust forward. 'Where's Mr Magee?'

'Who's the woman?'

'It's his wife –'

But Malone and Caroline had jumped into the back seat of the unmarked car. Clements, behind the wheel, the ubiquitous parking ticket still behind the wipers, swung the car out into the traffic to a clamour of horns from others who thought they owned the road. He did a swift U-turn, turning Malone's stomach, and they were heading back uptown and out towards Surry Hills and Police Centre.

Caroline had sprawled against Malone in the back seat; she recovered her balance. 'Does he always drive like this?'

Malone smiled at her admirably. 'Do you ever lose your cool?'

'You'll find out,' she said and settled back in the seat, staring straight ahead.

'You may need a lawyer, Caroline. You want to contact one when we get to Police Centre?'

'I'll see,' she said, still staring straight ahead.

At Police Centre there were few officers in the Incident Room; they all looked up as Caroline Magee was brought in. Clements had called Greg Random on the car phone and he came into the room behind them:

'Mrs Magee, thank you for coming.'

'No pleasure of mine,' she said and looked around at the four strike force officers, three men and a woman, who stood in the background like football replacements. 'Do you all interrogate me?'

'No, just Inspector Malone and Sergeant Clements. Both very experienced and very hospitable.'

'I'll bet,' she said and followed Malone and Clements as they led her towards an interview room.

Once inside the room Clements turned on the video recorder and gave the usual warning. 'You sure you don't want a lawyer here with you?'

'Not yet.' She settled herself in the chair across the table from them. She had put on her jacket, arranged the collar of her shirt over it. 'I'll decide when I know what you're charging me with.'

'Caroline,' said Malone, determined to keep the interview on as even a keel as possible, 'we're not charging you with anything at the moment. A lot will depend on how you answer our questions. Now, your maiden name was Briskin. You are related to Shirlee Briskin – she's your mother?'

'You'll have to ask her.'

He grinned. 'Nice one, Caroline. We'll do that – they're bringing her in now.' He waited for a reaction, but there was none. He went on, 'Her and your brother Corey. There's also another brother, right? Phoenix? He's in hospital. Anyone else? A sister, whose name we don't have yet . . .'

'Am I supposed to be helping you with a family history?'

'No,' said Clements, the support bowler, 'no, Mrs Magee, what you're doing is buggering us about.'

'Very hospitable,' she said, but her smile was friendly, she was still at ease. 'Yes, that's my family.'

'And,' said Malone, 'they were in the kidnapping of your husband? They were the ones who carried it out?'

'Inspector –' She took her time, looking directly at Malone; as if he were the more hospitable officer. 'How can I be accused of kidnapping my husband? We're still legally married, not divorced.'

Malone wasn't sure of the answer to that one. 'You, or your family, demanded ransom from Kunishima Bank.'

'Who told you that? Errol told us this morning that it employs Japanese gangsters, *yakuza*. You believe what the bank told you?'

'No,' said Clements, 'we believe what we've found out.'

'And what's that?'

'That the kidnappers murdered your husband's maid, Juanita Marcos. That's why the inspector and I are on this case, Mrs Magee. Because of the murder, not the kidnapping.'

Clements had turned the questioning at right angles; he had taken her round a corner and faced her with something she didn't want to know. For a moment she looked ugly, but she remained motionless. 'I had nothing to do with that.'

'Not you, maybe. But maybe one of your brothers.'

Malone had learned enough about women to know their uses of silence. They use it with more finesse than men; they can use it cruelly or lovingly or as an invisble wall. Caroline Magee all at once was on the other side of a wall.

Malone waited, then at last said, 'Well?'

No answer; she was another woman.

Clements also waited, then he switched off the recorder.

'I think you had better get a lawyer, Mrs Magee.'

Mobile phones have widened communication, thickening the herd instinct. Getaway drivers are now in instant touch with bank robbers to warn of danger. Unwanted lovers get the instant flick without having to wait for the two-day post. Funerals now can be arranged before the body is cold.

Shirlee Briskin had a built-in awareness of danger that would have made her an ideal presidential bodyguard. By accident, or because of her awareness, she was at the front window of her house when the four police cars came cruising down the street, looking for her house-number, and pulled up, like a white wedding procession come for the bride.

She had made two swift calls to Corey's and Darlene's mobiles, something she could not have done if she had had to go through their office switchboards, before she answered the ring-ring-ring at the front door.

She looked at the three police officers, two men and a woman, as if they were door-to-door salespeople. 'Yes? What do you want?' She didn't turn her head, but out of the corner of her eye she saw the armed officers going up beside the house towards the rear. She also saw Mrs Charlton already at the side fence on sentry duty. 'What's wrong? Is my son Pheeny worse?'

'No, Mrs Briskin. You are Mrs Briskin, right?' She nodded. 'We'd just like you to come with us for some questioning.'

'What about?'

'The kidnapping of Mr Errol Magee.'

'Who?' Then light dawned; or so it seemed. Judi Dench, one of her favourites, couldn't have done better. 'That businessman? You must be joking!'

'I'm afraid not,' said the sergeant in charge of the detail; he was showing a lot of patience. 'Just come with us –'

'Am I being charged with anything?'

'Not yet. Please, Mrs Briskin? No fuss.'

She considered, as if buying something they had offered. Then she nodded, 'I'll get my coat and handbag.'

'I'll come with you,' said the policewoman.

Shirlee looked her up and down, as if deciding whether to trust her in the house, then she nodded and led the way towards the front bedroom.

'This is ridiculous,' she said as she pulled on her coat, looked in the wardrobe mirror to check that her hair was neat.

'Possibly,' said the policewoman; she was young and learning which ropes you used for hanging. 'We'll bring you back if everything's okay.'

'They're not gunna turn over the house or anything, are they?' The blue hoods had been burned, along with the Versace dress and jacket, by Corey early this morning; the ashes were buried in the back garden. 'I like everything to be neat.'

When she came out of the house, taking care to close the front door and lock it, and walked down towards the front gate surrounded by ten police officers, some still putting away their guns, Mrs Charlton was out on the footpath, tongue at the ready:

'Something wrong, Shirlee? Pheeny's okay? You're not in trouble?'

'Just some speeding tickets, Daph. Corey's been booked.'

'All these cops for speeding tickets? With guns?'

'They're practising, Daph.'

She got into the back seat of the lead police car, said to no one in particular, 'Bloody busybody.'

'Life's tough, Shirl,' said the sergeant in the front seat.

'Shir- *lee*,' said Shirlee and settled back for the ride. She hoped Corey and Darlene had taken her warning and fled. She was dead scared, but it didn't show. She was neat, steam-pressed for combat.

When she arrived at Police Centre the first person she saw was *that* inspector, Malone. The second person she saw was her elder daughter, sitting comfortably in a chair as if she came here regularly.

'Chantelle? What are you doing here?'

'Chantelle?' said Malone.

'It's a nickname,' said Caroline Magee. 'A joke. Mum, they think we kidnapped Errol, my husband. That's another joke. She's never met him,' she told Malone.

'Of course it's a joke!' snapped Shirlee. 'Her husband? How could we kidnap her *husband*? You kidnap strangers.'

'You've read up on kidnappers?' said Malone.

'Nice try, Inspector,' said Caroline and gave him a nice smile. 'Just relax, Mum. Our lawyer will be here soon.'

'Our lawyer?' said Shirlee. 'Mr Bomaker?'

'Who's he?' said Caroline.

But then Caradoc Evans arrived before Mr Bomaker had to be explained. He came in briskly, as he always did, as if he had a string of clients waiting and he was running down the line of them. He didn't look at the two women, but went straight to Malone.

'Scobie, what's going on? I'm Mr Magee's lawyer, but I get a call his wife wants my appearance. His *wife*? I didn't know he had one.'

Caradoc Evans had come out of the Welsh coal valleys thirty years ago. There he had studied law and played rugby and got drunk, all with equal enthusiasm. He had poked fingers in eyes, bitten ears and twisted testicles as a rugby forward: all good preparation for a career in law. He had come to Australia, turning his back and lungs against coal dust and the drunken singing of hymns on Saturday nights, and established himself as a no-holds-barred defender of the criminal. Yet, Malone knew, he was not crooked and would have poked the eye and bitten the ear and twisted the testicles of any crim who had tried to bribe him. He loved the law because it was a worthy opponent.

Malone introduced him to Caroline Magee and Shirlee Briskin. Evans was impressed; he liked women, especially good-looking women. 'I'll talk to Inspector Malone first, then come back to you. Do you want me to represent both of you?'

'Yes,' said Caroline. 'My mother and I think the charge is ridiculous.'

Evans had heard that more times than a rugby referee's whistle. 'We'll see. Excuse me.'

He went back to where Malone stood waiting for him. 'What's the charge?'

'There's no charge so far,' said Malone and took Evans out into the corridor and explained the situation. 'We think they were both involved in the kidnapping of your client.'

'Magee? And I'm here to defend *them*?' Evans shook his head, as if he had been stomped on. 'What are you doing on a kidnapping case? Homicide?'

'There was a murder,' said Malone and gave more details. 'This is turning into a circus, Doc, if Mrs Magee wants you to represent her. You've never met her before?'

'Never. She's a nice-looking piece of goods. You think she had something to do with the murder?'

'Not directly, no. And maybe her mother didn't, either. There are a daughter and son missing and another son in hospital. It was a family party.'

'Where's Magee?'

'Back at his apartment, he's pretty well stuffed by the last couple of days. You'd better talk to him first before you start representing Mrs Magee.'

Evans leaned against a wall. He was built like a boulder, even to his bald head; he would have been nominated at birth as a front-row forward. But in the chipped, blunt features there was shrewd intelligence; in court he was always one step ahead of the competition. He cocked a scarred eyebrow at Malone:

'I'll call him now, get him up here. Stuffed or not.'

'Be my guest,' said Malone and went to look for Greg Random.

He found him in the Incident Room with Clements and

the senior officer of the strike force, Inspector Garry Peeples. 'Caradoc Evans is here.'

'We're beaten, licked,' said Random with mock gravity. 'Welsh intelligence and philosophy. Unbeatable.'

'Balls,' said Malone. 'Are you pessimistic or patriotic?'

'Both. It's being Welsh.'

Garry Peeples, like Malone, was an ex-fast bowler: a breed bred for hard work. He was taller than either Malone or Random, had the build of a weight-lifter and the look of a man who wondered why he bothered about public safety. 'You think this – Briskin? – family, you think they did the killing and the kidnapping?'

'Sure of it, Garry. Whether they killed the maid –' Malone shrugged. 'But the kidnapping – yes.'

'Who else could have done it?' asked Random. 'His girlfriend, Miss Doolan? The *yakuza*?'

'No,' said Malone, committing himself. 'The Briskins did it, the kidnapping. But it's not going to be easy to get Mrs Magee or Mrs Briskin to admit it. It floored me for a moment when I found out Mrs Magee was a Briskin. But then things began to fall into place. But first, we'll have to see what sort of advice they take from Doc Evans.'

'Jesus,' said Garry Peeples, looking as frustrated as a bowler who had just had three catches dropped off his bowling, 'I remember when I first started on the beat, all we had to deal with was a pub brawl or a break-and-enter and the occasional wife-bashing. Life's getting too complicated.'

'Keep working your way up the ladder,' said Chief Superintendent Random. 'Life at the top has no complications. So long as you keep three copies and bless the Commissioner's name . . . Ah, here's Mr Evans, as honest as daylight saving. How are things, Caradoc?'

'Couldn't be better, Gregory. You saw last week's news? We beat the English 14–10! That'll settle the nabobs of Twickenham back on their smug arses. We're slowly working towards the Disunited Kingdom ... My client, Mr Magee, is on his way.'

'So who'll you be representing?' asked Malone. 'Him or his wife and mother-in-law?'

'He'll be surprised when he finds out he has a mother-in-law. They are often surprised when you know about them.'

The three married men nodded in agreement.

'In the meantime,' said Evans, 'I'm a touch judge, on the sidelines.'

Malone looked at Peeples. 'These bloody rugby types. I've got a son who's infected. Thank Christ the Welsh don't play much cricket – they'd be singing bloody hymns at the tea interval.'

'The way you Aussies are playing in India, you could do with some hymns,' said Evans, enjoying himself immensely.

It was the sort of chat that keeps tradespeople, no matter what their trade, afloat. Without the diversion of it they would drown in responsibility or sometimes the horror of their trade.

Caroline Magee and Shirlee Briskin were kept apart. They were taken into separate rooms and given coffee and biscuits. Both women were composed, seemingly at ease. Clements looked in occasionally on each of them as they sat with policewomen and came back to Malone shaking his head.

'It's not gunna be easy. They come out of the same mold – an earthquake wouldn't budge them.'

Then Errol Magee arrived. He was accompanied by Kylie Doolan, hanging on to him like an anchor that was losing its grip. With them, as security, was a young male officer Malone recognized from the strike force. He realized that he had, for the moment, forgotten about the *yakuza* threat to Magee.

'What the hell's going on?' Magee looked as if he had just got out of bed; which he had. 'What's Caroline doing here? Where is she?'

'I told you –' said Kylie.

'Shut up,' he said, and took his arm out of hers.

'Don't talk to me like that!'

'Mr Magee,' said Malone, taking Magee's other arm; the last thing he wanted was a domestic to upset the scene, 'let's go in here. No, Miss Doolan, not you –'

He led Magee into a room off the Incident Room, followed by Evans, Random and Peeples. Kylie let out a gasp, but didn't attempt to move as Peeples closed the door in her face.

Magee pushed back his hair, which was not in a ponytail. He was in jeans, what looked like a pyjama-top, a suede jacket and Reeboks. He was in casual wear, but he looked anything but casual. The skeins of nightmare were still around him.

'I can't believe Caroline is involved in all this. We didn't get on, I mean while we were married, but Christ – *kidnapping* me?'

'We'll leave your wife out of the picture for the moment,' said Random; it was hard to tell whether he was sympathetic towards Magee or not. 'We'd like you to look at her mother, Mrs Briskin –'

'In a line-up, you mean? I told you, the mother, all of them, they all had blue hoods on all the time. I never saw their faces –'

'You will have to put her in a line-up if you want her identified,' said Evans.

Random looked at him. 'Are you representing her now?'

'No, I'm giving you free legal advice.'

'Errol,' said Malone, 'would you recognize her voice?'

Magee looked dubious. 'I might. But let me get one thing straight – are you telling me Caroline was in on all this?'

Malone went out on a limb, a not unfamiliar perch: 'We think she might have organized the whole thing. What she didn't organize was the murder of your maid Juanita. That's when it became serious.'

'It was bloody serious being kidnapped! Jesus –'

'Sorry. Yeah, sure it was. But –' Malone gave him a rundown on the Briskin family. 'They fit your description. A mother, a daughter, two sons. It was probably the sons who grabbed you and on their way out of your apartment ran into Juanita. Whoever, whatever, Juanita's dead.'

Magee considered a moment, then nodded. 'Yeah, you're right. I'm sorry about that – her, I mean.' He didn't sound very sincere nor concerned, but Malone made no comment. 'I don't know Caroline's family. When we were together, she'd get letters from them, but she never showed them to me. Then we split up –'

'She ever mention her father?'

'Not that I recall. Tell you the truth, I wasn't really interested. I'm not a family man. My own folks are dead.' He spoke as if he didn't miss them.

'Righto, we'll have you listen to Mrs Briskin's voice.' Malone looked at Evans. 'That okay, touch judge? You're not going to put your flag up?'

Caradoc Evans grinned. 'I'm no longer on the sidelines. I'm Mr Magee's legal counsel. You want to try and identify Mrs Briskin's voice?'

'I'll try,' said Magee, but, to Malone's ear, all at once sounded reluctant.

Malone went out of the room, found Clements having coffee with Caroline Magee. 'You two getting on well together?'

'Like old friends,' said Caroline. 'He's been telling me about his young daughter.'

'He's a real family man. I see you a moment, Russ?'

Clements followed him out into the corridor. 'She's not a bad sort when you talk to her –'

'Russ, pull your head in, or I'll tell Romy and your young daughter. I want you to take Mrs Briskin into a room, there's one off the Incident Room. Have a little chat with her. I want our mate Errol to identify her voice.'

'Will that stand up in court?'

'Probably not. But have you got any other suggestions how we start nailing her and her family? It'll be something to kick off with. Then we start leaning on her.'

'If she's like her daughter, it'll be like leaning up against a stone wall. Okay, I'll try. What'll I talk about?'

'Tell her about your busted investments with I-Saw. Compare them with the ransom she and the family didn't get.'

'You're a real bastard, you know that?'

'I know. I enjoy it now and again. Chat her up, then when I knock on the door, bring her out. I'll have Magee there. Don't stop, just walk her past him and we'll see what reaction we get.'

Shirlee Briskin didn't object when Clements came into the room where she was having coffee with a young policewoman: 'Come with you, Sergeant? Of course. I was just telling Roma here how good it is you're getting more women into the police force. About time –'

Clements led her gently into the room off the Incident Room. 'What did you think about the Magee kidnapping? You read about it? Heard it on the radio?'

'Terrible! I agreed with all those talkers on radio – what do they call 'em?'

'Shock jocks.'

'Do they? I think that's a bit unkind. But what they said is true, nobody's safe any more, are they? Am I being interrogated – is that the word?'

'We never use it, Mrs Briskin. Only shock jocks do that.' Clements was as friendly as an insurance salesman. 'No, we'll be letting you go soon. What did you think of the ransom they were asking? Five million!'

'I know. Everything's going up –'

'And that was without GST.'

She laughed, comfortable and at ease; or so it looked. 'They tax everything, don't they? But it was no joke, was it? I mean, for him.'

Out in the Incident Room Malone had brought Magee close to the slightly open door, but out of line of sight. Magee appeared to be listening intently; then he shook his head. Malone stared at him: *you sure*? Magee shook his head again and Malone gave up. He knocked on the door, moved himself and Magee back to join Random, Peeples and Evans.

Clements brought Shirlee Briskin out of the inner room, walked her towards the door into the corridor, still chatting to her. She glanced at Magee and the other four men, but didn't pause. At the door she said to Clements, 'Is that him?' Then she was out in the corridor and gone from sight.

Malone looked at Magee. 'Recognize her? Her walk, her figure, anything about her?'

'No,' said Magee.

You bastard, you're lying. He had been reading faces, eyes, body language for twenty-five years. But all he said was, 'Righto, now we're taking you out to Hurstville, to the Briskin house. You might identify something there.'

'Is all this necessary?' said Evans. 'My client has said he doesn't recognize the woman.'

'Doc, we're just eliminating all the possibilities.' He was keeping control of his temper. Magee, for reasons he couldn't yet fathom, had screwed him. 'It's an inconvenience for Mr Magee, but we are trying to solve a murder. The murder of someone who worked for him, who made his bed, served him breakfast . . .' He was piling it on, looking at Magee, not at Evans. 'I'm sure you feel you owe her something, Mr Magee.'

Magee hesitated, then nodded. 'Of course. But first, I'll have to get rid – I'll have to tell Kylie to go back to the apartment. And what about my wife?'

It was the first time he had referred to Caroline as *his wife*. As if a relationship had been renewed, even if involuntarily.

'You have a couple of problems there,' said Malone, trying to sound sympathetic; he wanted to keep Magee on side. 'Sergeant Clements will look after them. We'll need to keep Caroline here till we get back, but Miss Doolan can go.'

'That won't be easy,' said Magee and for a moment showed a spark of wry humour.

'Chief Superintendent,' said Malone, 'will you mind Mr Magee while Inspector Peeples and I look for Mrs Briskin?'

'Certainly, Inspector,' said Random, deadpan.

Malone grinned at him, trying to get his own mood up. Then he and Peeples went out to tell Mrs Briskin that they were taking her back home.

'What if she demands a search warrant?' asked Peeples.

'We're not looking for anything, just doing a recce. If she asks for a warrant, that'll look pretty suspicious, won't it?'

'All women are born suspect,' said Peeples, another born chauvinist.

Malone let that pass, went looking for Clements and Shirlee Briskin. He found them in the room where they were having another cup of coffee. Shirlee looked at home, as if she might move in and tidy up the housekeeping. But she demurred when Malone told her what he wanted to do:

'I'm not gunna have the place over-run by cops,' she said, putting down her cup, putting down her foot. 'What'll the neighbours think?'

Malone grinned again, trying to keep it friendly. He didn't want to have to go through the chore of getting a warrant, even if that would only confirm his suspicions about the Briskin family. 'The woman next door? We'll go in an unmarked car. There'll be another unmarked car – Chief Superintendent Random and Mr Magee.'

'You're wasting your time,' she said. 'And his.'

'He doesn't mind.'

She considered for a moment; then: 'What about Chantelle? My daughter?'

'Mrs Magee?' He was having trouble marrying Chantelle and Caroline. 'She'll stay here. Sergeant Clements will look after her.'

'Are you charging her with anything? It's ridiculous, like I told you, saying she kidnapped her own husband.'

'There's no charge so far, Mrs Briskin.'

'So far?'

'A figure of speech, Mrs Briskin. Can we go? Inspector Peeples and I, two inspectors from Hurstville council.' He grinned again, the friendly man from the council, the ratepayers' mate. 'We'll handle Mrs What'shername. No gossip, no scandal.'

She looked them up and down, then picked up her handbag. 'Be friendly with my daughter, Sergeant.'

'Like her own father,' said Clements.

'Not like him, anything but,' said Shirlee and led the way out of the room.

As they were heading down towards the underground garage of Police Centre, Malone saw Paula Decker. He stopped, telling Peeples he would catch up with him in a moment, and pulled Paula aside. 'What are you doing up here?'

'I'm still attached to the strike force, sir. They called me in to help with the security on the two women, Mrs Magee and Miss Doolan.'

'Forget Mrs Magee, I think we'll be keeping her up here, charging her. You'll have your hands full with Kylie. How's she been?'

'Clinging to Magee like crazy. I think she's at last woken up to the fact that everything's gone down the gurgler. She's a greedy little bitch.'

'Get used to it, Paula. That's the way the world is going. Take care.'

'How's your luck holding, sir?'

'Just.'

Down in the garage Random was standing beside his own unmarked car with his driver and Errol Magee. 'Garry has just told me we're all from Hurstville council. No fuss, no gossip.'

Malone looked at Magee. 'You don't want Mr Evans with you?'

Magee did not look comfortable, but there was no antagonism

in him. 'He won't be necessary. He's seeing what he can do for my wife.'

Malone didn't press the point. He just nodded and went across to Peeples' car. Peeples was behind the wheel and Malone got into the back seat beside Shirlee Briskin.

'Comfy, Mrs Briskin?'

'No,' she said. 'I'm never comfortable with a seat-belt.'

The two cars drove up out of the garage into the bright sunlight.

Chapter Ten

1

Darlene Briskin had just come out of the strongroom in Rockdale when she got the message from her mother. She wasn't sure what had prompted her to carry her mobile with her in the office; maybe it was pessimism, which cloaked her like rough underwear. She took the message, understood its abruptness, then shut off the phone. She looked back at the strongroom's open door and wanted to laugh, even if it hurt. It was full of money and more was due any minute when the Armaguard truck would arrive. She looked at it all, at the uselessness of it to her, then she turned her back on it and went to the staff locker room. She grabbed her handbag and jacket and went out of the bank with just a nod to one of the girls and no word at all to the manager. She had just resigned, involuntarily.

She had never kept an account at the bank, wanting privacy. She went down the street to the credit union office where she kept her money. She closed the account, taking out $3822.48. She looked at it as she stuffed it into her handbag and smiled wryly; no, sourly. Her entire stake for the future, if she had a future.

She went round a corner, stood in a shadow (already acting instinctively?) and called Corey on her mobile. He answered at once, as if he had been waiting on her call.

'Where are you?'

'Not at work,' she said. 'I've just resigned. Mum called you?'

'Yeah. I've just resigned, too – though the boss doesn't know. What we gunna do?'

'You got the car? Okay, I'll catch a train to Sydenham.' Five or six kilometres down the line: the first stage to where? But she didn't think any further than meeting Corey. 'Meet me there.'

'What about Pheeny? They'll pick him up, for sure. Can he keep his mouth shut?'

'We'll have to risk that, we can't go to the hospital. The cops may already be there. They'll have picked up Mum – she said they were at the front gate. Oh Christ, Corey!' But she switched off the phone before she let him hear her weep.

Corey was waiting for her outside Sydenham station when she got there. He was parked right outside the station, giving the middle finger to other drivers as they hooted and yelled at him for blocking a traffic lane. He didn't care: their troubles were nothing compared to his.

Darlene got into the car beside him and they didn't speak till he pulled up five minutes later in a suburban street. Then she said, 'We've really fucked up, haven't we?'

'Wash your mouth out,' he said, but his grin had no humour in it.

'What happened? How did we ever get into this?'

'Chantelle. She conned us, told us we were better than we thought we were. We were like football players, we moved up three grades, out of our class.' He looked through the windscreen, up the street. Three Aboriginal kids were throwing a football to each other: that was where the image had dropped into his mind. 'Mum was dazzled by her. Her daughter, the one who'd made good in London.'

'Don't start picking on Mum. Or Chantelle, either. We could of always said No. The money got us in. Five million. Jesus, what I was gunna do with my share!'

He didn't ask what her dreams had been. They were gone now, like his own. 'I dunno I could of handled it, that much dough.'

One of the Aboriginal kids kicked the football too hard and it came bouncing down the street to hit the front of the Toyota.

The boy came trotting down, picked it up, then walked round to look in at Corey.

'You looking for someone?' He was about fourteen, thin, with beautiful dark eyes made old with suspicion.

'No,' said Corey, 'just taking a breather.'

'You're not cops, are you?'

Corey laughed, but it seemed to catch in his breast. 'Nah, mate. Just thinking about suicide.'

The boy's eyes suddenly whitened. 'Shit, don't think about it around here! We got enough trouble, the cops down here all the fucking time!'

'No, sport, I wouldn't do it on your doorstep.' Corey started up the car and pulled it away from the kerh. 'Shit, why did I say that? Fucking suicide!'

'Like he said, don't even think about it.' Darlene was silent for a mile or two, then she said, 'You're gunna have to get rid of the car. They'll have the registration, they could be out now looking for it with us in it. Head for Canterbury Road.'

'Ah shit, Sis, I don't wanna sell it –' But he had already turned the car, heading south-west. 'Where do we go?'

'Canterbury Road, it's all car salesyards.'

'No, I mean after that. Where?'

'I dunno.' She put her hand on his arm; she truly loved this brother of hers. He had done some stupid things, but she didn't believe he was *bad*. 'We'll think of something.'

The traffic was heavy, as if it were on the side of law and order and respect for road rules; which it was not. They could not speed, much as Corey wanted to. Drivers yelled at each other, horns were blown, fanfares of road rage. On pedestrian crossings people who didn't own cars ambled across at their leisure, provoking more abuse.

At last Corey pulled off on to a car lot where a big sign claimed: Best Toyota Buys In Town!

The salesman had been born spruiking; his mother's tit had overdosed him with confidence: 'Best buys south of Cape

York! Whatever you want, we've got it – what? You're selling?'

Corey and Darlene were out of the car, putting on dark glasses against the glare from metal and windscreens and sales talk. 'What'll you give us? Five years old, I been the only owner. You can see, looks just the same's the day I bought it.'

The salesman smiled, one of a dozen variety he kept handy. He was no older than Corey, overweight, good looks spoiled by good living. All that spoiled him was his spiky hair, which looked as if it was kept on by Velcro. 'You in the trade? You got the talk . . .' He walked round the car, shaking his head, nodding it, the expert who relied only on the eye. He came back to Corey and Darlene. 'Eight thousand.'

'Eight?' Corey looked as if he had been offered vouchers. 'Ah, come on, sport –'

'Take it,' said Darlene, who had seen the police car cruising by, taking its time as if looking for stolen cars on the lot.

'Sis –'

'Take it!'

Corey looked at her, puzzled; then he turned back to the salesman. 'Okay, eight thousand. I'd like it in cash.'

'We-ll –' The salesman pursed his lips. 'We don't carry much cash here. Too risky. I don't wanna offend you, you know what I mean, but the car's not hot, is it?'

Corey was offended. 'Look, I can give you my licence and the registration –' Then he stopped. 'Shit!'

'What's the matter?' said Darlene, but she knew.

'The registration – it's at home –'

'Sorry,' said the salesman, seeing another prospect, a sales prospect, and heading in his direction. 'Come back with the rego and we got a deal.'

Corey and Darlene got back into the car, sat staring ahead of them, at the future blank as a windscreen with sun on it.

As the two unmarked cars pulled up outside the Briskin house, Random's mobile rang. He got out of the car and went to one side to take the call. He listened for a minute or two, said, 'Okay,' and switched off. Then he called Malone aside.

'The Briskin girl and one of her brothers have scooted. Both walked out of where they work without saying anything to anyone – they've done a bunk. I'd say that wraps it up. The family did the kidnapping.'

'What about the one in hospital?'

'He's not going anywhere. Two of our fellers are keeping him company. He's kept his trap shut, except to say he's not saying anything till he sees his mum.'

Malone couldn't hide his grin of pleasure. 'Righto, we'll get Errol to identify the room where he was kept, then we'll charge Mrs Briskin. That might bring in the son and daughter who've buzzed off, depending on how loving they are.'

'You going to charge Magee's wife, too?'

'The whole family. A package deal, like at the Royal Easter Show.'

They went round the car and rejoined Magee, Shirlee Briskin and Peeples. As they went in the front gate Mrs Charlton appeared at the side fence, a genie at the first rub of gossip.

'More trouble, Shirl? Oh, you're from the council,' she said, recognizing Malone. 'Back again?'

'Sewer trouble.' Malone was light-headed, or light-hearted. This was his last Homicide case and he was going to close it successfully. 'We may have to dig up the whole street.'

'That right, Shirl?'

'It's on the cards, Daph. Better be ready for the night-soil man.' She flickered a grin at Malone, then marched up to her front door, key at the ready.

'What's that all about?' asked Random.

'Tell you later,' said Malone, grinning, and followed Shirlee into the front hallway. He stood aside for the others to follow him. 'Here we are, Errol. We'll take you through the house and see what you recognize. You weren't blindfolded all the time, were you?'

'No,' said Magee, looking at Shirlee.

She returned his stare, saying nothing. Malone glanced at her, saw the crumbling in her. 'Righto, Mrs Briskin? Can we start here at the front of the house and work our way through?'

'Do what you like,' she said sniffily. 'Just leave everything like you find it. Neat.'

'Perhaps you and I can wait in the kitchen, Mrs Briskin?' said Random.

She appeared not to have heard him, just stared at Magee. Then abruptly she turned and went down the hallway. Random raised an eyebrow at Malone and Peeples, then followed her.

'Was she trying to tell you something, Errol?' said Malone.

'What?' Magee blinked, then recovered. 'What would she have to tell me?'

'She's your mother-in-law,' said Peeples. 'They usually have a lot to say.'

'You being funny? She's got something on her mind, but I don't know what it is. She's my mother-in-law, yeah, but I've never spoken a word to her. Ever.'

Malone studied him a moment, then he said, 'Righto, let's start in here. Looks like the main bedroom.'

They went into the room and Peeples looked around. 'Like she said, neat. I don't think they would of held you in here, Mr Magee, not the front of the house. You weren't gagged all the time, were you?'

'No.' Magee looked around the room. 'No, I don't recognize any of this.'

'If you weren't gagged,' said Malone, 'why didn't you try yelling out? The woman next door would have heard you.'

'Have you ever been kidnapped?'

'No-o –'

Magee said nothing, his look was enough. Peeples, diplomatically, said, 'Okay, let's move on. There's another bedroom across the hall.'

Malone suddenly began to feel uneasy, for no reason he could name. He followed Magee and Peeples into the second bedroom, also at the front of the house. This, too, was neat; there were two single beds, coverlets as neat as coffin drapes. Two enlarged photos on a wall: football teams, young men with arms crossed ready to take on the world. Magee looked around, then shook his head, saying nothing.

'Righto,' said Malone, keeping his voice steady. 'There looks to be another bedroom behind this one. Let's try it.'

They moved down the hallway, Peeples leading the way. They went into the third bedroom, a room smaller than the other two at the front of the house. Malone stood in the doorway, watching Magee as the latter looked around the room.

This room, like the others, was almost impossibly neat, Malone thought. Lisa, at Randwick, kept a neat house, but it was a shambles compared to the Briskin house. This room looked almost unlived in. The solitary picture on the wall, a Hans Heysen print of gum trees and glaring sunlight, might have hung there, perfectly straight, since the day Heysen had painted the original. Malone, for no reason at all, all at once had the feeling he had walked into a vacuum.

Magee looked around the room twice, then turned back to Malone. 'No,' he said calmly. 'I don't recognize anything here.'

You lying bastard! But it was just a silent exclamation in Malone's brain. He looked at Peeples and the latter heard what hadn't been said.

'You're sure, Mr Magee?' said Peeples. 'Absolutely sure?'

'Sure,' said Magee. 'Absolutely.'

Errol Magee wasn't sure yet why he had lied. He had been shocked when they had told him that Caroline was probably the organizer of his kidnapping. There had been anger at what she had done; if she had done it. It was bizarre to think she had come home all the way from London to do such a thing.

He had been surprised and pleased when she had turned up two weeks ago. He had, in a moment of loose thinking, entertained the idea of asking her to go with him when he fled abroad; better her than Kylie. Seeing her again he had realized she had been a better part of his life, for all their differences, than any of his other women. That first night he would have asked her to stay, if Kylie, out at some fashion opening, had not been coming back to the apartment.

He had known vaguely that she had a family; letters had arrived regularly in London for her. But, not being a family man himself, he had asked no questions when she had advanced no answers. He still couldn't quite believe that she would organize a gang, a *family*, to kidnap him.

In the car riding out to Hurstville he had sat silent most of the time. He had started to think about Caroline's family and had been surprised again. He had *liked* them; well, anyway, the brother and sister who had spent most time with him. Did he really want all of them, Caroline included, sent to jail? Sure, there was the accusation that one of them might have killed Juanita, his maid, but was there any proof?

By the time they had arrived outside the Briskin house he had made up his mind. He would not seek Caradoc Evans' advice; the Welshman, for all his efforts to beat the law, was too honest. He would not, for instance, approve Magee's over-riding reason for not accusing the Briskins.

If the Briskins were indicated he would have to stay in

Australia to give evidence against them. And if he stayed, the *yakuza* would still be here in Sydney wanting their pound of flesh, his. It would be self-defence to defend the Briskins. It was a form of hedging, which his friends on the stock exchange, if he still had any, would understand, though they might not approve.

When they had left the Briskin house, Shirlee Briskin had followed them to the front door. He had remarked her composure, as if she had known all along that he would not point the finger at her and her family.

'Satisfied?' she had asked Inspector Malone. 'Putting me to all this bother, not to mention the embarrassment.' With one eye on the neighbour next door, still at the side fence. 'Are you gunna let my daughter go?'

'Of course,' said Malone, though Magee thought he sounded reluctant.

Mrs Briskin had looked at Magee. 'Are you gunna make it up with Chantelle?'

'Who?'

'My daughter. Caroline.'

He was walking on very thin ice here. 'I think we'll be talking about it.'

'Good. I've always wanted a son-in-law.'

He didn't want a mother-in-law; not her, anyway.

As they went down the front path, the four men walking close together to avoid stepping on the neat garden strips bordering the path, the woman next door called out: 'Everything all right?'

'Everything's okay, Daph,' said Malone. 'We won't need to dig up the sewers.' Then he added, 'You might go in and talk to Mrs Briskin. She's upset.'

'That was pretty malicious,' said Random in a low voice.

'I couldn't be happier,' said Malone and looked at Magee with what the latter took to be real venom.

Magee did his best to ignore the look. 'Are you taking me back to Police Centre? My car's there.'

'We'll do that,' said Random, taking over; it was obvious he was muzzling Malone. 'It's part of the service. You ride with me and my driver.'

As Inspector Malone got into his car, he looked back over his shoulder. Magee knew there was no mistaking the look: he had made an enemy.

'Inspector Malone never forgets,' said Chief Superintendent Random. 'Remember that, Errol.'

They drew away from the kerb. Magee didn't look back, or he would have seen Shirlee closing the front door as the woman next door hurried up the path.

There was casual small talk on the way back to Police Centre; then Random said, with no change in his tone, 'Why did you bullshit us? You know the Briskins kidnapped you. They know it, we know it, you know it.'

Magee's mind now was a computer, one guarded against viruses. 'All I did was tell the truth.'

'Tomorrow, keep the day free. We'll take you down the South Coast, you can have a look at the house there that's owned by the Briskins.'

Careful, careful. 'Is that necessary?'

'Everything's necessary in the pursuit of truth, Errol. I thought you'd appreciate that. Didn't I-Saw work only for lawyers?'

'You cops don't like lawyers, do you?'

'Democracy is made up of necessary nuisances. Ask any politician who believes in it.'

Magee saw the driver smile in the rear-vision mirror. He would have to beware of their mockery.

4

Shirlee Briskin waited ten minutes after the police and that Magee, her son-in-law, had left, then she phoned for a cab.

Daphne Charlton had rung the doorbell, but she had ignored it and after a few minutes Daphne had retreated next door.

But when she went out of the house to get into the cab, Daphne, damn her, was at the side fence, on cue.

'They weren't from the council, were they, Shirl? What's going on?'

'I'll tell you later, Daph. Just relax. Nothing's happened, nothing's gunna happen. I'm on my way to see Pheeny. Ta-ta.'

She got into the cab, in the front seat beside the driver; she was a true-blue Aussie. He was from Mongolia and hadn't a clue where the hospital was. She almost got out and into the back seat. Bloody multiculturism . . .

When the driver finally found the hospital, having searched for it as if it were a tin shed on an allotment instead of a complex of buildings on several hectares, Shirlee gave him the exact fare, waiting for change. He gave her a look he had inherited from Jenghis Khan, she gave him a look that women had patented a millennium before Jenghis Khan.

When she walked into Phoenix's ward she met two men coming out. They stopped, then one of them said, 'You Mrs Briskin?'

'Yes. Who are you?'

'Police officers.' She should have recognized them. They were big and had that look that she was sure policemen put on every morning with their uniforms or their badges. She was starting to think like Clyde used to. 'We've been keeping your son company.'

'And you're leaving now?'

'We just got word you're all in the clear. Your son's just got another visitor. It's been your lucky day.'

'Thanks for nothing,' she said and walked past them into the ward.

Phoenix did, indeed, have another visitor. 'Mr Bomaker, what are you doing here?'

'Giving Phoenix the good news!' Bomaker's glaze was cracking with excitement. But there was also some caution: 'They were cops, weren't they?'

'A misunderstanding, Mr Bomaker, that was all. What's the good news?'

'We're going to be in the money!'

'Keep your voice down.' Shirlee had looked around. Yesterday's patients had been replaced by new arrivals, all supposedly ill or injured. But now they were as alert as cattle dogs. 'How?'

'We did due diligence on our lady friend, the lousy driver –'

'Due diligence?' said Phoenix, his leg still strung up. 'What's that?'

'Enquiries. Don't ask –' Bomaker put his finger alongside his nose. Shirlee had always thought only bad actors in bad movies did that. 'Our lady friend is worth fourteen million! It seems her husband, the developer, has a record of being sued by builders and unhappy home-owners. He put everything he owns in his wife's name. She's rolling in it. Oh, the thrill we got when we found out about that!'

He's a fairy, thought Shirlee; but a good one. 'How much?'

'How much what?'

'How much will our share be? How much will Pheeny get?'

'It's hard to tell. Depends whether we go before a judge or a jury.' He looked at Phoenix as he might have at livestock. 'He's been affected emotionally, you can tell that. And psychologically – it's slowed his grasp of things –'

Shirlee said nothing. Pheeny *was* slow, psychologically.

'– with a bit of luck, half a million, I should think. If we get a jury, if some of them are greenies, they hate developers – who knows what they'll give us?'

Shirlee all at once felt better. She still wasn't sure why Errol Magee had denied recognizing her. Being a romantic, but a hard-bitten one, she could only assume that he was still in love with Chantelle, had done it for her sake. And now here was money, maybe more than her share of the ransom would have been, dangling in the air before her.

She took Pheeny's hand, suddenly aglow with warm feelings towards the world. She could imagine the look on Daph Charlton's face when she told her.

Then she took out her mobile and called Darlene. '. . . Corey's with you? Good . . . No, no worries, love. Come to the hospital. Everything's rosy.'

Chapter Eleven

1

'You're free to go,' said Malone.

Caroline Magee didn't rise from her chair, but looked up at Malone as if he had just told her it had stopped raining outside. 'Really? That's nice. So it was a lot of fuss about nothing.'

'Not quite. We haven't finished yet. We're letting you go for now, but cancel your ticket for London. We'll be talking to you again.'

She stood up, taking her time, turned to Clements. 'It's been an interesting chat, Sergeant. I didn't realize the police knew so much about money and the stock exchange.'

'I'm in training for the Fraud Squad.' Clements also stood up. He looked as if he had enjoyed the last hour. 'Look after yourself, Caroline. You'll be staying where?'

'Are you holding Errol?' she asked Malone.

'Why would we hold him, Chantelle?'

Her smile was wry. 'Didn't you ever want to change Scobie to something else? Cary or Justin?'

He had to admire her, but reluctantly. 'Fred. But Fred Malone didn't have the proper ring to it. Go back to the hotel, Caroline, not the apartment. We'll have one of our policewomen keep you company.'

She had been about to pick up her jacket and handbag, but she paused and looked at him. 'You still think the *yakuza* are a threat?'

'Till we find Mr Tajiri, yes.'

'I'll be safer in London, though I don't know why they should be interested in me.'

'For the same reason we are, Caroline.'

She didn't question that, but said, 'Is Errol still outside? I'd like to see him.'

'Why?'

'He's my husband.'

Malone glanced at Clements, but the big man showed no reaction. 'Okay, five minutes. Then I'm taking him back to the apartment.'

Magee was out in the corridor with the young strike force officer who had brought him to Police Centre. Caradoc Evans had gone, bound for the Central Criminal Courts where arguments waited to be flourished like leeks and other Welsh symbols.

When Magee saw Caroline come out of the inner room there was a sudden jumble of emotion in him. He didn't know what love was, otherwise he might have recognized it. He had never read that in medieval times love had been listed as a mental disease; he knew nothing of the later belief that it was a mutual selfishness. All he had ever felt for women had been in his balls; testosterone and money, not love, made the world go round. Yet now he felt a *need* for Caroline and it weakened him.

She took his hand and they moved down the corridor away from the three police officers. 'I'm going back to London, Errol.'

He had to ask: 'Did you organize for me to be kidnapped?'

Her gaze was direct, as innocent as that of a ten-year-old from Coonabarabran. 'No.'

He wanted to believe her; he *had* to. He kept his voice low: 'Then how did your mother and the others organize it?'

'You didn't say anything to the police?' Her eyes slid sideways towards Malone and Clements. She didn't turn her head, still held his hand. 'Why?'

'I had my reasons.' Maybe he would tell her later, when . . . But he was not sure what was going to happen *when*. The Turks and Caicos Islands were the other side of Mars. 'Did you know they'd done it?'

'Yes.' She was all honesty. 'As soon as I found out, I got them to let you go. It was a stupid idea, the whole thing –'

'Did one of your brothers kill my maid Juanita?'

'No. My sister said another man came into your apartment after my brothers had left with you. It could've been one of the *yakuza* who are supposed to be after you. They keep talking about a man named Tajiri.'

'Where was your sister?'

'It doesn't matter. It was the other man who killed your maid. My brothers aren't *killers* . . . Why are you looking at me like that?'

He had never thought he would say it: 'I'm wondering if I'm still in love with you.'

She kissed his cheek, pressed his hand. 'You never were, Errol. But thanks for the thought. What are you going to do? You going overseas?'

'Why would I do that?'

'Errol darling, what about the forty million?'

'If it were true, which it isn't, would you come and share it with me?'

She kissed him again, this time a little lingeringly. 'Try me.'

'Why did you come home when you did? After all this time?'

'I worked in a stockbroker's office in London, I knew what was going on out here. All those collapses, all those smartarse names going broke. I came home because I thought I might be some help for you, hold your hand, sort things out. But I was too late.'

He stared at her, then he heard himself say, 'I think I love you.'

She pressed his hand. 'We'll see, sweetheart.'

She hadn't called him that after the first six months of their marriage. But now it sounded – *sweet*? He was becoming sentimental.

Then Malone came along to them. 'Time to go, Mr Magee.

246

Detective Decker will be taking your wife back to her hotel. Detective Ormiston –' He gestured towards the young officer from the strike force. 'He'll meet us back at your apartment. I'll ride back with you in your car.'

'You're not letting up, are you? I've been the bloody victim here, in case you've forgotten.'

'We never do let up, Errol. Persistence is our motto. Take care, Mrs Magee. I may come out to the airport to see you off. If you're going . . .'

'I may not be going after all.' She smiled at Magee, gave his hand a last squeeze. 'Take care, sweetheart, as Inspector Malone advises everyone.'

Malone and Magee went down to the garage. As Malone fitted himself into the Porsche Carerra, he said, 'When I was young, I was in bigger women than this.'

'That's an old one. You don't like sports cars?'

'I regret we gave up the horse and buggy. I warn you, as a police officer, that I consider anything over fifty ks as dangerous driving.'

'I'll never get out of second.'

'I won't mind if you don't get out of first.'

Magee wondered, as he took the car up out of the garage, why Malone was so relaxed and affable. But at the first red light, while they waited, Malone looked at him and said, 'Why did you bullshit us, Errol?'

The light turned green, Magee resisted the temptation to put his foot down hard. 'Superintendent Random asked me the same question. I didn't lie, Inspector. I just didn't recognize anything out at the Briskin house. And I didn't recognize the old lady's voice. That's all. No bullshit.'

'Caroline organized it all, you know that.'

They were going down College Street, past Police Head-quarters where the only questions ever asked were political. The car was still in second, the traffic thick ahead of it. All that speed under me, thought Magee, and I can't get away.

'No, she didn't. I'm thinking of getting back together with her again. Would I do that if I thought she'd organized the kidnapping?'

'Errol, I could tell you a dozen stories of men who trusted no-good women. She's conning you. Believe me.'

'You're an expert on women as well as on criminals?' They were passing St Mary's Cathedral, where a new archbishop was due in a couple of months, one who was hard on sin and knew little about women. Magee knew less about sin than he did about love.

'I've met more women crims than you have.' Then they were going down Macquarie Street, past Parliament House where the law-and-order issue, like a weekly wash, was being given another thumping. 'I don't care a damn about your kidnapping, Errol. But I do care who killed your maid. I just wish you and Caroline would understand that.'

Magee looked sideways at him, saw the sudden tightness in the face, the jaw almost re-defined. For the first time he had a glimmer of a cop's approach to life and the preservation of it.

'I do understand, Inspector. But you're wrong, dead wrong.'

Malone didn't answer and Magee took the Porsche down to the bottom of the street and swung it down into the apartments garage. He waited while the steel lattice gate lifted. The media had gone, chasing another story. Magee took the car in under the gate, neglected to close it as Malone said, 'We're not wrong, Errol. You'll be the first to find out.'

Magee swung the Porsche in beside Kylie's car, a BMW sports. *That will have to go*, he thought as he stepped out of his own car. Then he heard Malone say, 'For Crissakes!'

Vassily Todorov, in full Foley's Flyers kit, had come down the ramp on his bicycle and slipped into the garage.

'Mr Magee!' Todorov jumped off his bicycle, a courier with bad news from the front. 'I have to talk to you! It is about Juanita, your maid –'

'Who the fuck's he?' said Magee.

'Your maid's boyfriend. He's after money –'

But then Malone had moved round the car and intercepted Todorov as the Bulgarian, furious, came at Magee as if he intended thrashing him. Malone grappled with him, pushing him away.

'Todorov, get outa here!'

'He owes Juanita – he owes me –' Todorov was splitting with rage, his plumed helmet wobbling as if the top of his skull was coming apart.

Malone began to push him towards the ramp. They struggled, but Malone, though older by several years, was the bigger man. He pushed, swung round, pulled Todorov up the ramp, the Foley's Flyer swearing in a language that Berlitz would never have taught.

Magee stood unmoving beside his car. Then a voice behind him said quietly, 'Mr Magee –'

He turned towards the voice. Nakasone stood there on the other side of a black Mercedes. He held a gun aimed straight at Magee: it was a Heckler & Koch P7, though Magee would never know that. It was fitted with a silencer and when Nakasone squeezed the trigger the small sound was lost in the yelling coming from the ramp.

Magee died instantly, the bullet through his right eye; he died without wonder, which is unusual. His mind had become as blank as a dead computer screen.

Nakasone, taking off his gloves, putting the gun and the silencer in his briefcase, walked quickly to the lifts, where the door of one was propped open. The door closed on him and the lift began to ascend as the yelling in the ramp suddenly stopped.

2

'I don't bloody well know!' Malone could hardly control his voice. 'I got rid of Todorov and came back down to the car

– and Magee wasn't there. I started towards the lifts, thinking he had gone up to his apartment . . . Then I saw him – Greg, I've got no idea who did him in. I can guess –'

'Scobie,' said Random, 'guesses aren't good enough. Okay, you think it was the *yakuza* – we *know* it was the *yakuza*. But till we pick up Mr Tajiri . . . Did you search the garage?'

'Greg, I'm not bloody stupid! Of course I searched the place. Then I went up to the ground floor, but the concierge said he saw no one go out through the front doors – he'd taken some woman's parcels up to her apartment –'

'Simmer down, mate,' said Clements. 'Nobody's blaming you –'

'And nobody's going to,' said Random. 'If that bloody Bulgarian hadn't shoved his nose in, Magee would still be alive. You write the report, Russ. No blame attached.'

'What about Todorov?' asked Clements.

'You mean was he in on the act? As a decoy?' Malone shook his head, which ached. 'As he'd say, he was just pedalling his own bike. Forget him. He was a pain in the arse, but that's all.'

The garage was as busy as a motor-racing pit. Cars were being moved for the Physical Evidence team to go about their work; Crime Scene tapes were strung about like sponsors' bunting; media hawks were hovering at the steel gate, which had been closed. Magee's body was already on its way to the morgue, past greed, past love.

'Where are Magee's women?' asked Malone.

'Upstairs,' said Clements. 'Paula Decker brought Mrs Magee down from the hotel. Miss Doolan's up there with Sheryl.'

'How are they?'

'I'm just about to go up and see. Can we leave all this in your hands, Chief Superintendent?'

'One of these days my Welsh patience is going to run out,' said Random. 'Give my respects to the ladies. Where do you go next?'

'To the Kunishima Bank.' Malone was pulling himself together. *I'm getting old*, he thought. The tussle with Todorov had been tougher than he was going to let Random and Clements know. 'We're still looking for Tajiri.'

As he and Clements rode up the lift, the latter said, 'How d'you feel?'

'Shitty. Pissed off. Wouldn't you be? I was that close to cracking Magee –' He held finger and thumb an inch apart.

'You really think so? I don't, mate. I watched him and his missus when they were together back at the Centre. He was never gunna finger her.'

Malone leaned back against the wall of the lift, sighed, then nodded. 'I've become cross-eyed over this case. It's time I moved on.' Then he looked directly at Clements. 'I never thought I'd say that.'

'I'll be saying it in a year or two. It catches up with us in the end.'

'What?'

'Human bastardry.'

Kylie Doolan opened the apartment door to them, looking expectant, as if she might be waiting for Errol to come back from the dead. She stared at the two detectives as if they were unexpected. 'Yes?'

'May we come in? We want a word with you and Mrs Magee.'

She stood aside and the two men walked in. Paula Decker and Sheryl Dallen rose from their chairs, but Caroline Magee remained seated. Malone tried to sense the atmosphere of the room, but couldn't. This was women's atmosphere, a fog in which he always moved carefully.

'We've come to give our condolences,' he said, words he had said at other times and which always sounded hollow in his mouth.

'I thought you were supposed to be protecting him!' Kylie had found her voice and her attitude.

It was nothing new to Malone and Clements. It was the latter who said, 'We were protecting him, Miss Doolan. Mr Magee was attacked by a man named Todorov, your maid's boyfriend – Inspector Malone was hustling him out of the garage when –'

'Shut up and sit down, Kylie,' said Caroline.

'Don't tell me what –' But suddenly Kylie did shut up and sit down. She looked around at all of them, then turned and stared out through the big glass doors as if looking for someone more comforting there.

Caroline still hadn't risen, as if she had become the chatelaine of Magee's castle. Which, Malone abruptly recognized, she was indeed. Kylie Doolan was on her way back to Minto or points obscure.

'No one is to blame, Inspector,' Caroline said. 'It was always on the cards. Do Miss Doolan and I still need protection?'

'No,' said Malone. 'Not unless you'd like Detectives Dallen and Decker to stay on, at least for tonight?'

Neither Sheryl nor Paula moved their heads, but their eyes were vigorously saying *No, no, no.* Clements grinned and said, 'Get your sister down here, Miss Doolan, she'll be the best company for you. You'll be okay back at your hotel, Mrs Magee.'

'I'll be staying here,' she said, 'till the funeral.'

Kylie abruptly stopped looking out through the doors. 'You're *what*? Jesus, who do you think you are?'

'I'm his wife, Kylie. There'll be things to attend to –'

'We'll see about that! We'll see what's in his will –'

'There is no will, Kylie.'

There was a sudden silence; Malone broke it with, 'How do you know?'

'I checked ten minutes ago with the lawyers.' She was still seated, still holding court. 'Don't be shocked. It will probably be me who'll have to tidy up everything.'

'So you won't be leaving for London immediately?'

'No.'

Malone was suddenly dead tired; he couldn't resist it: 'You'll spend more time searching the computers?'

Her gaze was steady. 'If needs be.'

It was time to go; Malone could feel himself becoming cross-eyed again. 'Take care, Chantelle. You too, Kylie.'

He jerked his head at Sheryl Dallen and she followed him and Clements out to the lifts. 'Did you question Kylie? Did anyone call here looking for Errol? A phone call or anything?'

'Nothing, boss.' Then she said, 'I'm glad he didn't take a shot at you. That'd be no way to retire.'

'I'm not retiring, I'm being promoted.'

'Same thing, as far as we're concerned. Right?' She looked at Clements. For a moment all rank was forgotten.

'Right,' said Clements and held the door open for Malone, embarrassed, to step into the lift.

3

'Remember,' said Nakasone, 'our stories have to be exactly the same. I've been here all morning, sometimes in conference with you about a replacement for Tajiri.'

'Everything is true except the facts,' murmured Okada.

'What?'

'It was something someone said of a Soviet trial in Russia in the 1930s. Our historians are following the rule.'

'You would not dare say that back in Tokyo or Osaka.'

'I'm at risk everywhere, Kenji. Here, back home, it doesn't matter. Okay, you have been here all morning. What if they question Miss Minato? She's a devil for facts.'

'She didn't see me go out or come back. Neither did the rest of the staff.'

'What if they had come looking for you?'

'I will say I must have been in the toilet. All we have

to do is corroborate each other, Hauro. For the sake of the bank.'

'Of course. But Mr Magee's death doesn't get the bank back its forty million dollars. Unless you asked him before you – er – wiped him off our books?'

'No jokes, please,' said Nakasone, who had no sense of humour.

For the next hour Okada sat waiting the inevitable: the arrival of the police. He was not surprised that when they came they were familiar men: Inspector Malone and Sergeant Clements.

He pressed the button under his desk when they were announced and Nakasone came in from his office as the two detectives entered. Okada rose. 'Inspector, back so soon? More due diligence?'

'Very much so, Mr Okada. Mr Nakasone.' Malone glanced at the latter, then looked back at Okada. 'Your client Mr Magee is dead. He was shot just over an hour ago, in the garage of his apartments. I'm sure it's been on the radio.'

'We haven't heard it – we never listen to the radio, Inspector. Naturally, we're upset about Mr Magee. Murdered? Dreadful.' He shook his head at the way of the world. 'We were looking forward to sitting down and talking to him. About solving our problems.'

Clements turned to Nakasone. 'You heard from or seen Mr Tajiri today?'

'Tajiri? Why would I see him today? He has been sacked, paid off. You haven't talked to him yourselves?'

Don't push it, Clements advised him silently. 'What's been your programme this morning?'

'Programme? I was here, working, have been since seven-thirty. I had a conference with Mr Okada. I am in the process of finding someone to replace Tajiri.'

'You can vouch for that, Mr Okada?' said Malone, switching the bowling.

'Of course, Inspector. Are you suggesting we might have had something to do with Mr Magee's death?'

'It crossed our minds that someone from Kunishima might have.'

'Inspector, may I remind you that Mr Magee owed our bank forty million dollars. His death won't return our money. Unless he has had a stab of conscience and made a will in our favour, told us where the money is.'

'There's no will,' said Clements. 'But he might of told his killer where the money is, just before he was shot.'

'He might have done that,' said Nakasone, wondering if he had given Magee more time there might have been a return. But, of course, there had not been enough time . . . 'So far no one has told us if he did.'

'And you haven't a clue where Tajiri might be?' said Malone.

'Not a clue,' said Okada.

'We'll want a list of all your employees,' said Clements. 'We'll have officers back here within twenty minutes to question them. Tell them, all of them, not to go out to lunch.'

'We'll tell them, Sergeant,' said Okada. 'We'll do everything we can to help.'

'To get your money back?' said Malone.

'We have to balance our books, Inspector.'

'So have we. We'll be back, gentlemen,' said Malone, bowed mockingly and led Clements out of the office.

Nakasone looked at Okada. 'I think we're safe, Hauro.'

'Are you a religious man, Kenji? No? I didn't think so. I'll pray for both of us. And poor Mr Magee. But don't quote me.'

Going down in the lift Malone and Clements said nothing to each other. But outside in the sunlight Clements said, 'You're not happy.'

'I'm bloody *un*-happy. Wouldn't you be? My last case and I look like finishing up with two, *two*, unsolved murders.'

'Not unsolved, mate. We know who did them. One of the Briskins and Mr Tajiri. We'll solve 'em eventually.'

'We?'

'Well, someone.'

Chapter Twelve

1

And so history, as it does, has slid on through its regular pattern of a hundred opinions, half-truths and winners and losers. By the time you read this:

Caroline Briskin is back in London with Greenfield & Company, doing some day trading on the side, building her own small fortune. She has a lover, an Italian soccer player with the English Premier League who has his own small fortune in his left boot.

Kylie Doolan lives in a small flat in Paddington and works as a general dogsbody for a bald-headed dress designer. Occasionally she goes back to Minto for Sunday lunch with Monica and Clarrie and her two nieces. She still has hopes of marrying money.

Kenji Nakasone and Tamezo Tajiri are back in Osaka, helping elderly corrupt politicians understand who is helping them. They have no conscience but a strict sense of duty towards the *yakuza*.

Hauro Okada is still in Sydney, still running the Kunishima Bank. He sits high in his office above the city and the view of the harbour and thinks now that he will retire here amongst the barbarians, certain that if he goes home, he will be out of place in what's happening to Japan. As he may be out of place here in Sydney. But, as the barbarians say, no worries, mate. It's a form of survival.

The Briskins now lead a crime-free life; they gave it up for Lent and it has just gone on. Shirlee manages a florist's shop; the bunches of flowers are arranged neatly, never a petal on the floor. Darlene works for a solicitor in the city, sometimes co-ordinating work with the office of Caradoc Evans; she has a boyfriend, a computer expert, but she has no intention of marrying him, at least not till her mother dies. Phoenix has recovered from his injuries, but, under his mother's instructions, walks with a limp and still draws the dole. The class action against the negligent, but rich, woman driver is scheduled for the end of the year.

Corey is the one least well-adjusted. He is back as senior mechanic for the transport company, but he has changed, his workmates say. What they don't see is his conscience. He still suffers from guilt, a non-compensatory disease, over the killing of Juanita Marcos and Constable Haywood. The local command, out of Homicide's domain, were still working on the Haywood murder, but had no leads and Corey hoped they never would. To his surprise he remembers Errol Magee almost with affection.

I-Saw went under and was buried, not with decency. Jared Cragg has moved on to another IT company. Daniela Bonicelli and Louise Cobcroft now work for the Kunishima Bank. Vassily Todorov is still pedalling furiously through life, but, seemingly, with no destination.

The forty million dollars, gathering interest at 4 per cent, is in a secret account in the Shahriver Bank in the Turks and Caicos Islands. The pass word is *bungee*, a leap of imagination that no one, so far, has made.

When it came time for Malone to leave Homicide, his promotion to superintendent in the Crime Agency having come through, he insisted there should be no farewell dinner. He hated fuss and functions and his staff, graciously but reluctantly, respected his wishes. On the final day there was a finger-food lunch and Clements, Phil Truach and Sheryl Dallen all said a few words and Malone replied with even fewer. Then he went into his office, sat down and wanted to cry.

Late in the afternoon it was time to leave. He had cleaned out his desk and brought in a small suitcase to cart away the memories of more years than he wanted to remember. When he walked out into the main office those still in the big room were watching a soap opera on the television set in one corner.

On the screen, in the background two women, a man and a dog, all with lots of hair, were looking towards the camera, tears in their eyes. In the foreground an elderly woman, with more hair than a yak, was crying. In the immediate foreground was a young blonde woman whose tear-irrigated face suggested it could grow rice.

'What's happened?' asked Malone.

'She's leaving,' said Truach.

'Who?'

'The dog,' said Truach and switched off the set.

It was time to go. He got to the security door, opened it with some difficulty and looked back. 'Take care,' he said.

'You, too,' they all said. 'Take care.'

2

And now tonight it was dinner at Level 41.

'He'll have a heart attack when you tell him,' said Claire.

'He's not paying,' said Lisa. 'You and Mo and Tom are.'

'You're worse than the capitalist bosses. Screwing the workers.'

'You sound just like Grandpa Con. Russ and Romy will be there.'

'I hope Dad doesn't ask who's paying. You know what he's like.'

But Malone didn't ask. Not even when they were all shown into a private room. He even kept his composure and his pocket didn't clench when the waiter came to Lisa and said, 'Champagne all round, ma'am?'

'All round,' said Lisa. 'It's the Krug?'

'Yes, ma'am. Your son suggested Porphry Pearl, but we're out of it.'

Tom grinned around the table. 'I heard Dad say once that that used to be the drink when he was taking girls out, before he met Mum. A dollar-ninety-five a bottle.'

'And worth every cent,' said his father, 'if the girl said Yes.'

'Oh God,' said Maureen, 'he's going to tell us about his bimbos!'

'He's a dead duck if he does,' said her mother.

Malone looked around the table. At Clements, Romy, Jason, his son-in-law, at Claire, Maureen, Tom and finally, the light of his life, Lisa. God, he decided, had been looking in his direction most of his life.

'Some people are born lucky,' he said and raised his glass. 'I was one of them.'

Kirribilli

August 2000 – April 2001